Nine Missing Girls

ALSO BY STEENA HOLMES

BERVIE SPRINGS SERIES
Book 1: Engaged to a Serial Killer
Book 2: The Twin

STANDALONES
The Sister under the Stairs
The Girls in the Basement
Nine Missing Girls

NINE MISSING GIRLS

STEENA HOLMES

JOFFE BOOKS

Joffe Books, London
www.joffebooks.com

First published in Great Britain in 2026

Cover art by Nick Castle

ISBN: 978-1-80573-481-9

AUTHOR'S NOTE

These short stories follow Detective Meri Amber — a woman shaped by shadows, driven by loss, and haunted by the sister she couldn't save.

If you've read *The Sister Under the Stairs* and *The Girls in the Basement*, you already know the beginning of Meri's journey. She's someone with a special gift — a drive to find those forgotten, and she never forgets a smell (and she's addicted to sugar-free Halls). Each case she takes in these short stories peels back another layer of who she is and why she does what she does: finding those who are missing.

Her search for the missing isn't just a profession — it's a vow, a promise. Every girl she finds brings her one step closer to understanding what happened to her own sister . . . and to the man who took her. And every time she's too late, it only pushes her to do better, to be better.

These stories don't just explore the crimes Meri uncovers — they reveal the truths she can't walk away from.

Because for Meri Amber, the missing are never just names on a file. They're echoes she can't ignore.

PS: If you haven't read *The Widow's Basement* (another case from this collection) yet, you can read it for free from my website: www.steenaholmes.com. It is the 'last' case file to read after you've read all of these.

MERI'S RULES

From Meri Amber

I don't believe people just vanish. Not really.

Someone always knows something. Someone always sees. They just don't always speak.

These cases? They're not just checkboxes on a department board. They're the weight I carry. Girls who go missing. Women who disappear. Echoes I refuse to let fade. And they're all from different times in my life.

You might've met me in *The Sister Under the Stairs* or *The Girls in the Basement*. Those stories scratched the surface. What you're about to read digs deeper — into the girls I've found, the truths I've uncovered, and the cracks in my own past I can't seem to seal.

I've been searching for my sister for twenty years.

Every missing girl is a mirror.

Every scream behind a wall could be hers.

Even though my sister's story is over, now that I've not only found her but her abductor, that doesn't mean I stop.

These cases give you insight as to why.

—Meri

* * *

The Rules I Live By

Not the ones they teach at the academy. The ones that keep you alive.

1. **Always listen to the quiet ones.**
    The loud ones want to be seen. The dangerous ones wait.
2. **Victims remember details they were told to forget.**
    You just have to ask the right question, the right way, at the wrong time.
3. **Trust is currency — and everyone's for sale eventually.**
    What they don't say is worth twice as much as what they do say.
4. **If something feels off, it is.**
    Intuition is a scream in a whisper.
5. **No one just disappears.**
    They're always somewhere. The trick is knowing where they don't want you to look.
6. **The eyes never lie.**
    Even when the mouth does.
7. **There are no coincidences.**
    Patterns don't lie. People do.
8. **Truth is rarely buried deep — it's just covered in shame.**
    Dig through the lies, and you'll find it bruised and breathing.
9. **Every survivor has a tell.**
    It's in the flinch, the silence, the too-smooth story.
10. **There's always something in the basement.**
    And it's never just boxes and dust.

1.
A HOUSE OF DOLLS

RULE #1

Always listen to the quiet ones.

The loud ones want to be seen. The dangerous ones wait.

CHAPTER 1: THE TIP

I have a love-hate relationship with anonymous tips.

They are often vague and unreliable, and I've stopped counting the number of times people use the tip line to punish a neighbor or nemesis for something they've done.

Over the years, I've received hundreds of tips. Some have helped. Many have not. Some have led me on wild goose chases. Some get me one step closer to finding my sister. Many are a waste of time, but I can't ignore any of them because of the infamous "what if" scenario.

What if the one I ignore is the one that is real?

What if the one I ignore is the one to solve a case?

There's something about the voice on this morning's tip line that worms its way into my thoughts and won't let go.

"They're in the dollhouse," the voice whispers. "Just like before. You missed one, Detective."

No name. No number. Just that message, along with a rustle of wind or a breath before it ends.

I've replayed it three times so far. Each time, the same chill slides down my spine.

I missed one. Missed what? A clue? A perpetrator? A victim? What did I miss?

Now, standing in front of the collapsed gate of 118 Sycamore Lane, I wonder if I should've let the unease pass. I've got no warrant and no partner to watch my back. Just a gut feeling and a voicemail challenging me to right a wrong I didn't know I made.

The house before me sags like it's exhaled its last breath. Weeds curl up around the porch columns like bony fingers. The windows are filthy, opaque with years of dust and spiderwebs, and above the porch, a wooden sign barely legible through peeling paint reads, The Dahl House.

Locals call it The House of Dolls.

It's been empty since the '90s, when Victor Dahl, a once-renowned toy craftsman, disappeared shortly after his daughter's unsolved disappearance. I looked up the old case files and almost wish I hadn't. People said Victor Dahl went mad with grief, and after seeing the photos of all the dolls he'd carved in his daughter's likeness, I can believe it. Rumor has it he still lives there, his ghost haunting the premises after his heart gave out.

There are a lot of rumors about him and this house, a lot of myths, legends, and whispered secrets people are all too willing to share.

I've never really cared much for folklore, but I do care about girls who go missing and never come home.

I step through the broken gate and walk toward the porch, each footstep a deliberate choice. My hand grips my flashlight. It's mid-morning, but the trees around the property blot out the sun.

The porch creaks with my weight. The front door moans open with a single push.

Inside, the house smells like mildew and old wood with a hint of something sickly sweet, like rotting fruit masked with lavender. My nose itches at the scent, and I reach for a sugar-free Halls I'd stuffed into my pocket earlier.

The foyer stretches in front of me. The place is a mess with doll parts scattered everywhere — limbs, heads, glass eyes in jars.

A child's music box plays somewhere deeper in the house, the tune warbling and out of sync.

Of course, there's a child's music box playing after all this time.

I don't flinch. It's probably the wind moving the box to make it play.

I grab my phone and click on the voicemail again. "You missed one, Detective."

My breath catches, and it's not because of the message but because of the doll standing at the end of the hallway. A three-foot-tall doll wearing a blue cotton dress, with strawberry-blond hair and a freckled face that looks disturbingly familiar.

My eyes are playing tricks with me. They have to be.

I step toward the doll, the wood floors creaking beneath my feet. The only sound in the house is that haunting music box, and I almost swear the lips on the doll twitch.

I blink. I blink again.

This is the most realistic doll I've ever seen. It's not plastic, and if it's porcelain, it's a porcelain I've never encountered before.

Once I'm in front of the doll, I reach out and lightly touch the hair, my fingers recoiling as I realize it's real hair. Human hair. I swallow hard. The long lashes, so dark and full, can only be real, too, and the fingernails are painted with a sparkly pink polish that hasn't chipped or even faded.

There's something about this doll that is unsettling, but I can't pinpoint why.

I kneel for a closer look. On the doll's dress, a small name tag has been sewn into the collar. *Aimee.*

My heart drops, and my mouth dries up as the palm of my hand hits the wood floor. I know this name. I know this girl. I've read her missing persons file.

Aimee Linwood was reported missing over two years ago. She was riding her bike home from ballet practice and was never seen again.

And now, here she is. Or at least something that wears her name and face. The question is why. Why here? Why now? Is this what I'm supposed to find — this doll in the image of a missing girl?

I stand, brush dirt from my hand, and head toward the room next to me. It's littered with doll parts, and lining the walls, sitting in chairs, and lying on floors are actual dolls.

Dozens of them. All watching. All waiting.

I turn my camera on and take a video, sweeping the room slowly so I don't miss anything.

This isn't a collection. It's a mausoleum.

I just walked into the graveyard.

CHAPTER 2: THE FILE THAT SHOULD HAVE STAYED CLOSED

The evidence room is a room I'm more than familiar with. In all my years here, it hasn't changed. It's still cold. Still windowless. Still hums with a low, constant buzzing from old fluorescent lights and even older secrets.

I sign my name in the logbook, barely recognizing my own signature beneath the rows of younger, newer detectives. Then, I wait. The clerk brings me a box, one of those old gray ones with duct-taped corners and a faded red sticker.

Closed — March 2017.

I carry it to the back corner table and sit. No one looks my way. They never do.

I open the lid and reach for the folder lying on top. I flip through the statements and papers and go right for the photos. My breath hitches at the sight of twin girls, aged nine — Mila and Morgan Barrett.

Their story haunts my sleep, features in my nightmares, and always has me hesitating before I open a storage closet.

They were found locked inside one such closet inside their home, severely malnourished, bruised from head to toe, broken in body and spirit, and surrounded by handmade dolls.

It's the dolls that invade my nightmares.

Those girls didn't speak for weeks. Not to me when I first found them, not even to the social worker who was there to help them and keep them safe.

Eventually, their aunt came forward and took custody of them. The parents were convicted of child endangerment and cruelty. The neglect, the lock on that closet door, and a house filled with dolls crafted from scraps of fabric and human hair were enough to incarcerate them for the rest of their lives.

Nor could they ever explain why one of the dolls had a small paper heart sewn to its chest with the words, "She's not like us anymore."

The parents never offered the name either. They're both dead now, died while in prison, and I've never been more satisfied with how that case ended.

I flip through to the next report and sigh. There are regular reports of the girls' progress toward healing, but according to this, Morgan ran away a year later. There's no update on whether she was ever found or whether she returned to her aunt's house on her own.

The soft click of my pen echoes in the room, and I scribble one word in the margin of the file. "Dahl?"

I pull out my laptop from my bag and search for overlaps with any other cases around the same time Morgan ran away. The only thing I find is a report about Mila. A few years after her sister left, her aunt died, and Mila had been placed into a private group home, just fifteen miles from Sycamore Lane.

The same year Aimee Linwood disappeared.

A sour taste fills my mouth, and I reach for my cell and make a call.

"Can you get me any incident reports connected to 118 Sycamore Lane for the past ten years?" I ask. "Especially anything involving trespassing, loitering, or disturbances."

I hang up before I am asked why.

I continue through the file, going through some pages I skipped earlier. I pick up one at random, a drawing Mila made. She'd drawn dolls over and over again any time she'd been given a paper and crayon. She drew hundreds of them, all faceless, all nameless. I always assumed she was drawing her nightmares.

One always stuck with me. Mila had drawn a house, but instead of windows, she drew eyes, and instead of a front door, it was a mouth, and instead of flowers in the garden, there were dolls.

I asked her about it. She still wasn't speaking then, but she did scribble a note. I search the folder for that note and find it at the very back.

"That's where the dolls sleep when they're bad."

I'd dismissed it as imagination, but now, I'm not so sure.

I pack the file up and return it to the clerk before heading to my car.

The house still torments me, and I think about that doll I found. Aimee.

I pull up the pictures on my phone and zoom in, searching for one key visual. I'm still waiting on forensics to determine who the hair belongs to, but it's the bright, sparkly pink nails that I'm focused on.

My stomach churns as I realize the truth of what Mila had been trying to tell me.

The nails had dirt under them, like she'd tried to claw her way out from the ground.

CHAPTER 3: THE WATCHER
IN THE TREES

By the time I return to 118 Sycamore Lane, it's just after dusk.

I park two houses down this time and walk the last stretch under the cloak of thick, whispering branches. The street is essentially abandoned.

The Dahl House doesn't just loom. It waits even now. Probably more so now than before. A shudder runs down my spine.

My boots crunch over gravel and leaves. There are no birds, no crickets, just the brittle silence of a place deliberately forgotten.

I stay off the porch this time and circle around the side of the house.

There's a footprint in the soft mud near the cracked foundation.

It's smaller than my own, but it's fresh and faces the house, instead of away.

Someone is here.

I crouch beside it, my breathing shallow. The footprint definitely belongs to a child. The arch is narrow, the heel worn smooth. There is no distinct branding on the sole.

I slowly rise, my gaze scanning the tree line, my senses alert. That's when I feel it. Not hear. Not see. Feel. Like breath on my skin. Like a light caress along the crook of my back.

Someone is watching me.

I turn, my flashlight arcing through the woods behind me, but there's nothing. No glowing eyes, no darkened shadows, no light-colored clothing that stands out.

Absolutely nothing.

I still feel it, though, like someone is staring directly at me. My skin prickles, and I wish I had come with some backup.

"Who's there?" I call out, stepping toward the woods, my voice steadier than I feel.

The only answer is the whisper of wind weaving through the branches.

Then, there's a flicker of movement, high in the trees.

I stop, raise the beam again, and see a shape. Whomever it is, they move fast, skittering down the tree until it disappears into the darkness.

I don't give chase despite wanting to. I know better than to chase shadows until I understand what they want. Instead, I cut back to where the shoe print had been and see the outline of an old root cellar. My breath fogs the air as I reach the heavy wooden door half-buried in ivy and damp rot. There's no lock, thankfully, and I yank it open and step inside.

The scent of mildew is strong. So is something else, something sweet and cloying. Like before, rotting fruit masked by lavender sachets. It's strong and intentional, a stark reminder of the smell from inside the house.

My flashlight scans the cramped cellar and catches on something.

A folded blanket, recently used.

Nearby, crumbs litter the cement floor, along with a cracked plastic bowl. Beside that bowl is a doll, its face painted with smeared makeup, cheeks blushed with childlike effort, lips colored a garish red.

Someone is living here, just like I suspected, and they're not just hiding.

I crouch beside the blanket and pull out a pair of gloves from my pocket. I don't want to contaminate the scene more than I am. There are boot prints ranging in all sizes, but mainly smaller than my own.

Then, I hear a scraping noise from behind the far panel off to my right.

I freeze.

There's another scrape. I hear a voice, quiet, raspy, like it hasn't been used in a while. "She said you'd come back. The one who looked like the girl with the twin."

My skin tightens. "Who said that?" I ask, rising slowly, my hand near my holster.

There's no response.

"Who said that?" I ask again.

"The one who left. Aimee."

My stomach drops. "Aimee Linwood?"

There's a pause, then the sound of a hand brushing stone.

"She said we weren't real unless we stayed still."

"Where is she now?" I ask, my voice soft despite the tightening of my muscles. Why did I come alone?

"She broke. He couldn't fix her." A pause. "So he made another."

The voice is close now, just behind the panel.

I move slowly, careful not to alarm whoever is on the other side. "What's your name?" I ask.

There's no answer.

I press my hand to the panel. It creaks as it opens. A girl steps out. She's pale and filthy, every area of skin covered in a thick layer of dirt. She's also as thin as a whisper. At first glance, I have no idea how old she is, maybe early teens, maybe mid-twenties. Her hair is a wild tangle, nested and matted. Her torn dress is streaked with what I think is mud and discolored by age and wear.

But it's her eyes that score a hole into my soul, and I know I'll see her eyes for years in my nightmares. They are large. Hollow. Dead.

"You're not him." That's all she says. Her voice has no inflection, no emotion.

"No," I say. "I'm Detective Meri Amber."

She gives me a brief nod. "He said you'd come. He left the doll for you."

"What doll?"

"The one with your eyes."

Chills race across my skin as I kneel. "Can you tell me who you are?"

The girl tilts her head, as if thinking. Her smile is thin and so very, very, wrong. "We don't use names down here."

My heart pounds so fast and hard that I find myself placing my palm against my chest and pressing down.

"I need to find Aimee. Can you help me?" I ask.

The girl looks away. "Aimee tried to speak. She said the dolls weren't real and that they were girls, but he said real girls lie." She looks down at the floor as she says this.

"Who is he?"

The girl touches her lips. "If we say his name, we can't leave."

Reaching into my coat, I slowly pull out a small mirror from my pocket and hold it up to the girl. This is a trick I learned years ago when interviewing traumatized children.

"Do you see yourself?" I ask. It takes everything in me to keep my voice soft and approachable. Scaring her is the last thing I want to do.

She flinches, then slowly nods. "I think I used to be her."

The sadness in her voice just about breaks me.

"And what happened to her?"

"He turned her inside out," the girl whispers. "He made her prettier. Quieter. Told her she'd never be alone again."

A rush of bile rises up my throat. "I want to help you," I say, "but we need to get you somewhere safe. Will you come with me?"

The girl hesitates. "Not yet," she says. "I want to show you where they sleep."

"Who?"

"The broken ones. The ones who stopped pretending."

Her cold fingers reach for my hand, and her grip is tight. She leads me deeper into the cellar, where the dirt smells wetter, darker.

Where the dolls are buried. Where the truth lives beneath layers of cotton and painted smiles.

Where someone has been watching for far too long.

CHAPTER 4: WHERE THE DOLLS SLEEP

The girl leads me down a narrow, low-ceilinged hallway framed with rotting wood and cobwebs. Her bare feet don't make a sound on the dirt floor. Meanwhile, the thrumming of my heartbeat is a thud in my ears. Every inch of the air is damp with secrets.

"This is the nursery," the girl whispers, her fingers trailing along the wall. "He brings us here to make us better."

The beam of my flashlight casts long shadows that dance over peeling wallpaper, exposed beams, and old toys piled in the corners, each one broken in a different way. There's a small child-sized door with pink paint barely showing beneath the grime. The hair on my arms rises at the sight of a crude, hand-drawn heart faded and stained on the door.

The girl stops, her posture stiff, her hands fisted. "He doesn't let us go in without permission, it's locked, but sometimes . . . after the music plays . . . the door opens."

"What kind of music?"

She gives me a slight shrug. "A lullaby. It plays on a music box, the one with teeth."

My skin prickles. "What do you mean teeth?"

"It has a mouth," the girl says, matter-of-fact. "It bit Morgan when she turned it too fast."

I can only nod, not trusting my voice.

The girl opens the child-sized door slowly and flicks a switch. The room is small, no more than eight by eight feet, lit by a single, buzzing overhead bulb.

I'm about to say something when I notice the shelves on the walls. They're filled with dozens of dolls that are all perfectly dressed, perfectly posed, perfectly . . . eerie.

I feel drawn to them and step farther into the room, my boots stirring up dust thin as powdered bone. These dolls will haunt me for the rest of my life. Their skin is made of fabric, their faces molded with wax and painted in flesh tones. Their hair — human hair — is carefully stitched onto their scalps. The details on each face are unique as well.

One has freckles that remind me of Morgan Barrett.

Another has a scar above its lip, a detail from Aimee's file.

And another . . . I lean in closer and see my eyes staring back at me. A dagger-like shiver runs down my spine.

I move back, fighting the urge to cover my mouth. This isn't a nursery. It's a reliquary, a tomb for the forgotten, arranged like museum pieces to be admired.

I turn, and my gaze settles onto another doll sitting on a center shelf. It's wearing a faded pink tutu, its face blushed like a ballerina. A cracked name tag hangs from its neck, painted in looping red letters.

Linnie.

Like a hand is gripping my lungs, I can't breathe. These dolls aren't tributes. They aren't mirrors and memories and museum pieces.

They are replacements.

I notice other details I glossed over previously. Each doll has its mouth stitched closed. Some have missing fingers. Others have hollow eye sockets stuffed with cotton balls and stitched over with black thread.

I gag.

Against the far wall is a desk covered in junk. I find sewing needles, wax molds, scalpels, and thread. At the back corner is a Mason jar full of baby teeth. Next to it sits a can of adhesive labeled *SkinFlex*, and beside that is a notebook.

I push the horrors that run through my mind as far away as I can and open the book where I find page after page of diagrams, anatomical notes, and sketches of girls. There are even instructions on how to bleach fabric to match the tone of real skin.

It's the personalized notes that churn my stomach.

Third batch: Skin texture still wrong. Tried actual samples.
Aimee's hands are too stiff. Need younger clay. Linnie had better joints.
If they don't speak, they last longer.

I turn the page and find a Polaroid of Aimee stuck between the pages. I gasp slightly. She's strapped to a bench, her eyes open, her face painted.

I turn away, one hand pressed to the wall to steady myself. The rage building within me pulses behind my eyes.

Everything here is about one thing and one thing only.

Ownership.

Whoever is doing this controls and erases these girls.

I pull in a deep breath and swallow back my cry of anger.

That's when I see the hooks. I make my way there and read the labels so carefully placed above each hook. *Morgan. Aimee. Linne.* Two are empty. The fourth isn't. Hanging from that hook is a doll slumped like a marionette waiting for its strings as it hangs from its shoulders. The limbs are twisted at wrong angles, but her expression is serene.

I force myself to photograph everything. I need evidence. Proof. Not just for the courts but for myself, to remind myself that this isn't a nightmare, that it's all real.

I step back into the hallway to find the girl, but she's gone.

There's no sound, no movement within the low corridor that stretches out into darkness. Panic surges through me.

"Hey," I shout. "Where are you?"

There's no answer. The only sound I hear is footsteps above me. They're soft and deliberate but heavier than that girl could make.

I draw my weapon and climb the stairs into the kitchen. The light is low, the house unchanged, but the back door stands wide open.

Outside, the trees shudder in the wind.

I step onto the porch, sweeping my light across the yard. It flickers then catches on something just beyond the railing, something scratched into the wood with a blade.

Still missing one.

My breath stutters in my chest. I turn, light from my flashlight dancing across the broken porch, back to the tree line, where I see some movement.

A pale face in the branches.

I blink, and it's gone.

I back away from the porch, my weapon high, pulse pounding. I'm being watched.

CHAPTER 5: THE FINAL DOLL

I'm sitting in my car, Dahl's notebook lying on my lap, each page crawling with madness disguised as craft. The handwriting becomes more erratic the more I read, as if the act of creation peeled something loose inside him.

Finally, at 2:47 a.m., I call in the only person I trust with this.

Detective Rhys Mercer, my former partner and occasional thorn. He's the one who sat with me the night the Barrett twins were found.

He answers on the first ring. "It's never good news when you call this late," he mutters.

He sounds tired but not like I woke him. More like too-exhausted-to sleep-tired, which is exactly how I'm feeling.

"I think I found Morgan," I say.

No hello. No how are you. No catching up because none of that ever needs to be said between us.

The silence stretches.

"Alive?" he asks. There's no inflection in his voice. He's neither hopeful nor disappointed.

"I don't know," I admit. I tell him what I found, who I found. "All I know is that if that girl in the cellar isn't Morgan, she knows where she went."

"How can you be sure?"

I pause. "She mentioned Aimee. She said he couldn't fix her."

"Jesus." His voice drops. "I'm on my way. Have you called it in?"

"Not yet."

He doesn't ask why. He simply says, "I'm on my way. Report it. I'll be there before they arrive."

* * *

When Rhys arrives, we don't speak. He pulls out a duffel bag, opens it, and shows me the lights, cameras, and body armor inside. I hold up the notebook, now in a sealed bag, and grab an evidence kit.

The air feels thicker tonight, not just with dampness but with memories neither one of us can let go.

I lead the way to the basement.

It's empty.

No dolls. No pink door. No girl.

"What the . . ." I pull out my phone and flip to the images I'd taken to prove what I'd seen.

Rhys glances at the photos, then at me. "So he cleaned up while you—"

"Sat outside. The mother—" I stop, seeing something on the far wall. "Do you see this?" I ask him, pointing at the barely noticeable seam.

He nods.

Together, we push, and a section of concrete gives way.

The pink room is still there, but the dolls lining the shelves are all gone. There's only one strapped to the lone table in the middle of the room. Her eyes are closed. Her lips are painted, and her hair is curled.

It's Morgan.

Only older, early twenties, and frozen in time.

"Holy shit," Rhys whispers, stepping forward.

I reach her first and press two fingers to Morgan's wrist. There's a pulse. It's faint, but it's there.

Together, we tear at the straps holding her down. Rhys calls it in while I attempt to comfort the still girl. Morgan doesn't speak. She doesn't blink, but her breath is shallow and fast.

"She was here the whole time," I say, rage rising like bile. "He kept her here and made her into one of them, and I missed her."

Rhys stares around the room at the paint cans, makeup, cotton padding, medical tape, and craftsman's tools turned surgical. "Holy hell," he says.

I lightly touch Morgan's face, my finger coming away crusted with thick foundation. Beneath the makeup, I can barely make out the swelling and bruising.

What did that asshole do to her? Did he try to fix her after breaking her over and over again?

I snap dozens of photos, my hand trembling.

In the corner of the room is a mirror. I ignore it until I see someone else in that mirror, someone other than myself and Rhys. Someone standing behind us with a sardonic grin on their face.

I spin.

There's no one there.

I turn back to the mirror and see a shadow retreating into the wall.

"Someone's still here," I whisper.

Rhys is already moving. He lifts Morgan into his arms, and we leave the room as quickly as possible. When we reach the top of the stairs, something hard slams on the attic floor above.

We both freeze.

"I have to see," I say.

"You don't."

"There was a message that said we are missing one," I whisper. "There's another girl."

Rhys shakes his head. "Backup will be here shortly."

"It might be too late by then."

Rhys hesitates, then nods. "I'll wait in the car with Morgan. You get five minutes."

The attic stairs are narrow and steep, the kind that don't creak unless you're meant to be heard. The air grows colder the higher I go. It's laced with the scent of dust, old cotton, and a hint of decay.

I reach the attic door and slowly ease it open. The room is filled with dozens of mirrors, each one warped. All are mismatched. Some are stained with fingerprints and lipstick kisses. In the center of the room is a glass case that holds a full-sized doll wearing a pale blue nightgown similar to one that I have at home. The hair on this doll hangs in a curtain of black silk, and my throat tightens.

This doll looks like me.

Same eyes. Same mouth. Same scar on the chin from falling off my bike in fourth grade.

On the mirror behind the case is a message scrawled in lipstick:

Now we are complete.

CHAPTER 6: THE DOLLMAKER'S LEGACY

The ambulance pulls away with Morgan inside, her body still slack but breathing, barely tethered to consciousness. Rhys stands silent beside me on the lawn, watching the red and blue lights disappear into the tree line.

Neither of us speaks for a long time. The house looms behind us, its broken windows like hollow eyes.

"You want to tell me what the hell that was?" he finally asks, his voice low and steady.

I can't answer, not right away. I'm still seeing my own reflection in the mirrored case.

My double. The doll in my nightgown.

A weight presses against my chest like a second heart, wrong and pulsing.

"He's dead, Rhys," I finally say. "Victor Dahl died years ago."

"Then who's been building these things?"

"I don't know." I shake my head and sigh. "Or maybe I do."

His gaze narrows. "What are you saying?"

I arch my back and hear it *pop-pop-pop*. "I think someone took up where he left off. Maybe a protégé. Maybe a survivor. Maybe . . . someone worse."

"Worse?"

I nod. "Whoever it is, they know me. Intimately."

"You sure the girl in the cellar wasn't Linnie?"

"I'm sure," I say. "Linnie's long gone. She was the first doll. The prototype. That girl . . . she's someone else. Maybe one of the foster kids. Maybe someone we missed, but she's not a child anymore."

I remember the way the girl moved — too quiet and too practiced. Like she'd been playing a part for so long, she didn't know how to be anything else.

And then there's the doll, the one made in my image. Every scar, every detail. Even the eyes were painted with a fleck of gold in the right iris.

Only someone close would know that.

Too close.

"You think someone's targeting you now?" Rhys asks.

I don't answer.

"I think the next doll would've been me," I finally say.

Rhys swears under his breath. "We need to burn that house to the ground."

I nod. "We will but not yet."

I reach into my jacket and pull out the notebook, and flip to the last page. It's a list of names. Some have been crossed out.

Morgan is there. So is Aimee. So is Mila Barrett, the surviving twin.

So is my name. That one makes me pause.

But there's one more name scribbled in the margin:

Hannah Vale.

Rhys reads it out loud. "That name mean anything to you?"

"Not yet," I say.

But it will. I can feel it.

*　*　*

Two days later, I'm at my desk with three monitors glowing bright. Dahl's case notes lie on the table in front of me. There's a map of missing girls pinned on one of the screens.

I zoom in on a cluster of disappearances in the last five years, all of them within a hundred-mile radius of Sycamore Lane. All girls between eight and fourteen. All from foster care.

There's been no media coverage. No investigations.

They all just vanished.

And every single one bore a resemblance to someone else.

A sister. A social worker. A detective. A dollmaker's daughter.

I stare at the image of the mirror again, the one written to me in lipstick. *Now we are complete.*

It wasn't just about me. It wasn't meant just for me. It's about the story. The cycle. The perfect collection. I don't know who took them, but I'll find out. That's a promise.

I stand, go to my filing cabinet, open a drawer, and pull out a folder I know all too well.

River Amber.

My sister. My shadow.

A sick knot twists in my gut. What if she hadn't vanished? What if she'd been chosen? Not for who she was but because she looked like someone else?

I shudder and run my fingers along the edge of the folder, and for the first time in months, maybe years, I'm afraid.

Not for myself, but for the girls no one is looking for. The ones turned into dolls. Frozen. Forgotten. Loved by no one but the ghosts who made them.

I turn off the lights and close my office door.

"I'm coming for you," I whisper into the dark.

The End

2.
THE BIRTHDAY ROOM

RULE #2

Victims remember details they were told to forget.

You just have to ask the right question,
the right way, at the wrong time.

CHAPTER 1: THE CAKE THAT
NEVER SPOILS

The call comes in as a welfare check on a quiet property in the hills. Neighbors have been complaining about music at odd hours. Lights have been flickering in the attic, and children come and go at all hours. The kind of nothing that sometimes turns into something you can't scrub from your hands. I take it anyway.

The Whitcomb Retreat sits at the end of a gravel lane bordered by birch and alder, a Victorian with too many windows and a porch that sags like a tired smile. A wooden placard swings on rusty chains — *WHITCOMB FAMILY THERAPEUTIC RETREAT*. Beneath it, hand-stenciled in lavender, is *Renew your beginnings*.

I park on the gravel driveway and make my way across, scanning the area. The door opens before I can even climb the porch stairs and knock. A woman stands there. She's in her mid-fifties, with hair pulled into a loose bun, and an unsettling calm that makes my nerves itch. She's wearing a beige linen dress with a waist-length cardigan over it, bare feet, her palms up in greeting.

"Mrs. Whitcomb? I'm Detective Amber," I introduce myself.

"Yes, I'm Lillian Whitcomb. Can I help you?" She clutches the end of her sweater.

"We've had reports from your neighbors about noises and seeing young girls running around the property late at night. They think you keep girls here overnight without parental supervision."

She blinks a few times. "Keep girls? What an odd thing to say. We support families. Short-term residencies for milestone work."

"Milestone?"

She shrugs. "Yes." She looks at me as if I'm an imbecile. "Milestone events such as birthdays. They can be particularly difficult for trauma survivors."

"Difficult how?"

"They mark time, and time marks loss."

She steps back to let me in. The foyer smells like lemon oil and something sweet underneath that I can't place. The house is staged rather than lived-in, with artful stacks of books, a vase of wilting peonies, and a bowl of wax fruit solemnly dusted.

She leads me through rooms clipped from a cottage magazine, with soft throws and dim lamps and lacking anything sharp. Family photos trail up the staircase — sepia, then Polaroid, then digital — each labeled in neat script. *LIAM, 12*, is the last. The boy reappears in every frame, candlelit cheeks and a gap-toothed grin, arms slung around a younger mother and a father. The woman looks like a much younger Lillian.

"Your son?" I ask.

Lillian's mouth twitches. "He died before his thirteenth birthday."

"I'm sorry."

"Everyone is," she says gently. She continues climbing.

There's an open door on the second floor to a sewing room with rows of ribbon hanging on a wall shelf. On the sewing table, I spot a smear of pink frosting. I don't comment.

The stairs to the attic are narrow and mean, built for luggage and secrets. A chain hangs through the ceiling hatch with a plywood tag painted *CELEBRATION ROOM.*

"You hold sessions up there?" I ask.

"Occasionally," Lillian says with a shrug. "Birthdays can be healing when we rebuild them."

"Rebuild?"

"Rituals overwrite pain. If the twelfth was broken, we craft a gentler twelve."

She's speaking in riddles, and it's all I can do to bite my tongue.

She points toward the chain, and I take that as my invitation to proceed. I tug, and the hatch gives way with a wooden cough. A sickly sweet swash of warm air spills down.

I climb. The attic opens into an A-frame room banded with beams and string lights. Paper streamers droop in faded pinks and blues. A party table runs the length of the room, set with paper plates, paper hats, and a plastic knife shaped like a candle. Foil star stickers cluster on the walls in random patterns.

At the far end is a small cake, the white frosting smooth, perched on a milk-glass stand. Twelve candles sit in two neat rows of six. There's also a little music box beside it, key unwound, the lid closed, *Happy Birthday* painted in an earnest script.

I cross the room slowly. Glitter covers the floor. I notice a table with hats. This room has been set, used, and reset again.

"How often do you . . ." I search for the right word. "Hold these parties?"

"It all depends on need," Lillian says. "I try to catch families before the date passes. It's worse if they miss it."

"Who was the last birthday for?"

Her gaze slides away, not to the cake but to a corner table covered with a pink cloth. Before I can move, she palms the music box and winds it twice, a therapist's sleight of hand. The tune spills out slow and slightly off, like a bent key. *Hap-py birth-day to —* Then, there's a skip, a stretch, and a note that shouldn't live there.

"Children like predictability," she says, "but they also like novelty."

I stay silent, my eyes on a child-sized chair scraped raw along the front rung where feet had swung for too long. The floor beneath shows grooves, little half-moons carved by back-and-forward motion until the wood learned the movement.

"Where are your guests?"

"Resting. Today was . . . intense."

"Because of a birthday?"

"Because of a memory," Lillian explains. "Would you like to meet her later? The girl."

"What's her name?"

"Nora."

I stare at the cake, taking in what she'd said. "Can I see your intake forms?" I ask, fully expecting her to say no.

"Is that necessary?"

"It would be helpful."

She leads me back down the narrow stairs, her hand steady on the rail. In the foyer, she turns left and enters a paneled hall I hadn't noticed, then heads down to a cool half-basement lined with file cabinets, string tags fluttering like small flags. A dehumidifier rattles in the corner.

The sweet-sour smell is more pungent here, cut with bleach.

Red flags go off in my brain.

Lillian opens a drawer, rifles through it, and pulls out a slim file marked *NORA, 12*. Inside are two forms — *Parent/Guardian Consent* and *Milestone Plan* — both signed by Caroline M. The signatures seem right until I take another look.

The *C* in Caroline is perfect on one and rushed and almost panicked on the other.

"Caroline's her mother?" I ask.

"She's a caregiver," Lillian says, her smile flattening.

"Where's Nora's last name?"

"Sealed," she says, her lips thinning. "At the family's request."

I flip to the back page and read the session notes.

Arrived tearful. Resistant to candles. Music box calmed the effect. Redirected to wish practice.

"What's wish practice?"

"Articulating the wish you needed at a specific age," Lillian says softly. "Then practice blowing it into the dark. Sometimes the girls need to repeat it."

"How many times?"

"As many as it takes."

I shut the folder and hand it back. "Are these all the guest files?"

"They are."

"Can I see Nora, your current guest?" I ask.

Lillian hesitates. "She's sleeping. Birthdays are exhausting."

I look around again and then leave my card on the file cabinet. "I really must insist," I say.

"Why?" I hear notes of panic in her otherwise neutrally crafted tone.

"Because the cake's wrong," I say.

Finally, Lillian looks unsettled. "In what way?"

"Twelve candles, two rows of six." I keep my voice even. "But the frosting has twelve rosettes around the edge, thirteen piped in the middle." I pause. "Someone here doesn't know how to turn twelve."

I climb the stairs without waiting for her reply. At the top, I glance back toward the ceiling hatch. From above, the music box ticks two stubborn notes and quits, like a song that refuses to end the way it was taught.

CHAPTER 2: THE GIRL
WHO TURNS TWELVE

Lillian leads me to a sitting room off the library where I can meet her guests and ask all the questions I need in order to leave as quickly as I arrived. It's a sunny room surrounded by windows. It feels safe and cozy.

She returns with a tray of tea and cookies, placing it on the table. She pours me a cup, but I leave it on the table, untouched.

I was expecting to only meet Nora, but Lillian introduces me to Maddi first. The young girl wears a sweatshirt two sizes too big and keeps the hood half up, as if it might hide her from me. Instead of sitting, she hovers by the arm of the couch, her eyes moving between the door and the mantel clock.

"Hey, Maddi." I keep my voice soft. "I'm Meri. I just want to ask a few questions."

Maddi nods without commitment.

"Did you have a birthday here?"

A microscopic flinch. "We don't call it that."

"What do you call it?"

"A reset."

"What happens in a reset?"

Maddi's fingers pinch the sweatshirt hem, rolling the fabric. "Streamers. Cake. You blow out twelve candles even if you're not turning twelve."

"How old are you?"

"Fifteen." Beat. "I mean, fifteen again. It's confusing."

"I'm sure it must be. Can you tell me about the reset? You mentioned streamers. What color were they?"

"Blue," she says immediately. Then, quieter, she adds, "I think."

"What song played?"

She frowns. "'Happy Birthday.' But . . . it was wrong."

"How was it wrong?"

Maddi's breath stutters. "It stretches like taffy. You can't sing with it. Your voice gets stuck."

"Who lights the candles?"

"Miss Lillian." Another beat. "And sometimes Nora helps."

I make a few notes, letting the quiet grow between us.

It doesn't take long for Maddi to raise her hood. "The knife is plastic."

"What knife?"

"The one you cut the cake with. It looks like a candle. That's funny, right?" She swallows. "It's so you remember it's just pretend."

"Does it feel pretend?"

Maddi looks at me then, straight on, a flash of anger under glass. "My parents made me come."

I nod. "Parents have that habit of making you do things you don't always want to do, don't they?"

Maddi swallows hard. "It feels like you can't breathe when the lights go off," she whispers, "and the song keeps going even after you blow."

I thank her and scribble the details — *blue streamers, plastic candle-knife, wrong song.*

I try to hide my surprise when the next girl arrives. How many are there?

"June, this is Detective Amber, she has a few questions for you." Lillian introduces us before she leaves to stand in the doorway, hovering.

June sits cross-legged on the armchair like a cat and answers in decisive bursts, which I copy.

"Streamers?" I ask.

"Pink."

"Cake?"

"Vanilla with strawberry in the middle."

"Candles?"

"Twelve. Always twelve. No matter what."

"Music?"

"Music box. It skips."

"Who's there?" I'm quite enjoying the quick back and forth.

June's mouth flattens. "If you close your eyes, only the song. If you open them, Miss Lillian and sometimes the mirror."

"What mirror?" I lean forward at this new piece of information.

She shrugs. "The shiny part on the cake stand. You can see yourself if the candles are tall."

"What do you wish for?"

"You're not supposed to tell."

"Did you feel better after?"

June hops down, a small, precise movement. "Miss Lillian says you do. So . . . yes." Her *yes* is a lie.

The third girl, Priya, is smaller, younger, and carries a stuffed bear whose fur has been petted into a wave. She answers in facts like they are the only safe thing left.

"Streamers?"

"Yellow."

"Cake?"

"Chocolate."

"Knife?"

"Plastic."

"Song?"

Priya's lips move. She hums a bar, then stops and glances toward the door, then hums another. The sound is warped, the fourth note stretched, the sixth note lifted like a question. I write that down, unsure if it's important.

"Who stands closest to you?" I ask.

"Nora," Priya says, then adds, as if reciting, "She is very good at birthdays." She leaves the room, head buried into her stuffed bear.

Lillian hovers in the hall. Her smile is hospitable. Her eyes count everything.

"Are there any others?"

Lillian shakes her head.

"Then I'd like to speak with Nora now." It may sound like a question, but it's not, and Lillian hears the demand.

Lillian's smile falters. "She's resting after yesterday."

"I'll be brief."

"She gets disoriented when strangers push." She's clutching her hands together now.

"I'm not pushing."

I also won't take no for an answer.

"Nora?" I call out. I heard the creak in the floorboard out in the hallway a few moments ago.

When Nora appears, it's hard to tell her age. She watches me with huge eyes and stands with her hands folded like she's finished praying.

I glance over at Lillian just for a moment and notice the frown before she hides it.

"Hi, Nora," I say, adding a softness to my voice.

"Hi, Detective." Nora's voice carries the polite edge of someone who has heard too many adults insist they were helpers.

"Will you join me?"

Nora chooses the unsupported middle of the couch, her back straight, feet flat, palms placed. A perfect posture you could build a ritual on.

"I hear you're good at birthdays," I start.

Nora's mouth quirks. "I am good at remembering."

"Tell me about one."

"Which one?"

"The last you were in."

Nora considers. "We used blue streamers first," she says, "but they looked wrong in the afternoon, so we switched them to pink. The cake was white because chocolate stains. Twelve candles. It smelled like almond, not vanilla." Her gaze slides past me. "The music box skipped on the fourth beat, but Miss Lillian kept smiling so we didn't fix it."

"What did the girl do?"

"She blew the candles. She tried to wish for thirteen." Nora's mouth flattens. "That never works."

"What did she wish for instead?" I ask even though I doubt she'll answer. Wishes are secrets carried in the wind.

Nora's eyes soften briefly. "To go home."

I hide my surprise. "Did she?"

"Guests don't stay," Nora says.

That's not quite an answer.

"Do you like the song?" I ask.

Nora tilts her head as if listening down a hallway. Then she hums "Happy Birthday" very softly. On the fourth note, she stretches it, exactly as Priya had. On the sixth, she lifts it a half-step too high, and in the last phrase, she inserts an extra breath, the tiniest hiccup before *dear*.

I keep my hands folded in my lap. Inside, my body is vibrating, but I'm not sure why. "Why that version?"

Nora looks at me, unblinking. "That's how the box plays it."

"Boxes don't choose songs."

"People do," Nora agrees with the smallest smile, "and sometimes people become boxes."

Lillian drifts in like a cloud. "Is that all, Detective? Nora has therapy in ten minutes."

"Almost." I keep my gaze on Nora. "What does twelve mean to you?"

Nora's composure slips for a moment. "The last good year for some of us."

"For Miss Lillian?"

Nora shifts for the first time. "For everyone who didn't make it to thirteen."

The room cools almost immediately.

"Did you like your last birthday?" I ask very gently.

Nora's lashes lower. "I turned fourteen," she says, confirming her age, "but I blew out twelve candles."

Just like everyone else.

"What did you wish for?"

Nora's mouth opens and closes. When she speaks, her voice is thinner. "To forget."

If only it were that easy.

"Did it work?" I ask.

Nora's eyes lift to mine, and for one bare second, the practiced calm falls away. "No."

Lillian's hand cups Nora's shoulder. "Thank you, sweetheart."

Nora stands. "You should check the attic window," she whispers. "Sometimes the breeze moves the streamers even when the hatch is closed."

"Why would it be closed?"

"So the candles don't go out," Nora says before leaving.

Lillian waits a beat. "You're making them nervous." Her words, laced with a mixture of anxiety and disapproval, don't affect me.

"They're already nervous," I tell her. "Your rituals are precision machines, but machines don't care who they cut."

Lillian fixes me with a steely gaze. "You think you've found cruelty because the song is off?"

"I think I've found a room that's been used too many times to keep pretending it's therapy," I say, "and I think one of your girls knows how to tune a music box whether you want her to or not."

"That's quite a conclusion."

Outside, wind scrapes the birch leaves together like paper. From somewhere above, too faint to be a coincidence, too deliberate to be a draft, I hear the music box tick four notes — one long, one high — and stop.

"I have a few more questions, if you don't mind."

CHAPTER 3: THE MOTHER'S HANDS

Lillian Whitcomb's hands tell me more than her words do.

She keeps them busy. Earlier, she fiddled with her desk, cleaning up files, obscuring names on folders she didn't want me to see. Now, she's pouring tea, straightening the edges of her sweater, and smoothing the invisible wrinkles in her linen dress. They're slender and pale, but her knuckles are thick, as if they've gripped too hard for too long.

"You've met Nora," she says, like we've just shared polite introductions at a garden party and aren't inside a locked retreat where every girl pretends to be twelve.

"Yes," I say. "She's . . . memorable."

A small smile tugs at her lips. "She's one of my successes. When she arrived, she wouldn't speak for days."

"Now she hums the birthday song."

Lillian's gaze flickers. Her hands still for exactly one second before folding neatly in her lap. "Music is therapeutic."

"Music can also be a trigger."

She leans back in her chair and crosses one ankle over the other. "You hear what you want to hear, Detective Amber."

She's not wrong. I've built my career on it.

We move from the sitting room to her office, tucked behind the library on the main floor. The windows are open, letting in the birch-scented air. There's a faint layer of dust on the sill, but the furniture gleams. Everything in here is just imperfect enough to look lived-in, but it's a set, and Lillian is the stage manager.

"Tell me more about the birthdays," I say.

"Re-storying," she corrects gently. "We give the girls a safer twelfth birthday than the one they remember."

I flip open my notebook. "What happened at their real twelfth birthdays that they need this re-storying?"

Her eyes sharpen. "What happens to anyone's real twelfth birthday, Detective? Puberty, uncertainty, loss . . ." She waves one hand, airy and dismissive. "We can't stop life, but we can rewrite it."

I let the silence stretch. Most people rush to fill it. Lillian just folds her hands again. The skin around her nails is too pink, like she's been scrubbing them with something stronger than soap.

"Where did you learn this technique?" I ask.

"It came to me . . . after Liam died." She gestures toward a framed photograph on her desk. The same boy from the hallway pictures — Liam, frozen at twelve. In this shot, his hair is longer, curling into his eyes. He's holding a cake with crooked candles and looking up at someone out of frame.

"Your son," I say.

"My everything."

"How did he die?"

The question lands like a coin dropped in still water. Her mouth moves, but the answer is not the one I expected.

"He drowned," she says finally. "Lake at our summer home. I wasn't there."

Her hands tremble. She reaches for her tea, maybe an attempt to cover the movement with a sip.

"Was it his birthday?" I ask.

Her gaze meets mine, steady and dry. "It was going to be."

That explains the room. The cake. The candles. The rituals that never let a girl age past twelve.

"Do you ever run these birthdays for boys?"

Her eyes shutter, blocking me out. "Girls need it more."

I shift gears. "Do you keep all your records downstairs?"

"Of course," she says, curiosity piqued by my question. "But I've already shown you Nora's file."

I give her a slight smile, the kind that says I know you're hiding something. "I'd like to see the rest of them." It's a huge ask, and I'm fully expecting her to fight me on this.

"That's not possible."

"It is," I say. "You just don't want me to."

She exhales slowly. "Do you have a warrant?"

"I will get one." It's a promise, not a warning.

Her hands curl around the armrests now, white at the knuckles. "Then I can't help you."

"Not true." I lean forward. "You've already helped me. More than you probably intended. I know these girls aren't here for therapy. I know your rituals are rehearsed. I know Nora's been in that room more than once and not always as the guest of honor."

Lillian's smile returns, brittle and precise. "You think you've uncovered something dark, but you'll see, Detective. The ritual is love. Sometimes love is the only thing that keeps them alive."

Her words crawl under my skin. "Keeping them alive isn't the same as keeping them safe."

Lillian purses her lips. We both know we're done here.

I stand, thank her, and step out into the hall. My eyes drift to the staircase, to the family photos, to Liam's frozen smile. Twelve forever.

As I reach the front door, movement catches my eye — a hand withdrawing from behind the library curtains. Small, pale, a flash of pink nail polish.

Nora.

She's been listening.

She heard everything.

CHAPTER 4: THE CANDLE
THAT WON'T GO OUT

The warrant's still hours away, but something about that place has been needling me, and I can't let it go. If I wait any longer, Lillian will have all the time she needs to strip it clean.

It's dark, and the gravel drive crunches under my boots, loud in the quiet. The retreat looks softer now, moonlight washing the yellow siding to silver, the porch sagging into shadow. The house is void of any lights.

I head to the back door, which, surprisingly, is unlocked.

Inside, the smell hits me with a punch. Bleach, along with the smell of something rotten. I lift my shirt neckline to cover my nose for only a moment as I head toward the back set of stairs I'd noticed earlier.

The steps groan under my weight. Each step feels like it's broadcasting my presence to every corner of the house.

At the second-floor landing, I pause. The hatch to the room above is already open.

I climb.

The attic is exactly as I saw it earlier — sagging streamers, paper plates on the long table, the glass stand holding the white cake with its two neat rows of six candles.

But there's something new.

One candle is lit.

The flame dances lazily in the still air, except there's no breeze to feed it.

Crossing the room slowly, I shine my light along the floor, watching for tripwires and cameras. My boots crunch faintly on the glitter. The candle's burned halfway, wax pooling at the base, but the flame doesn't shrink.

It's warm in here — too warm.

Circling the table, my eyes scan the baseboards. Just past the corner chair, where the wall meets the floor, is a seam. The narrow, hair-thin line looks like the outline of a door that doesn't belong.

I crouch and run my fingers along it. The seam's cold. My nails find a shallow groove, just enough to pull, and the panel shifts with a low creak.

A dark space yawns beyond, the smell stronger now — wax, sweat, fear. I shine my light inside.

It's a crawl space just tall enough for someone to crouch. I shine my light and realize the walls are covered in scratches, numbers etched in jagged lines — twelve, twelve, twelve, twelve over and over. There must be hundreds of them. In the far corner, a storage trunk sits under a sheet.

Crouched, I enter and I pull the sheet away and open the trunk. Inside are hair ribbons, party hats, paper plates, and melted candle stubs. Each item is tagged with a name and a date. The earliest is over twenty years old. The most recent is dated yesterday.

There's a small Polaroid of Nora tucked at the bottom. She's wearing the same clothes she had on this morning, standing in front of the cake. She's almost smiling. Her hands are clenched in her lap. The caption in neat handwriting reads: *NORA — fourteenth birthday*.

Fourteen.

I hear a sound then. Not from behind me. From inside the crawl space. A small, ragged breath.

I sweep the flashlight across the wall.

A vent. It's too small for anyone to get through.

But behind it are eyes. Wide and unblinking.

The voice is barely a whisper. "Don't blow them out."

The eyes, the voice, they are gone. Did I imagine it? A chill runs over my body, and as I back away, the hair on my neck rises. My instincts are screaming at me to leave, but I force one more sweep with the light.

On the wall above the vent, written in thick, waxy red letters, are three words.

MAKE A WISH.

CHAPTER 5: MAKE A WISH

I don't remember climbing down the ladder. The music starts again before I even reach the stairs, faint at first, then clear enough that I hear the long fourth note, the high sixth, the breath before *dear*.

It's coming from the parlor.

I follow the sound, curious as to why the music box is playing from the parlor after just seeing it upstairs in the attic. I need to leave. I should leave before anyone sees me, but the pull to know more is too strong. I check my phone, hoping, praying, the warrant has come through, and sure enough, there's the email.

The parlor door is partially open. Lillian stands by the fireplace, lighting a match. Twelve candles glow on a cake perched on a pedestal in the middle of the room. Nora sits cross-legged in front of it, her hands folded neatly in her lap, her eyes fixed on the flames.

"You're up late, Detective," Lillian says without turning. She doesn't sound surprised that I'm there.

"So are you." I step into the room, my hand near my holstered gun. "We need to talk about the attic."

Lillian glances at me, her eyes calm, the match burning low before she drops it in a dish. "You've already seen it. I've already explained what it's used for."

"Sure. You host the birthday parties up there. I'm more interested in the crawl space."

Nora's gaze flicks to mine.

Lillian folds her hands, mirroring Nora. "The girls need a safe twelfth birthday, Detective. You saw the files earlier. You read Nora's. Every file has a similar story. They're here for help."

"Helping them means locking them in the walls?"

"They're not locked," she says, her voice sharp enough to slice. "They're *kept* safe. The twelfth is a year they can return to when the world wants to push them forward before they're ready."

"That's not safety," I say, doing my absolute best not to lose it on her. "That's control."

Her mouth curves. "And what's police work if not control? You keep the bad things out. I keep the bad years out. We're not so different."

I step closer to Nora. "Is that what you want? To stay twelve forever?"

Her lips press together. She doesn't answer.

"Nora," I say softly, "I found the Polaroid. You were fourteen."

Her shoulders tighten like a wire pulled too far. "She said if I blew twelve again, I could forget."

"And did you?"

Her eyes lift to mine. She doesn't blink. "No," she finally whispers.

Lillian's voice slices between us. "She doesn't need your pity, Detective. She's had enough broken promises."

I turn to her fully now. Earlier, in her office, I'd seen a name written on a folder Lillian had tried to hide from me. "What happened to Samantha Leary?"

Lillian's gaze stays steady. "She made her wish."

"What was it?"

A pause. "To go home."

I am really hating these non-answers. "And you kept her here instead."

"I gave her a home."

My pulse hammers. "Where is she now?"

The air shifts.

"She's still here," Nora says.

The candle flames dance in a draft that shouldn't exist. I feel it too, cool and deliberate, curling around my ankles.

Lillian doesn't move to stop me when I cross to the wall. She only watches, her hands clasped tighter now, knuckles whitening.

I bang my palm flat against the plaster. There's a hollow thud.

I turn back to Nora. "Tell me."

She stands, her eyes glassy but her voice steady. "You blow twelve. You make a wish, and if you wish to stay, you get kept."

"And if you wish to leave?"

Her gaze drops to the cake. The candle flames shiver.

"You go in the walls," she says.

CHAPTER 6: THIRTEEN

I call it in.

While the operator confirms the warrant updates, I stay in the parlor and refuse to look at the cake. The twelve flames hiss softly, alive, breathing.

Lillian watches me with that serene therapist face that always reads like a dare. Nora stands behind her chair, her hands clasped, her eyes fixed on the carpet.

"Officers are en route," the dispatcher says. "Hold scene."

"Copy." I hang up.

"Detective?" Lillian folds her hands in her lap. "May I tell you what this looks like from my side of the couch?"

"No." I edge around the table until I'm between her and the door. "You can tell it to your attorney."

"Birthdays were safe in my house," she says anyway, her voice almost soft, "even when nothing else was. My son knew he could make a wish once a year and be heard. That's all I gave these girls — a place to be heard."

"You gave them a script," I say, "and then punished them for forgetting their lines."

Nora lifts her head, a small movement that makes the room tilt. "Miss Lillian doesn't punish," she says.

"Doesn't she?" I look at Nora. "Because I didn't write 'make a wish' in wax above a vent, and I didn't scratch twelve into a crawl space wall a hundred times."

Nora's gaze skitters across the room and lands on the music box on the mantel, an identical twin to the one upstairs. It's painted with the same cheerful script that makes my teeth grind. She doesn't reach for it, but I see the impulse ladder up the tendons in her neck.

Lillian's voice lands like a velvet paperweight. "Nora, sweetheart, would you like to go to your room?"

"No," I say. "She stays."

Sirens arrive as a faraway ribbon of noise and grow into something more immediate. Tires on gravel. Radio crackle. The house inhales.

I open the parlor door.

Uniforms sweep the foyer. Officer Valdez leads, her eyes scanning, her mouth set. She nods to me, sees the cake, but doesn't look long. Some details are splinters. You learn not to grab them head-on.

"Attic and basement," I say. "Crawl space off the birthday room. Another in the storm cellar."

Valdez posts two at the front door, one at the stairs, and one with me. Lillian sits very still while we talk around her like she's furniture. Nora does the same.

"Amber?" Valdez lowers her voice. "You want to move them out of here while we clear?"

"No," I say. "I want them to hear it."

"*It* being . . ."

"Proof."

I don't let myself say bodies. That word gets inside your lungs. We climb. The second-floor landing creaks under our weight.

Inside, the room looks the same — sagging streamers, plates, and glitter grit — but the candle that was burning earlier is gone. In its place, a tiny crater of wax looks like an empty eye.

"Here," I say, crouching by the baseboard seam.

Valdez kneels beside me. I slide my fingers into the shallow groove and pull. The panel opens.

Lights sweep the crawl space. The wall comes alive with numbers — twelve, twelve, twelve — etched until the paint surrendered. The trunk sits under its sheet. Valdez flips it open, and we observe ribbons, hats, wax, and the tagged names like toe tags that never found bodies.

"Jesus," she whispers.

"Keep going."

I stand and swing my light to the far corner, where the vent lives like a little mouth. The grid is rusty. The screws are old but not frozen. Someone has turned them before.

I unscrew the vent and place the grate aside. The breath that comes out of the dark is cool, damp, and deliberate.

"Nora?" I call out, knowing she can hear me. "Do you know what's behind this?"

She doesn't answer from the ladder, but I hear the faint sound of bare feet on wood. She's come up.

I don't turn. My light is a straight line into black.

"Hello?" I call into the vent.

Three knocks. A pause. One more knock.

The vent answers. Sometimes, houses play along. Or it could be the wind.

Valdez exhales something that could be relief or dread.

I hear a sound behind me. Both Lillian and Nora are standing there, Lillian's arm around Nora's shoulder.

Lillian says nothing. Her silence feels like a choice she made years ago.

I slide my hand into the void and feel brick within arm's reach, then air, then something low and rough like a beam. The space isn't deep, but it's somehow wrong. It has been built by someone who didn't believe in straight lines.

"Gimme the pry bar," I say.

Valdez hands it over. I work the edge into the seam. The wall shakes, and the beam groans, resists, and then yields. Something flakes across my wrist — white dust or old paint or a thousand birthday wishes ground to powder.

The final panel gives way with a sound like a rib cracking.

I lift it free.

Behind it is a cavity the size of a coffin. There's a mattress, a bowl, and a ribbon tied to a nail. I smell wax and something copper.

And there's a handprint on the floor. Small, from a child, pressed into the soot of a melted candle.

Valdez angles her flashlight. "Christ. You think—"

"Look," I say.

The wall bears new scratches, fresh enough that the edges are still sharp. Not just twelves this time. Letters. Three near the vent, a struggle of curves and lines, two on the other side.

S L E then *E P.*

SLEEP.

No. Not sleep.

I blink twice, and the word fixes itself, as if the room had to decide what it meant.

KEEP.

"Detective?" Valdez is behind me now, voice careful. "We're going to need to seal this so we can investigate."

Lillian's voice interrupts in a register I haven't heard yet. "Stop."

Valdez looks over her shoulder, clearly surprised.

Lillian presses one hand to her stomach like she's holding something in. Her face has dropped its polish.

"You shouldn't open it anymore," she says. "It doesn't like drafts."

My skin knows fear better than my brain, and every nerve stands. I keep my flashlight steady.

"It?" I ask.

"The wish," she says. The word isn't ridiculous in her mouth. "If they wish to stay, we keep them. If they wish to go . . ." She nods toward the wall. ". . . they go."

"They go where?" Valdez demands.

"Into the walls," Nora answers, looking small, her young body unnaturally still. "That's how you leave."

I don't realize I'm moving until I'm beside her, my hand on her shoulder, my voice as soft as I can make it. "Nora, did you ever put someone in here?"

Her mouth opens and then closes.

Rule Three unfurls in my chest like a reminder: I have to ask the right question, the right way, at the wrong time.

"Tell the truth," I say. "Not what you were told. What you remember."

Nora's chin trembles, and she glances at Lillian. Lillian looks at me and says nothing. That silence cuts this room into before and after.

"I locked the second door," Nora whispers.

A beat where silence reigns. I look to Valdez, unsure if she heard the same thing I just did.

"What second door?" Valdez asks after giving me a brief nod.

Nora points at the far wall of the crawl space, where my light hasn't touched yet. I sweep the beam of my flashlight. There's a seam so faint that anyone would miss it if you weren't looking for it. It's in the ceiling.

"Get me the short ladder," I say to Valdez. We then position it under the crawl space, and I climb up.

We wedge a panel loose and stick my light into the area, shining it around. Cold air spills over my face as I pull myself up. The area is a coffin-sized cavity. Ahead of me, there's a hole. I make my way over there, careful to stay on the wood beams, and find a shaft that drops three feet into a horizontal run between the walls.

I return to the opening and drop back down. "What did you do, Nora?" I ask, wiping my hands of the dust and cobwebs.

Her voice is small, but exact. "She kept choosing other girls. I told her that if I stayed twelve for her, would she stop? She didn't. So I . . ." She swallows and drops her gaze. "I turned the lock and took the key, and I put it in the cake where the candles go. I thought if no one could open it, no one would go in anymore."

A cold flare runs along my ribs, one that pulses with anger. "And did she stop?" It takes everything in me not to look toward Lillian. I notice Valdez moves closer to the woman, however.

Nora nods once. "For a while."

"Who was in there when you locked it?"

Nora's breath fogs the ladder rung. "Samantha," she says.

The name finally takes full shape in this house.

Valdez covers her mouth.

Lillian leans against the wall, and for one honest second, the grief is human and unperformed. Then, it's gone.

"Get the crime scene up here," I tell Valdez. "And keep someone on her." I point toward Lillian, unable to look her in the face.

It's hard to wait for the team to come in and take over. Even harder to wait until we have proof. But eventually, someone comes my way holding on to something frail and delicate in their gloved hand. It's a chain. At the end is a locket clogged with wax. I'm handed a small knife and manage to open the clasp.

Inside is a water-damaged photo of a girl with braces and a gap between her front teeth. I don't need the initials to know who it belongs to. On the back are the initials *S.L.*

I return to the parlor where Lillian and Nora sit. Nora's face pales when she sees me. I hold the locket up. "Recognize this?"

I ask the question to Lillian, but I'm watching Nora. She glances over at the woman, and if I've ever wondered whether love and harm can live in the same body, I don't now.

They can. They have. They do.

"Miss Lillian?" Nora asks, her voice almost empty.

Lillian nods once. She doesn't say anything, but she doesn't have to.

"Cuff her," I tell Valdez.

Lillian doesn't resist. When the metal clicks, she exhales, like she's been waiting for the nightmare she created to end, and now it finally has.

I take out another item I was given upstairs, a small music box with *S.L.* scratched into the wood, and set it on the coffee table. I wind it once, then twice. The song stumbles where it always stumbles, but on the fourth note, I tap the comb with my pen, and it shifts a hair's width. The next phrase comes clean.

"Boxes don't choose songs," I say, mostly to myself. "People do."

Nora watches my hands. "Will you change it back?" she asks.

"No," I say. "We're done playing it that way."

Valdez takes custody of the music boxes. She bags and tags them. Officers move Lillian to the cruiser.

I walk Nora to the porch. The night air has that clean after-rain smell, like you could be forgiven for anything if you ask right now.

"You did a terrible thing for a reason that made sense to you," I tell her. "That's not the same as being safe. It's not the same as being free."

"Will she come back?" Nora asks.

"Who?"

"The wish."

I don't say anything at first. She's not just talking about the girl she locked away, the one dead in the crawl space, the body the crew upstairs is waiting to remove, once Nora is out of the way. She's talking about herself, too, the girl she used to be.

"Maybe," I admit, deciding to focus on her real question. "When she does, we'll listen to what she really is. Not what someone told her to be."

Nora nods like she's adding that to a rulebook no one sees.

CHAPTER 7: THE THIRTEENTH CANDLE

A week later, the house is a crime scene with a padlock and an orange notice. The county has an opinion about what to do with it. I don't. I stand on the sidewalk and watch my breath in the early cold.

Valdez texts me a photo from evidence of wax with a fingerprint. Not Lillian's. Not Nora's. Unmatched for now.

On a Tuesday, a package arrives at the department, addressed to me, wrapped in brown paper with no return address. It's light as a secret. Inside is a single birthday candle burned down to the nub, the wick stained black, the wax soft. There's also a note in small, neat handwriting.

Wish granted. Try thirteen.

Rule Two holds, like it always does. *Victims remember the details they were told to forget.*

And sometimes, the house remembers, too.

The End

3.
THE GIRL BENEATH THE GLASS

RULE #3

Trust is currency — and everyone's for sale eventually.

What they don't say is worth twice as much as what they do.

CHAPTER 1: THE CONSERVATORY BLEEDS GLASS

The call comes in just after dawn when the sky is still stained with the pale pink of sleep.

I haven't had coffee yet, not that I need it to wake up. All that took was two words from the dispatcher during the call to jolt my heart awake.

"Glass conservatory."

A beautiful estate high up in the hills north of town, it was once a home for adolescent teenagers and is now a trauma recovery center. That place haunts my nightmares.

According to the dispatcher, a local renovation team found bones in a crawl space beneath the floor in the glass conservatory.

I pull up to the estate twenty minutes later. The property looms like something out of a forgotten fairy tale, its white pillars flanking the entrance. Most of the estate has been well looked after, refurbished over the years, but the conservatory reminds me of an eerie skeleton, its curved metal beams reaching skyward like twisted fingers. Thick vines claw up its sides, curling through gaps with glassless windows. Even in the early daylight, the place swallows sound. No birdsong. No insects. Just a hush that presses in too close.

"Detective Amber." Officer Nina Valdez waves me over from the tape line. "You're going to want to see this for yourself."

I duck under the yellow tape and follow Valdez into the ruins of the conservatory. The scent hits me first — damp, musty earth. It's the kind of smell that only exists when something has been sealed for far too long.

The first thing I notice is the floor. 'It's caved inward near the center. It's not fully collapsed but broken in a jagged starburst, almost like it was by design. Tools and shattered boards lie scattered around the perimeter where construction obviously abruptly stopped.

"Tell me what I'm looking at," I say to Valdez.

"The conservatory has been closed for a number of years, as you know. Thanks to . . ." She glances at the notebook in her hand. ". . . a private funder, which has yet to be disclosed to us. They started to restore the place. A local crew were the lucky ones to find, well, that." She gestures toward the hole.

I look around, but I don't see anything. No body bags. No tarped covering a large mound. "Where's the body?"

Valdez points to the hole. "Under there. The renovation crew dropped a beam straight through the floor. Cracked the ceiling of a chamber beneath." She pauses. "It wasn't on the original blueprints."

I kneel at the edge and peer down. The crawl space isn't empty. There's a single room with a low ceiling. White tile walls have been stained with time. In the center, slumped against the wall, is a woman's skeleton. Long hair still clings to the skull.

I squint, catching light reflections on the floor. "Is that . . . a mirror?"

"Looks like a one-way pane. From down there, it just reflects, but from up here . . . you could watch everything."

My skin chills. A hidden room with mirrored glass. A viewing chamber. Someone built this deliberately.

"Any ID?" I ask.

Valdez hesitates. "Not on the body, but . . ."

She hands over a clear evidence bag. Inside is a faded photograph, its edges water-damaged and curled with age. A face stares back — sharp eyes, dark hair, and young.

I can't help but gasp, surprised by the name written in black ink.

Hannah Vale.

I turn the photograph over and look at Valdez. "That's not Hannah Vale."

Valdez shakes her head. "Correct. We're not sure who that is in the photograph. The photo was dropped off this morning at the precinct. It was left at the front desk in an envelope with your name on it."

With my name on it? That doesn't make any sense.

"By who?" I ask.

Valdez shrugs. "No ID. No return address. Just the photo and your name."

A boulder drops in my heart as I turn the photograph over and stare at Hannah's name. I think back to the Dahl case with the creepy dolls. There was a notebook, and on the last page was a list of names. Some were victims with their names crossed out. Others . . . perhaps they were intended victims? My name was on there. As was Hannah Vale's.

Since then, I've looked up Hannah Vale. She had been declared missing, and I've made it my goal to find out what happened to her.

Apparently, someone has decided to help me. Maybe they don't think I'm looking hard enough or fast enough.

A breeze shifts through the ruins, scattering dried petals and dust across the tile.

There's a thin rusted cot in the corner, a single dirty tennis shoe off to the side, and a drawing taped to the tile wall, half-erased by moisture.

It isn't just a hiding place.

It's a prison.

Valdez clears her throat. "Amber, there's something else." She hands me an evidence bag containing a piece of torn cloth — pale blue silk threaded with lace. "This was found clutched in the skeleton's hand."

Something in the back of my memory stirs as I look at the cloth. There's a monogram stitched in faded pink on one corner — *S.B.*

Furiously, I go through my mental file folders and try to place the initials with a name. It doesn't take me long to realize what S.B. stands for.

Sara Beckett.

That doesn't make sense. Sara Beckett's body was already found and identified.

But if Sara died down here, then what exactly had the coroner signed off on a decade ago? And why or how had someone linked Hannah Vale to this after all this time?

My mind is already racing, but I know one thing.

The answers are down there.

Beneath the glass.

Still waiting to be found.

CHAPTER 2: THE GIRL WHO VANISHED TWICE

When I return to my vehicle, I find a folded note sitting on the passenger seat. My name is written on the top, and a time and location on the inside.

So here I sit, at an old greenhouse café on the edge of town, all creeping vines and warped glass. Half the tables are empty. The other half is full of people staring deep into their mugs.

Except for one person. She gives me a hint of a smile as I walk toward her.

Hannah Vale.

No longer missing, good to know.

Her fingers are wrapped around a chipped teacup, and she doesn't say anything until I join her at the table. She pours some tea into a waiting cup for me and then sighs.

"You left a photograph for me," I say.

Hannah's face is unreadable. Her dark eyes are hollow around the edges but alert. Too alert. What has this woman been through?

"I wanted to make sure it got to the right person," she says. "Did it help?"

"It raised more questions than answers," I say, deciding to be honest. She left it for a reason, and I need to know why. "I don't believe we've met before, but you knew my name?"

"Oh, we've met. You've just forgotten." Hannah sips her tea. "You also stopped looking."

I wrap my palms around the teacup, enjoying its warmth as it seeps into my skin. "You'll need to be clearer than that."

She nods. "I know. I was sixteen. You came to the group home." She pauses, giving me time to remember.

"I've visited a lot of group homes," I tell her.

"Big Mama met you at the door."

I blink, and the memory hits me.

"I was in the hallway," Hannah continues. "You looked right through me."

"I'm sorry I didn't notice you."

She shrugs. "You were there because of Sara," Hannah says, almost whispering.

I pull my notebook from my jacket pocket and set it down on the table. "What happened to her?"

"She went missing." Hannah's voice is flat. "And then someone made her disappear again."

I lean in. Something tells me there's more to be told, and if I want to hear it, I need to pay careful attention.

"Did you know you were declared missing?"

Hannah nods. "Prefer to keep it that way too, if you don't mind."

I tighten my lips. "Why now, Hannah? Why bring this back after ten years?" I ask.

"Because someone rebuilt the floor." Hannah stares out through the café's fogged glass. "Someone tried to seal her in again, and I couldn't let that happen."

"You knew the room was there," I say slowly, trying to figure this out.

"We all knew."

That earns my silence.

Hannah draws little circles with her finger on the table as she continues to stare out the window. "We weren't supposed to go near it. They said it was part of the foundation, but I heard things and saw things through the cracks in the glass. Sara was in there long before she vanished. When they said she ran away . . . I knew they were lying."

I let that sink in before I reach for my pen. "Who's 'they'?"

Hannah's gaze flicks back to me. "You need to prove yourself first." There's a hardness in her voice I immediately recognize. She's been betrayed too many times in the past.

"Then why come to me at all?"

"Because you're the only one who wrote her name down," Hannah says. "The only one who cared for more than a minute, and I thought maybe, just maybe, you'd still want the truth."

My jaw tightens as I push the words I want to say away. "If you knew, then why didn't you report it years ago?"

"I was sixteen. No one listens to girls like me."

The silence between us thickens.

Hannah pulls something from her coat pocket. A folded square of yellowed paper. She slides it across the table.

It's a sketch of the room beneath the conservatory. It's crude but accurate. It has the mirror, the cot, the tile, and a girl in the corner curled up.

I turn it around. On the back, in small, shaky letters, is "We see her but we don't help her."

"Did you draw this?" I ask.

"No," Hannah says, her voice small. "Sara did. She hid it. I kept it."

I take another sip of my tea. "You're saying Sara knew she was being watched?"

Hannah nods slowly. "She told me once that the mirror talked to her at night."

A waitress stops by and asks if we'd like more hot water. Neither one of us replies.

"Help me," I say once the waitress is gone. "Help me find out who did this."

Hannah gives a hollow laugh. "You think this ends with a name? It doesn't. You'll find records missing. Interviews erased. Dead ends paved over with fake smiles."

"Try me."

Another beat of silence.

Hannah rises. "I'll call you when I'm ready." She starts to walk away, but pauses. "You asked me why now," her voice a ghost of a whisper. "Because I saw the papers. That photo you held at the press conference last year, the one of the girl in the yellow jacket?"

I freeze.

"She had Sara's eyes."

Then Hannah is gone, and she leaves behind a sketch, a ghost, and the sudden, suffocating weight of everything I missed ten years ago.

CHAPTER 3: THE BURIED CASE

Something is wrong. These files, the ones for Sara Beckett, they're not what I remember.

Later that afternoon, I'm sitting in the records room at headquarters, my shoulders pressed against the metal shelf behind me, legs curled tight beneath the battered desk that still bears a gouge from some long-ago evidence chain mishap. The fluorescent lights over my head are doing their usual stuttering waltz with darkness, occasionally blinking out entirely only to gasp back alive and flicker with renewed desperation.

The folder in front of me is slim, too slim. I know at a glance because I remember the weight from when I worked the case ten years ago. The label is in my handwriting, all caps and no nonsense. *BECKETT, S.* The paper is yellowed, soft at the corners, and I flip it open with a flick of my thumb.

As I read, my blood pressure rises. My fury builds at the base of my skull, radiating out in a way that makes the world blur slightly around the edges of the page. The official report is too tidy.

Sara Beckett, age seventeen, ward of the state. Last seen outside the group home at dusk. Found three days later in a wooded area bordering the riverbank. Cause of death: accidental fall. No signs of trauma. No autopsy required.

That's not what I remember.

I can see her face when we found her, the dark lines on her arms, the crescent bruises that looked like the imprints of desperate fingers. I remember the shallow cut on her lip, barely scabbed, fresh.

None of it is in the file. Not a single mention.

The next section is interviews, and even these are sparse — the social worker who was babysitting the evening shift, the groundskeeper who was trimming hedges and 'didn't see or hear anything unusual,' and a single fellow resident, one Ivy Markham, who describes Sara in three brisk sentences as 'nice, quiet, maybe a little weird.' There's no mention of anyone else, no suggestion that Sara had friends or enemies, no hint of context or depth.

I flip forward, back, but that's all there is. I distinctly remember there being so much more. What happened to it?

There's no mention of Hannah Vale. No record of anyone else living in the room next to Sara's, either.

"She said she was interviewed," I mumble softly.

I pick up my phone and call Officer Valdez. She answers on the first ring.

"Can you do me a favor?" I ask. "I need the intake roster from the Millridge Adolescent Home from ten years ago. A full resident list."

"You know that the name changed years ago, right? In fact, the home itself closed down, and they started a new adolescent trauma center. What are you looking for?"

"Not what — *who*. Ivy Markham. She's not the one I'm really looking for, but . . ."

There's a pause. "But if she's not in their records, there might be others missing as well."

I nod. I knew she'd get it. "I want to know what else has been buried, but we have to tread carefully."

I hang up and stare at the open file in front of me. One thing stands out — a scanned signature that stops me cold. Detective Marshal Hodge, I would know his handwriting anywhere, from the familiar slant of his aggressive capital letters and the way his "G" loops twice. My old supervisor, my mentor, always wore his perpetually coffee-stained tie and had a nicotine-yellowed mustache.

I remember exactly what he said when he pulled me off this case, his breath smelling of peppermint gum masking whiskey. "Let it go, Amber. That one's done."

Who gave him that order? And why does Hodge's handwriting seem shakier than I remember?

I close the folder with a soft thud and stand, my chair squeaking against the linoleum. Time to find someone who'll talk off the record, someone whose fear has had a decade to fade.

The precinct hallway smells like burnt coffee and industrial cleaner. I walk fast, my shoes clicking against the linoleum as I head for the one person who might still talk to me about Hodge.

Lena Ruiz works in Records now, but ten years ago, she was Hodge's admin. If anyone knows where he disappeared to after retirement, it's her.

I find her at her desk sorting through a stack of misfiled case numbers. She glances up when my shadow falls across her paperwork.

"Amber." Her voice is flat. "Heard you were digging in cold storage."

"Just doing some light reading." I lean against her desk. "You ever keep in touch with Hodge?"

Her fingers pause on a manila folder. "Why?"

"Old times."

Lena snorts. "You were never sentimental." She eyes me like she's deciding whether to throw me out. "He's got a cabin up near Pine Ridge. Fishing." She takes a piece of paper and writes something down before handing it to me. "He changed his number a few years back," she says.

"Thank you." I pocket the paper.

"Don't mention it. I mean that. The last thing I need is the old man bitching me out because I shared his number."

I give her a wave before climbing the stairs and leaving the building. The precinct parking lot is nearly empty when I step outside, the air thick. The damp cold seeps into my bones. My breath fogs in front of me as I dial. It rings four times before a familiar gravelly voice answers.

"Amber." Hodge doesn't sound surprised. "How'd you get this number?"

I lean against my car, the metal biting through my jacket. Hodge was never one for small talk, and honestly, neither am I, so I get right to the point. "We need to talk about Sara Beckett."

There's a long pause. I hear the click of a lighter and the slow exhale of smoke. "That case is dead and buried."

"Not anymore." I press my fingers against my eyelids until colors bloom. "The file's been sanitized. Hannah Vale's interview is missing. Your signature's on the closure."

Another drag of his cigarette. "Meet me at O'Malley's in an hour. Come alone."

The line goes dead before I can respond. Typical Hodge.

CHAPTER 4: THE MAN WHO
KNEW TOO MUCH

I step into O'Malley's, the door's bell jangling weakly against the low murmur of conversation and the clink of glasses. Light from stained bulbs washes over the worn wooden bar, and there's a tang of stale beer and fryer oil in the air. At the far end, Hodge perches on a cracked leather stool, his gaze locked on the flickering hockey game overhead. He's just as intense as he used to be on stakeouts.

Time hasn't been kind to him. An oxygen tank hisses softly at his side, and his hands tremble like leaves in a breeze, but those steel-gray eyes remain piercing. He spots me before I'm halfway to the bar.

"I knew it'd be you," he rasps, his voice rough as gravel.

I slide onto the next stool, the polished wood cool beneath my palm. "You heard about the greenhouse skeleton?"

"That's all they're talking about in here. You dragging in trouble again, Meri?"

The neon sign above the bar casts a crimson glow across my jacket as I pull it off. "You shelved a case."

He doesn't flinch.

"You buried a girl," I continue, softer now but sharp enough.

Hodge draws in a slow, rattled breath. "I didn't bury anyone."

I press on, my voice low. "You signed off on the Beckett report."

He bows his head. "I signed what they put in front of me."

"And you pulled me off that case. Told me to stop digging."

"Because I knew where you'd end up if you didn't."

A heavy silence settles, broken only by the distant roar of skates on ice from the TV. Finally, I ask, "What are you getting at?"

He exhales wearily. "That group home . . . it had backers. Private donors who wanted no fuss. One funded an experimental juvenile therapy wing. They needed compliant kids, kids nobody would miss."

"Like Sara," I whisper.

He nods, his eyes dark. "When she started vanishing for hours, they couldn't risk bad press. When she died, they made it look like an accident."

"And Hannah?"

He shakes his head. "Hannah got too close. I questioned her, but that never made it into the files."

I stand, anger and betrayal twisting through me. "You knew all this and did nothing."

"I was trying to protect you," he rasps. "You were green. You cared too much."

My fists clench. "You let them build those rooms, Hodge."

He closes his eyes. "I stopped asking questions they didn't want answered."

My voice falters. "She was a kid."

He meets my gaze, sorrow in his eyes. "So were you," he says softly. "You're still chasing ghosts, Meri. They don't like that."

I turn to go, my boots scraping the floor.

His voice follows me out. "Watch your back. If Hannah's come back into the light, you're on their radar again."

Once in my car, I yank my notebook free and flip to the blank page I've been too scared to fill. In deliberate strokes, I write:

Hannah Vale

I underline her name twice and scribble three questions:

What did she endure?
Who was watching Sara?
Why now?

My phone buzzes. A text from Valdez reads, *Ivy Markham died in 2019. Found hanging in her garage. Ruled a suicide.*
Was that all? I text back.
Found a missing person report two months before.
Who filed that report?
Hannah Vale.

CHAPTER 5: MIRROR GIRLS

The Rosehall Trauma Recovery sits on a bluff outside town, with white brick and windowless hallways. Inside is too quiet and too sterile.

The receptionist looks startled when I show my badge.

"I'm following up on an old death connected to a former patient," I say. "Sara Beckett. Admitted ten years ago. I need access to any existing records."

"I'm sorry," the receptionist says, visibly uncomfortable. "Our archives only go back five years. Anything from when it was the Millridge Adolescent Home was digitized . . . or is unavailable."

"What does that mean?"

"They were part of a legal dispute when the facility changed hands. Lots of files got sealed."

I raise an eyebrow. "You don't still have backups?"

A long pause. Then she says, "You'll need to speak to Dr. Amanda Rue."

Dr. Rue is soft-spoken and sharp-eyed. She's in her late fifties with a silver-streaked bun. Her posture says she's spent a lifetime being underestimated and has enjoyed it.

"I remember Sara," she says without hesitation. "And Hannah. And Ivy."

I blink, surprised that she volunteers the extra names without any nudging on my part. "You knew them?"

"I didn't work directly on the experimental cases, but I reviewed the internal reports. Sara was bright and a little volatile. She was one of the first candidates."

"For what?"

Rue hesitates. "Sensory mirror therapy."

I stiffen. "What does that mean?"

"They believed trauma could be reduced by forcing patients to confront their mirrored selves while isolated in a neutral space with minimal stimuli. The conservatory was built for that. It was originally just for observation."

Something in Dr. Rue's voice tells me she didn't approve of their methods of observation.

"But it became something else."

Rue nods grimly. "It became more of a means for punishment than observation and healing."

She gave me just enough to read between the lines. My stomach turns. "And no one stopped it?"

"It was monitored and approved. The rationale was emotional recalibration."

I lean forward. "How many girls?"

Rue frowns. "Three that I know of, but there were more. Sara, a girl named Tamara, and Mila Barrett."

I write the names down. "What happened to Tamara?"

"She died here. Suicide. It was quiet. Her file was sealed immediately."

"And Mila?"

Rue's eyes flick away. "She survived, but she was never the same."

"Is it possible to speak with her?"

"She left the state. Last I heard, she changed her name. She wanted to forget everything. I doubt she'll talk." She pauses. "I wouldn't."

"You say that, but they want to talk . . . when they think someone's actually listening."

She pulls out a thin, unlabeled folder. She hands it over without a word. Inside are copies of therapy logs, observational sketches, timestamps, and a page of notes scribbled in blue ink.

Subject 2 displays mirroring distress. Spoke to "the watcher" through the glass.
Subject cried when left in the room for longer than 3 hours.
Drew the observer's face. Not part of the stimulus.

A chill creeps over my skin. The drawing is paper-clipped to the last page — a narrow male face sketched in pencil.

"Who's this?"

Rue's voice is quiet. "That's not one of ours."

"Do you know who it is?"

"No," she says, "but I've seen him before. He was in the security logs just once. Logged in as an 'equipment repair technician.'"

I turn the drawing over. In the corner, scrawled in a different hand, is a number.

It's a case file ID that matches one I haven't seen in years, one forever etched in my brain.

It's a case from a rest stop for a missing girl. A truck was parked too long. No prints. No witnesses.

I don't remember the name of the girl, but I remember the man who was never caught. Andy Rawlings.

My pulse jumps. I finally have a face for the name I've been searching for all these years.

I carefully fold the drawing and tuck it into my jacket. "Thank you," I say to Rue, my voice trembling. I need to pull it together.

"I hope it helps."

I nod and walk out, the wind slapping my face as I step into the parking lot. I pull out the sketch one more time and memorize it. "I'll find you," I swear.

I don't care how long it takes, but I will find the man who kidnapped my sister.

My phone buzzes with a new text. No number. Just a photo of Sara. She's younger and smiling. Reflected faintly in the conservatory glass . . . is me.

I'm in the background, distant and unaware, in uniform. Ten years ago.

CHAPTER 6: THE ROOM
THAT DIDN'T EXIST

The conservatory has been emptied out. Police tape flaps in the crosswind, caught on broken glass and half-splintered wood like a last warning, but the rest is stripped bare. I hover on the threshold, memories of the last time prickling through me, then step into the glass carcass.

I can taste the horrors still sticky on the walls. The floor yawns open where Sara fell, the crater circled with a ring of soot and crumbled tile.

The sublevel is damp and tiled. The walls, yellowed over time, the lines between the tiles stained a hundred shades of bile.

I make for the cot first. The mattress is bare, rusted springs jutting out. Underneath, the floor is a constellation of burns. Cigarette, maybe, or matches. Some old, some fresh.

I recall the diagram from the autopsy reports — where the burns mapped onto Sara's arms, her calves, her back. How many of these marks belonged to her and how many to whoever came before?

I sweep the room, slower this time. I run my hand over the mirror wall, still intact though warped from the heat. On my side, it's just me, a thin ghost, but I know what's behind it — the observation room or what's left of it. I tap once, twice, and the echo bounces back like a heartbeat. The mirror is thick. Soundproof. Someone wanted privacy for their experiments.

But the mirror isn't the only thing off. I circle the room, tracing the edges with my flashlight, and stop at the far wall. There's a seam, a hairline crack running vertically through the tile. It's not a door. More like a panel cut precisely and camouflaged with grout.

I press my palm to it, and it shudders. There's a spring catch, maybe, or something behind it that doesn't want to be found.

My heart stutters. I take a breath and lean in, using my shoulder for leverage. The panel yields with a sigh and swings open.

Behind it is another smaller room. The ceiling is barely high enough for a person to stand upright. There's no cot, just four walls, a floor, and the stink of old rot. The light from my phone barely touches the corners. I edge forward, careful not to touch anything.

That's when I see her — folded into the farthest angle, knees to chest, arms wrapped tight around herself even in death. What's left of her is shrunken and brown, preserved by the lack of air and sun. Her hair is gone. Hospital scrubs, discolored and brittle, cling to her bones.

No one mentioned a second body. No one thought to check for more than one.

I take a picture, then another. My hands are shaking, and I can't stop them. Not from fear, exactly, but from the way it all fits so perfectly — the secret room, the hidden girl, the burns on the floor. This was never a treatment center. It was a test site, a maze, and someone designed it to keep its secrets even after the last scream faded.

Backing out of the chamber, I'm careful not to touch the remains and let the panel close itself again. Air rushes in behind me, thick and sour. I take a minute against the wall, trying to settle the tremor in my legs, then sweep the rest of the room for anything else. Evidence. Motive. A clue about who built this place and who the second girl was.

There's nothing, just the echo of my own breath, but as I head for the ladder, my foot catches on a tile that's raised a fraction of an inch. I crouch and press, and it rocks under my weight. I slide a fingernail into the gap and pull up. Beneath is a small metal box, the kind you would use for cash or keys. Or, in this case, a recorder. I pop the latch. It's old, analog, and covered in a patina of dust and ash.

I rewind the tape inside and hit play.

At first, there's just silence. Then, I hear static along with the whine and pop of a cheap microphone. There's a voice, older, male, clipped with authority. *"Begin session."* Footsteps. A chair dragging. Then, a soft female voice mumbling something I can't catch. She's crying. The man's voice is calm and impassive. *"You are here for your own safety."* More crying. *"If you want the light, you'll have to earn it."* The recorder whirs, and the session ends.

The next track is a scream — wet, animal, desperate. Then, silence.

I play the next. Female, again, but different. Empty, flattened. *"Please let me out,"* she says. *"I said I'm sorry."* Silence. *"Please."*

The man, patient as ever, says, *"This is part of the process. You'll be grateful when it's over."*

There's something in the way he says it, something final. I feel sick.

I fast forward. More sessions, more screams.

In one, the female whispers, *"He's not supposed to be here. He watches from the window when they're gone."* Pause. *"He's not like them."*

The man sighs. *"You're safer with me than with him."* Then a crash, the sound of fists on metal, the recorder skittering across the floor, and then nothing. The tape ends.

I sit back, the box heavy in my hands. How many girls disappeared into this place, how many ended up like the one in the alcove, how many walked out and never spoke again? I take one last look at the now closed, seamless panel and the mirror, both sides of the story sealed off from each other. Then, I go to the ladder and climb out, my hands shaking the whole way.

CHAPTER 7: THE PAST

I need to contact Valdez, but there's no reception down here. Halfway up the steps, I pause. A thought, stubborn like a splinter, just won't let go. The room, the skeleton, the cot . . .

The cot.

I didn't check beneath it.

I retrace my steps, my shoes skidding on the dusty linoleum, and kneel by the rotting mattress. My flashlight throws shadows that skitter like insects. The light reveals a tangle of cobwebs, a chipped doll's shoe, and, pressed tight between cold steel and damp wall, something thin and rectangular, barely visible in the beam.

I reach in, my fingertips barely brushing against what's hidden. I gently pull it out and hold it gingerly. It's a photograph, yellowed with neglect, edges scalloped and torn, one corner looking like it's been nibbled on. The surface is warped, but the image is clear. Three girls, rigid and formal in summer gowns, stand in the hard winter sun. Sara is on the left with her angled jaw, unruly hair, and a smidge of shadow beneath her eye. Her smile sits on her face like a question, uneasy and unsure.

I don't recognize the other two girls. Their features are slightly blurred, like a thumb has rubbed against the face over and over. The girl in the middle stands slightly taller than the others. The third girl . . . she's the mummified victim I found.

There's a hint of mischief in her eyes that tells me she was a fighter. She leans toward Sara, her arm draped behind her in an embrace that seems more staged than sincere. There is no warmth in the contact, only the compliance of children who have learned obedience from necessity.

It is not the girls that draw my gaze, though, but what's in the background.

My stomach rolls, churns, and heaves as I rock back on my heels.

A man looms just inside the frame. He is dressed in the drab uniform of a groundskeeper or maybe a night warden, clipboard clutched to his chest, cap tilted to shadow his eyes. He appears to be directing the girls, his attention focused on something just beyond the lens. The photographer? The next pose? Another girl? His face is turned, but the nose is a beak, the jaw too square, the profile unmistakable.

Andy Rawlings.

That's twice now, and I don't believe in coincidences. What is he doing here? He's a truck driver. Everything I've ever found on him insists he's always only been a truck driver, so why is he here in that uniform?

My hand trembles, and the photo rattles. I press it flat against my palm, the paper thin as a scab. I flip it over on instinct. In the upper margin is a date: *June 12, 1995*. Beneath it, in a hand that is precise but oddly childish, three names. *Sara. L. Tessa.*

Tessa must be the first victim we found.

I pull out an evidence bag from my pocket and secure the photograph, but something about the scene doesn't sit right. I scan the floor, tiled, old, and warped by damp, and then spot a rusty streak arcing from the headboard to the wall, long dried but recent enough to suggest a struggle. The mattress is torn at the edge. I wedge my fingers in and pull. Something gives, and a thin trickle of debris spills out.

An item tumbles free — a tape cassette, label faded and half-peeled, the ink bled into anonymity. My heart sinks.

I turn it over, searching for a marking, a word, a name. There's only a crude smiley face drawn in blue ballpoint and the date, just a week after the photo. *6/20/95.*

I pocket the tape, knowing whatever is on here isn't good.

A shudder runs through the conservatory, just a draft or a settling of ancient beams, but it feels like a reaction, as if the house doesn't want me trespassing, like I'm discovering too many of its secrets.

My knees crack as I force myself to stand. With one last sweep of my light, I leave the conservatory. I want to run, but I make myself walk, slow and deliberate, down the length of the hall.

At the end, I hesitate. Valdez mentioned another room I haven't checked yet.

The room is empty except for a metal shelf and a scattering of children's drawings tacked to the wall in no particular order. I approach, half expecting a jump scare, but they're only crayon and cheap construction paper. The images of stick figures, houses, and a dog are crude, but in every one, there is a black shape hovering nearby — sometimes a person, sometimes a blob, sometimes just a scribble with eyes. I count six of these drawings, and on the back of each, the same name, printed in childish block letters: *L.*

I step back, a cold sweat prickling under my collar. If I had time, I would start a full inventory, but the urge to leave is now a command. I hurry to the ladder. I climb, then pause at the top, take out my phone to snap a quick shot of the evidence bag, and send it to Valdez along with a note of what I've found.

I let the silence stretch as the photo takes its time sending. The building is utterly still. My skin buzzes, as if every cell is tuned to a frequency just above human hearing. There are other girls, other rooms, other voices waiting in the dark. I am sure of it now. Sara's story is only the overture. I am standing at the threshold of a much larger pattern, a lattice of cruelty and neglect, and with every new fact, the whole thing vibrates closer to collapse.

My phone vibrates in my hand. Valdez's text is blunt and urgent, as if she's afraid I'll disappear before I can read them.

Team and I are on our way. FYI, you were right. The records were scrubbed, but I found something in the original building plans. Wait till I arrive. We're looking for an access tunnel behind the utility panel in the subbasement.

I close my eyes, holding the phone tight. It's not over. Not even close. The conservatory isn't just a crime scene. It's a map, a message from the dead to the living, and the living are finally listening.

CHAPTER 8: THE GLASS CONFESSION

I wait at the café again. Same corner table. Same chipped mug. Same window with the foggy glass pressed with my prints, the city's pulse beyond it, dull and insistently gray.

The waitress recognizes me and slides a biscotti onto my saucer with a smile. "Place might not look like much, but it's the food that brings you back."

She's right. I'll definitely be back.

This time, I came with a purpose. I told Hannah to meet me. No pretense, no sideways glances or cryptic texts.

She walks through the bell-chimed door in a peacoat two sizes too large and a scarf draped around her neck, beelines straight for my table. She doesn't even pause at the threshold, doesn't bother with the little rituals the rest of us use to slip unnoticed into public places.

She slides into the seat across from me and folds her hands. She looks older than I remember. Maybe it's the lack of eye makeup, or maybe some essential thread has snapped loose inside her since we last spoke.

I wonder if I look the same to her.

"You found it," she says, and the way she says *it*, I feel the pronoun sag with the weight of everything that word can mean — case, secret, grave, body, truth.

I keep my hands wrapped around the mug even though the coffee's gone cold. The silence between us is thick and unfinished, like mortar waiting for bricks. I let it stretch until I see Hannah's fingers twitch, clearly a nervous tell.

"There were two girls," I say. I don't try to soften it, and I don't say their names.

She nods once — a confirmation, not an apology.

"You knew," I say, accusation and defeat braided together in my throat.

"I did." She doesn't flinch. She looks at me with those pale, restless eyes, and I realize she's been rehearsing this moment since before I ever knew her.

"Why didn't you tell me sooner?"

"Because you weren't ready to believe it then." She shrugs, a small, deliberate gesture. "You needed to see the ghosts for yourself."

I want to ask if she always talks like a fortune cookie or if she saves this voice just for me.

"You let me walk into that room alone." I don't bother to hide the anger.

"I had to. You would've dismissed it if I told you the truth upfront. Everyone else did."

My voice drops to a whisper. "So you fed me just enough to keep me chasing."

"I guided you."

"No, you manipulated me."

Hannah doesn't deny it. She just looks at me without blinking until the space between us is so taut I can feel my pulse in my gums.

"You're angry," she says.

"No shit."

She laughs. The brittle sound cracks the shell of her composure for a second. "That's better than numb."

I want to tell her that I stopped being numb the moment I saw the second pair of shoes years ago, half-buried in the garden bed behind the Delrose house. I want to tell her about the dreams, the ones where I find more and more shoes, an endless parade of empty leather leading me down into the earth.

She doesn't get to tell me how I should feel, but I don't say that. I don't say anything. I just sit there and try to remember how to breathe evenly.

Hannah watches me with the patience of someone who has already mapped out the next five moves. Her right hand drums on the table — two quick taps, then a pause, then three more taps, like Morse code for an SOS.

She reaches into her coat again and pulls out a folded envelope. "This is the last piece," she says, sliding it across the table.

I open it slowly. Inside is another photograph, same style and same age-worn edges, but this time, the image chills me more than anything I've seen. A man stands beside a van parked outside the therapy facility. Early morning. Mist still clinging to the trees. The van is unmarked. The man's uniform — plain coveralls, frayed at the collar — bears a name tag.

Rawlings.

I stare at it. "Andy Rawlings."

"You know him?" Hannah asks.

"I've been chasing him for years," I whisper. "He's a long-haul trucker. He's suspected in multiple disappearances across state lines, but no one could pin him to anything."

Hannah nods slowly, as if confirming something in her own mind. "He was there. Not just once. Multiple times. They let him in like he belonged."

"What was he doing?"

Hannah's voice drops to a whisper. "Taking inventory."

My stomach twists. "Of the girls?"

She nods. "They kept track of which ones responded best to isolation and which ones broke. He watched the tapes. Sometimes . . . he requested certain sessions."

My fingers tighten around the envelope. "And no one stopped him."

"No one wanted to."

I shake my head, my breath short. "How are you still alive?"

"I ran, and I stayed hidden, but I kept watching."

"Why come back now?"

Hannah hesitates, then leans forward. "Because they've started again."

My blood freezes.

"They're building something new. A facility. Quiet. Private donors."

I stare down at the photo again. "Is Rawlings involved?"

She shrugs. "I haven't seen him."

I close my eyes for one brief second, then look back at Hannah. "Why me?"

"You were the only one who hesitated when they closed the Beckett case. You asked the right questions . . . even if you never followed them all the way."

"I was green. I didn't know how to fight."

"Now you do."

I stare at the photo one last time. Rawlings' face is blurred, but I know it's him. He's watching the facility the way someone might inspect livestock.

"I don't know if I can stop it," I say.

"But you'll try," Hannah says softly. She stands, pulls on her coat, and turns away.

I call after her. "Will I see you again?"

Hannah doesn't look back. "You already have."

And then she's gone again. Just like before.

I remain at the table long after Hannah disappears into the morning mist. I hold the photo of Andy Rawlings in my hands like it's radioactive. My fingers tremble, but not from fear. From fury. I've always believed justice is a straight line — painful and maybe slow but direct. You dig. You follow. You uncover the truth and bring it to the light. That's what I told myself after every dead-end case, every girl who slipped through the cracks, every time a parent begged me to "please just look one more time."

But Hannah's words echo through my skull like a warning I can no longer ignore. "They've started again."

How many times have I walked past the truth? How many monsters have worn maintenance uniforms and walked through open doors?

I think of Sara begging on the tape. Of the second girl, still nameless, still crumpled in the dark behind a sealed wall. I think of Ivy Markham hanging in a garage. Of Mila Barrett vanishing into silence. And I think of all the times I let myself believe that a clean report meant a clean conscience.

It doesn't. It never will.

A scream rises in my throat, raw and splintered, but I don't let it out. Instead, I fold the photo of Rawlings and slide it into my notebook. I don't know what I'll do with it yet. Turn it over to the feds? Go after him myself? There are protocols and procedures, but they didn't save Sara or the girl with no name. Maybe this time, I won't follow them.

My phone buzzes in my pocket. A new number. No message. Just an image. A grainy and tinted green still frame from a security camera. There's a side profile of a man standing outside a new building — modern, steel, and clean. A medical symbol is painted on the side. In his hand is a clipboard, on his hip a key card.

I don't recognize either the building or the symbol.

I stare at it for a long time. Then, I close my notebook, stand, and walk out of the café. I don't know where Hannah will go next, but I know where I need to start. This time, I'm not going to ask permission. I'm going to kick in the door.

CHAPTER 9: THE REFLECTION YOU MISSED

I stand above the sealed room beneath the conservatory, alone in the predawn stillness.

The forensic team has cleared the scene — the bones cataloged, the room photographed, the evidence boxed and stored — but something still pulls me back.

I walk slowly through the ruin, boots crunching over broken glass. I reach the edge of the open floor and stare down into the hole like it might stare back.

For a long moment, I don't move. Then, I descend the ladder again, one rung at a time, until the hush of the underground swallows me. The space feels different now. Hollow. Cold. Grieving.

I turn to the mirror. My face stares back at me — tired, pale, my eyes lined with months of sleep lost to dead ends. Wait. In the corner, there's a reflection that doesn't belong.

Not the skeleton. Not the cot.

A piece of an old photo was propped in the corner of the sealed chamber. I hadn't seen it before. No, I'm certain it wasn't here before.

Someone else has been here. Someone other than my team.

Dust coats the surface, but I wipe it clean. The photo is of me. I'm in my rookie uniform, notebook in hand as I stand just outside the group home gates, oblivious that I'm being watched.

Beside me, blurred by time but unmistakable, is Hannah Vale. She's watching me with a curious expression.

She was there the whole time. She saw me arrive, watched me leave, and waited for years until I came close to the truth again. And now . . .

I don't know if this is closure. It doesn't feel like an ending. If anything, it feels like something is just beginning.

I climb out of the hole, the photo tucked into my jacket pocket.

Outside, the morning sun is just breaking across the horizon, scattering shards of light through the broken glass above me.

I stand in the wreckage. Not whole. Not healed. But awake and watching now.

Just like someone once watched Sara.

The End

4.
THE WIDOW'S GAME

RULE #4

If something feels off, it is.

Intuition is a scream in a whisper.

CHAPTER 1: THE WIDOW

Someone is watching me.

I linger in my car at the edge of the long gravel drive. The farmhouse looms at the end, a patchwork of white siding gone gray at the edges, its windows staring back like dark hollow eyes. The moment I kill the engine, a curtain shifts and light shines through.

Someone is watching and waiting for me.

The widow meets me at the door before I can knock. "Detective Amber." Her voice is thin but steady. She's in a cardigan two sizes too big, the sleeves swallowing her hands. The lines around her mouth are carved deep, but her eyes aren't red from crying.

"Mrs. Hale," I say, because names matter. "You called."

She steps aside and motions me in. The house smells of lemon cleaner.

On the coffee table, a stack of paper waits. Each sheet is deliberately folded once. Beside them are envelopes.

The widow hovers until I sit, then lowers herself across from me like she's afraid the couch won't hold her.

"They started three weeks ago," she says. "First on the porch then in my mailbox, and last night . . ." She swallows. "One was in my kitchen on the counter. I lock my doors, Detective. I live alone. My husband is dead and yet . . ."

I open the envelope and slide the top note free. The handwriting is jagged and rough. My assumption is that a man wrote this.

Marjorie, we can't keep her hidden forever.

I glance up. "This your husband's writing?"

Her mouth trembles before it hardens into a line. "Yes."

"You just said your husband is dead, Mrs. Hale, did you not?"

"That's correct." She doesn't blink, and she doesn't look away.

The silence stretches long enough that I can hear a clock tick in the kitchen.

I set the note back down, careful not to smudge the ink. "Where did you find this one?"

"On the counter," she repeats, almost like she's daring me to call her a liar.

The other notes are the same, with short, sharp phrases, some accusing, some pleading.

You promised, Marjorie.
They'll come looking.
She was just a girl.

"Is it possible someone forged these?" I ask.

She shakes her head. "No. It's him."

I wait to see if she'll rush to fill the silence. She doesn't.

Instead, she folds her sleeves tighter around her fists. "I can't explain it. Walter was many things but cruel enough to play with me from beyond the grave? No. That's not him, but those . . . He wrote those."

The farmhouse creaks in the wind. Outside, the gravel shifts.

I carefully sift through the stack again. The paper's thin and lined, torn along a spiral binding.

"Do you still have his old papers? Letters? Journals?" I ask.

"No." Her answer is quick. Too quick. "I burned them after the funeral. I didn't want his words following me."

"And yet here they are."

Her gaze flickers to the notes like she can't look for long without them cutting her. "I don't know what you'll find here, Detective. I just know I can't stay in this house another night if someone doesn't explain it."

I gather the notes into a neat pile and slide them into an evidence folder. "I'll look into it."

"Will you find out who's doing this?"

I stand. "That's the plan."

Her eyes lift to mine finally, her veneer cracking. "Then maybe you'll find out what really happened to that girl."

Immediately, her lips press tight, her eyes wide. I have a feeling she didn't mean to say that.

I pause at the door, my hand on the knob. "Which girl, Mrs. Hale?"

She doesn't answer, not that I expected her to.

The wind rattles the windows, carrying silence heavier than truth.

CHAPTER 2: SCRAPS OF TRUTH

The Hale place sits at the far end of a narrow country lane. Two neighbors live within easy walking distance, three more if you like gravel in your shoes. People who live this far out notice everything, then pretend they don't.

The first house is a white ranch with a flag snapping on a short pole in the front yard. A yellow lab barks once, decides I'm not worth it, and flops back onto the stoop.

A man in denim wipes his hands on a rag and meets me halfway down his drive. He's in his late fifties. His sun-touched face says he's been outside most of his life and intends to die that way.

"Afternoon," he says, like we're about to talk weather and the price of gas these days.

"Afternoon. I'm Detective Amber." I show him my badge. "Do you know Marjorie Hale?"

"Everyone knows everyone out here." He jerks his chin toward the farmhouse. "How's she doing without Walter?"

"How did she do with him?"

His mouth twitches. "Walter was . . . a presence."

"Loud?"

"Loud, sure. Mean when he drank. Meaner the next day."

I nod, grasping what he's saying. "See anyone coming and going the last few weeks? Mrs. Hale mentioned she's had notes showing up on her porch."

He glances past me to the road, maybe thinking about what he's willing to share. "Don't know nothing about any notes." He scratches at the scruff along his jawline. "Saw a car pull into her drive two nights back. Didn't stay. Lights were on in the kitchen. Car backed out slow and took off."

"What kind of car?"

He shrugs. "Dark sedan. Older. Or just dirty."

"The driver?"

"Couldn't say. Headlights in my eyes. Possibly male. But he wasn't from out here." He lifts a shoulder. "We can tell."

They can tell? Interesting.

"You ever see lights by the barn at night?" I ask.

He nods. "Used to before Walter died. Lantern glow, like someone didn't want to flip a switch." He hesitates. "Sometimes I smelled earth turned over. Once I smelled something else. Maybe they burned trash."

His eyes flick to my face. He knows I know that's not what he smelled.

"Anything else?" I question.

"Marjorie's not a bad woman," he says. "She's just got a bad story. Big difference."

"What story?"

He shakes his head. "Not mine to tell."

I thank him and move on.

The second house is a double-wide trailer with geraniums in chipped mugs along the rail. A teenage girl answers in socks and an oversized sweatshirt that reads *STATE CHAMPS* across the front, her hair up in a lopsided bun.

"Hi. Your folks don't happen to be around?" I ask.

"Mom's at work. I'm supposed to say, 'no soliciting.'" She points to a sign beside the door.

"Good news. I'm not selling anything." I show the badge. "You know Mrs. Hale?"

"Kind of. She buys eggs sometimes. Gives out full-size candy bars at Halloween." The girl leans on the doorframe. "You looking into her husband?"

"Should I be?"

She shrugs.

"Actually, I'm looking into notes someone's leaving for her."

"Creepy." She glances toward the farmhouse, as if she can see it through the trees. "He used to yell, you know. Mr. Hale. You could hear it from the road if your window was open."

"He was that loud?"

She nods.

"Do you remember when?"

"Yeah, mostly Fridays." She looks down at her socks. "Once I saw Mrs. Hale at the grocery with sunglasses on when it was raining. My mom said don't stare."

"Anyone around here hold a grudge? Ex-employee? Family?"

"Mr. Hale didn't like people much," she says, "but Mrs. Hale . . . she talked to my grandma sometimes at church. She's nice."

"What did she say?"

"She said she 'prays for the Benton girl when the wind shifts.'" The teen shrugs. "I don't know who that is."

My pen stops for a beat. "Benton," I repeat.

"Yeah." She searches my face for a hint, but I school my features and keep my expression blank. "Weird, right?"

"Which church?"

"St. Margaret's."

"Thanks."

Sometimes I like talking to teenagers. They don't know enough not to say so much.

I take the long way back to the Hale farmhouse, not because I need the walk but because I want time to arrange what I've just been handed.

The Hale mailbox has a dent in the door where something hit it years ago, and no one bothered to fix it. I open it with a pen, not my fingers. It's empty. The inside smells like damp paper and rust. The flag squeaks when I lift it. There is no powder, no fibers obvious to the naked eye. I snap a few photos and bag a flake of paint from the inner lip. If someone's been planting notes, microscopic transfer will tell me more than a neighbor's memory.

I head back to the house, and the porch boards complain with each step. An old, dented metal ash can sits beside the steps. There's a couple of inches of ash and charred scraps inside. Someone dumped a bucket of rainwater on it recently. The sludge is gray soup with black islands. I lift the lid, cover my mouth against the smell, and sift with a gloved hand.

Paper clings to itself in wet layers. Most of it dissolves at a touch, but one scrap holds. It's a thicker, cardstock-type scrap. I tease it free and lay it on the step. The top edge is burned away, but the bottom shows narrow blue lines and a faint left margin. It reminds me of a notebook cover. On the back, there's a ghost of printing — *ton Middle Scho*. The burn takes the rest.

I bag it. The ash clings to the plastic like it's trying to spell something.

I circle around the house. A path threads through scrub grass to the barn — ruts worn by years then softened by neglect. The barn itself is a red rectangle fading to brown, doors padlocked with a new lock on old hardware. I peer through a gap where a wood knot fell out. Dust motes swim like slow fish. There's a workbench, a coil of rope, an empty feed bin, and, beneath the hard-packed dirt floor, a dark rectangle about the size of a shallow grave.

I stand there for a while, measuring what I can see and what I'm making myself wait to confirm. Then I walk the perimeter. There's fresh scuffing near the north wall where someone's shoved a wheelbarrow and a shovel leaning against the corner wall with clumps of dirt beneath it.

CHAPTER 3: BURNED MEMORIES

My phone buzzes with a call from an unknown number.

"Detective Amber?"

"Speaking."

A man exhales into the receiver, the sound of someone deciding how much to reveal. "I heard you were out by the Hales."

"Who is this?"

A pause. "A neighbor. Don't ask which one."

"Why's that?"

"Because it doesn't matter."

"It does to me."

He ignores that. "You should ask Marjorie about the girl from years back. Not those notes. The girl."

How does he know about the notes?

"What's her name?" I ask.

Click.

I stare at my reflection in the black screen. People don't hang up on me often, but when they do, they're either scared or guilty. Or both.

I pocket the phone and walk back to the porch. On the way, I see scuffs in the dirt near the side door — two tread patterns, one boot, one sneaker, overlaid like a stutter-step. The sneaker's small, maybe worn by a teen or a slight adult. The boot drags on the heel. Whoever wore it favored their right leg or was just tired.

On the porch, something catches the light between the boards. I crouch and slide my pen into the gap. A sliver of paper clings to the pen's metal clip when I pull it back, a thin, curled, soot-smudged piece. On it are ink letters, the tail ends only.

. . . ly B—

I bag that too.

Through the open window, the kitchen clock ticks as loud as a hammer.

Marjorie is in the back room off the kitchen, pretending to fold already-folded dish towels. She looks up and sees what's in my hand, and for a heartbeat, the practiced calm in her face drops a level.

"You burned some of them," I say.

"I threw them away," she says too fast. "Walter's words belong in the past."

"Was one of them written on school paper?"

Her eyes flit to the bag, away. "I don't know."

"Does the phrase 'Benton girl' mean anything to you?"

She swallows. Her knuckles whiten around a towel. "Who told you that?"

"Tell me about the name." I lift my chin, daring her to lie to me. I want to know what she's hiding. She didn't call me out here just to play games with me.

She wets her lips. "I'm not talking about that."

"About what?"

She squeezes the towel tightly, but doesn't say anything.

"You called for me, remember?"

I leave her with her towels and her bad story and drive back into town. The county office is open until five on Wednesdays. The clerk knows me. She slides the old property maps across the counter with a pen and a tired smile.

The Hale acreage runs from the road to the creek, with the barn sitting square in the middle. The floodplain cuts a ragged mouth along the back fence line.

In the hallway glass case, a sun-faded poster displays missing kids from the last three decades. I stand in front of it until the clerk clears her throat like a clock. It's the second row that has my attention. On the right is a girl with blunt bangs and crooked teeth and eyes that don't know how to play along with a camera.

HOLLY BENTON — Age 15 — Missing since 1998. Last seen near County 7 and Miller Creek Road.

Miller Creek runs behind the Hale property.

I take a picture of the flyer with my phone. Secrets don't stay buried. They rot their way back up, and sometimes, the creek helps.

CHAPTER 4: CRACKS IN THE STORY

Marjorie makes tea like it's a ritual holding her together. I watch her work in silence as she turns the kettle on, the blue flame low, two cups pre-warmed with the bags laid out on a folded dish towel. Her sweater sleeves slip down over her hands as she carries the tray to the table.

"Milk?" she asks.

"Black is fine."

We sit across from each other at the kitchen table. There are two chairs at this table, both worn smooth by years of sitting across from the same person.

"Did you talk to my neighbors?" Her voice trembles. She's clearly nervous about what I might have been told.

"I did."

"What did they say?"

"That you gave out full-size candy bars and that Walter was a presence." I let that sit. "They also said 'you pray for the Benton girl when the wind shifts.'"

Her hands still. The spoon hits the saucer with a ding she doesn't hide quickly enough.

"I think it's time we talk about her."

Her lips thin, and she remains silent.

I smile a little. "Marjorie, I once pulled a child's shoe out of a drain behind a truck stop because somebody told me there was a smell there twenty years ago, and they still couldn't shake it. I am here to help, but don't waste my time, all right?"

"You think this is a waste of time?"

"I didn't say that. I told you not to waste my time by clamming up and staying silent about the things you know you want to tell me."

Steam curls between us. The kettle ticks as it cools, and I wait.

When she finally looks up, her eyes are older than her face. "Walter wasn't a monster," she says.

"That's not what I asked."

"It's what you're circling."

"What I'm circling," I say, drawing an actual circle in the air with my finger, "is why notes in his handwriting are showing up on your porch weeks after he died and why a neighbor's kid knows you say the name Benton at church."

She folds her hands around her cup like she needs the warmth for support. "The notes are a cruelty."

I nod. I get that. "From whom?"

"I don't know."

"From where?"

"I don't know that either."

"Try this, then," I say gently. "Why now?"

She looks toward the back door, past the yard, to where the line of trees begins. "Because the ground is soft," she says.

"Marjorie."

I need more. She knows more.

"Because people remember, Detective," Marjorie says after letting out a sigh. "Maybe that's your answer. The world forgot Walter first. Then, it forgot me. They don't want to forget her."

"Her who?"

Her throat works. "Holly."

The word surprises her as much as it does me. It's out before she can catch it, and once it's in the air, we both listen to it.

"Holly," I repeat slowly.

She nods once, a small surrender. "The Benton girl."

This time, it's me wrapping a hand around my mug. "How did you know her?"

"I didn't," she says too quickly. "She worked weekends at the feed store. Everyone knew her face," she added, her tone softer now.

"That's not the same as knowing someone."

"I never said I knew her."

The kitchen clock ticks. I let the silence do its work. It always does.

Finally, she reaches for the sugar bowl. The spoon trembles over the cup and lands with a clink. "We had an agreement," she says.

"Who's we?"

"Walter and me."

"What kind of agreement?"

"I didn't ask about the barn, and he didn't ask about my sister."

I file that away. "What about your sister?"

"Dead," she says flat and fast, and I know I'm not getting more now. "It was a long time ago. I learned to leave closed doors alone."

And I've learned those doors need to be opened.

"Why did the agreement come about?" I ask.

Her mouth twists. "Why? Are you not married?" She pauses and gives me the space to answer, but I don't. "How do agreements in any relationship come about? You don't like something. You say something, but when they don't stop, you make the choice to stop noticing in order for some peace."

Interesting but true.

"And to keep that peace, what did you not look at?"

She leans back in her chair and stares at the ceiling like she's checking for leaks. "He had his place, and I had mine. He kept tools in the barn, and he kept bottles there too. He slept out there when he was loud. It was easier that way."

"And when he wasn't loud?"

"He apologized." She laughs once, a sound that doesn't know what to be. "You ever notice how sorry men are the morning after? You could lay their regret on a plate like ham."

"How did the Benton girl fit into this?"

"The Benton girl," she repeats like she's rolling a bead between her teeth. "She was in the newspapers for a while. People searched the creek. My church prayed. Then life . . . went on." She meets my eyes. "It always does."

"Unless it doesn't," I say.

Her gaze slides away first. "You're very good at this."

"Talking to women in kitchens? Yes."

She folds one sleeve back, then the other, exposing thin wrists. "I burned Walter's papers," she says, circling in again. "Letters he wrote me when we were young. Receipts. His old journals. I did it because I wanted to go on. That's my sin if you're looking for one."

"I'm looking for a girl," I say. "Not a sin."

"You won't find a girl in a stack of notes."

"Maybe not," I say, "but I'll find the person writing them."

She presses her lips together. "Maybe he's trying to help you."

"Who?"

"The person writing them," she says, impatience flashing then gone. "If they wanted to scare me, they'd write worse things."

"You sound like you've read worse things."

Her fingers tighten on the cup. "I sound like someone who has lived long enough to know when a threat doesn't intend to land."

I think about the ash can, the school paper, and the fragment lodged between porch boards . . . *ly B—*

I think about a dark sedan that didn't stay, and a neighbor who hung up when I asked his name.

"Let me ask you something practical," I say. "Do you keep a spare key hidden outside?"

She blinks. "No."

"Did Walter?"

"He kept a key under the old dog's dish."

"He kept the dog dish where?"

"Under the porch. It's cooler there."

I stand. "Can you show me?"

She hesitates, then leads me to the side door. The porch boards here are lower, closer to the ground, where a dog could retreat in hot weather. We kneel. She reaches into the dark between joists and pulls back empty fingers.

"It's gone," she says. There's real surprise in her voice.

"Could they key be anywhere else? In the house maybe?" I offer.

She huffs. "He always left it under here, where no one would look, but anything is possible, I guess."

I take this as permission to look and head back inside. I wander the kitchen, scrutinizing everything. Something sticks out from a drawer. It sticks as I pull, but once it's finally open, there's only rubber bands, pens, a pile of screws, a church bulletin folded into quarters, and a birth certificate sleeve with nothing in it.

There's a small *squeak* from the screen door as Marjorie walks back in. I'm closing the drawer when something catches my eye. At the back is a small composition book with a corner burned away, the black marbled cover bubbled.

"Don't," Marjorie says, too late.

I pick it up. Inside the front cover, in a neat teenage hand, is *Holly Benton — Lit. Comp. — Room 204*.

Nothing stays hidden for long.

My pulse kicks as I hold it up. "Where did you get this?"

Marjorie's chin lifts. "The creek brings things," she says. "I told you."

A good excuse.

"When?"

"Years ago. After a flood." Her words get softer. "There was garbage all along the fence after the waters receded. Shoes, garbage, plastic bottles, even half a bicycle. I found that book in the brush pile."

"And you kept it?"

She doesn't answer.

I close the notebook. It's swollen with water history. The pages are fused, the ink blurring into a storm across the paper. If there were words that mattered here once, the creek took them.

"You could have turned this in," I say.

"To who? Walter?" She shakes her head. "He would have burned it with everything else that made him feel seen."

"How would Walter feel seen by a dead girl's notebook?"

She looks at me like I'm asking the wrong questions. "Men like Walter don't like any reminder that the world remembers what they did."

The room seems smaller suddenly. Outside, the wind shifts, and for a second, I smell wet earth like a warning.

"Marjorie," I say softly, "did you ever see Holly Benton on your property?"

Her answer takes too long. "I saw a girl," she says finally. "I don't know what name she used to have."

Interesting.

"What name did she have here?"

Marjorie's smile is a crack. "Girls don't keep their names when men like Walter decide who they are."

I slide the notebook into an evidence bag and do my best to keep my thoughts off my face.

"We're done for today," I say, because if I stay, I'll push, and if I push, she'll break wrong. "I'll be back."

She doesn't walk me to the door. She stares at the place where my cup sits and says to the room, "He wasn't a monster."

"You keep saying that," I tell her. "It sounds like you're trying to convince someone."

"Who?"

"Yourself."

I let the screen door slap behind me.

On the porch, I write two words in my notebook and under-line them twice.

Holly Benton

The rule that fits this story is a drumbeat in my head. *Secrets don't stay buried. They rot their way back up.*

The creek knows it. The ground knows it.

So does Marjorie.

I need to go through Holly's file and do what I do best — look through the past to find a path in the present.

CHAPTER 5: OLD FILES, NEW SHADOWS

The precinct archive smells like dust and copier toner, the kind of air that settles into your clothes until you carry it home. The room is long, with fluorescent lights buzzing faintly and file cabinets lined along the wall.

I signed the log twenty minutes ago, but it was a new clerk managing the station, and they hovered before finally deciding I wasn't going to steal a box of ancient traffic citations.

Now it's just me, a stack of pulled folders, and the hollow quiet of unsolved things.

Holly Benton was only fifteen when she vanished. She was last seen at the feed store three blocks from her home. There were no signs of a struggle, no witnesses willing to admit what they saw.

The file is awfully thin. I've seen this all too many times. There's a missing girl with minimal leads and a search party that dissolved after two weeks.

I flip through the old reports, my pen ready.

The few witness statements I find are from a clerk from the feed store who says she clocked out at six. There's one from a neighbor claiming they saw her walking down Main Street with a backpack, and then another one that says they saw her hitching a ride near Route 19, but "couldn't be sure" it was her.

There's also a photo of Holly smiling with braces, holding a lamb at the county fair. It's printed on glossy paper, the kind that bleeds if you hold it too long. I snap a photo of it.

Next page is a surprise when I find Walter Hale's name written down. My pulse picks up until I realize the mistake that was made. Walter Hale was not a suspect. They didn't even do a formal interview with him. There's just a note that searchers checked the Hale property because it was "adjacent to creek land." No further follow-up had been recorded.

I lean back and stare at the line. That's it. A box checked. A dead end filed away under "nothing to see here."

I close my eyes for a second. This has been my life, case after case where too many men with secrets are overlooked by officers with pens running out of ink too fast. Do I blame them? No. Could they do better? We all can.

The hum of the lights folds over me, and for a moment, I see my own sister's face. River, her hair matted from the rain, her eyes full of every story she never got to tell. I also imagine Andy Rawlings' grin pressed against the window of a truck cab as it drove away. She's another girl who was overlooked because they didn't have enough manpower to properly search.

I shake it off and dig deeper. There's a note tucked behind the final page, a scrap like it was slipped in later. Different handwriting, ballpoint pen pressed so hard it tore the paper.

Check the barn. She's still there.

No signature. No follow-up reports. Just the note that had clearly been ignored.

I swear under my breath. Where the hell did this come from, and who put it there?

I copy the note word-for-word into my notebook. Then, I snap the file shut and take out my phone.

"Amber," comes the gruff voice on the other end. Retired Detective Ron Keller. He worked cold cases before I was assigned. Now, he fishes and complains about property taxes, and I try to catch up with him every so often. He's a good resource to have.

"I'm looking at Benton's file."

Long silence.

"You do remember her, right?"

"I remember them all. That one, there shouldn't be much in there." I hear the resignation in his voice.

"There rarely is, which is a problem. Here's the thing. I found a note at the back of the folder, like someone snuck it in there last minute. It's about the Hale property. Did you ever check it?"

"You think I'd remember that far back?" His tone is defensive.

"I know you do." He has a memory like an elephant. "Girl disappears, the neighbors whisper, and there's a barn on the edge of nowhere. You don't forget those details."

He sighs, and I can picture him running his hand through what little hair he has left. "You want the truth?" he asks. "We had a dozen missing that year. Girls running off, girls who never made it home from school. We chased every tip until we ran out of funding and patience."

"Funding and patience," I repeat flatly. "That's the excuse you gave to the parents?"

There's a long exhale on the other end. "Listen, Walter Hale wasn't a name we had reason to circle. He drank, and he yelled, but he wasn't on our radar."

"He is now," I say.

Another silence. "Be careful digging into ghosts, Amber. Sometimes the only thing you get for your trouble is dirt."

"I live in dirt," I tell him. Then I notice a name in the file. "What about the brother?"

"What about him? We looked into him, nothing panned out."

I hang up.

The file feels heavier when I slide it back into the box. I swear, Holly's weight is still inside.

On my way out, I sign the log again.

* * *

Back at my apartment, the room I never let visitors see waits for me. My map wall. It's filled with pins and red string. Newspaper clippings. A ghost gallery of girls, truck stops, and missing posters.

And Andy Rawlings' face, grinning from his driver's license photo, has followed me like a shadow for twenty years.

I pin Holly's picture, the one at the county fair, and step back. The pins ripple outward.

Different case. Different decade. But the pattern is the same.

I take a breath, press my palms flat against the desk.

Holly, Walter Hale, Marjorie — with her sleepless eyes — notes in a dead man's handwriting . . . Maybe it's not a coincidence.

Maybe it's a confession.

I sit, open my notebook, and scrawl, *Check Hale's barn. Find Holly's brother.*

The phone buzzes before I can close my notebook. Unknown number. Not a call, but a photo of a scrap piece of paper that's been torn out of a book and a single sentence written in what looks like a black marker.

You're looking in the wrong place.

The writing in this photo has the same jagged curve as the notes left for Marjorie.

The dead don't text, but someone who wants to be heard does.

And they know I'm looking.

CHAPTER 6: THE WIDOW CRACKS

The gravel crunches under my boots when I pull up to Marjorie Hale's farmhouse again. She's waiting on the porch this time, wrapped in that oversized cardigan like it's the only thing keeping her together.

"I didn't call you," she says as I climb the steps.

"I know." I hold up my phone. "But someone else did."

Her eyes flick down. "Another note?"

"Text," I correct. "This time they're modern enough to use a cell phone."

Her hand flutters toward her throat, trembles in the air, and then falls. "What did it say?"

"That I'm looking in the wrong place."

Her face drains, pale under the porch light. She whispers something I almost miss.

"What was that?" I press.

Her gaze snaps to mine, sharper now. "I said . . . maybe you are."

I follow her inside. The living room looks untouched, but the air feels different. There's a faint smell of smoke. Hmm. Everything is going to be exposed, so why try to hide it now?

I head to the fireplace. "What else did you burn?" I ask.

Her lips twitch. "Random junk."

My jaw tightens. "Can we stop this game, Mrs. Hale? You were the one who called first, remember? Stop making this harder than it needs to be."

"This is my life, Detective. I'm sorry if I'm not quite ready for you to destroy what's left of it."

I close my eyes but only for a second. "You've been holding something back since the first minute I walked in here. You said Walter wasn't cruel, but those notes and those words, they're cruel, Marjorie."

There's a sheen to her eyes, like she's trying not to cry. "You don't understand. Walter wasn't the one who needed to be cruel."

The sentence lands heavily. I want to say something, ask something, but I hold my tongue and wait her out.

She turns her back on me, and I notice the trembling in her shoulders. "Holly Benton," she says, barely audible. "She wasn't supposed to die."

My pulse spikes. I step closer but don't touch her. "Now you want to talk about her."

She nods once, quickly. Her hands grip the mantel like she might pull the wood loose. "Walter didn't mean to. That's what he told me. She came here, mouthing off, saying things she shouldn't have known. He snapped. She fell. After that . . ." Her voice breaks. "After that, there was no going back."

"And you kept quiet."

She spins then, wild-eyed. "You think anyone would've believed me? A wife saying her husband was dangerous after years of standing by his side? I'd have gone down with him, and for what? For a girl nobody looked for after two weeks?"

Her words slice, and for a beat, I almost see the younger version of her — trapped in her own silence, corners closing in.

I lower my tone. "So you buried her here."

Her lips tremble. "Not me. Walter. Always Walter. But the land remembers. The house remembers."

I glance at her hands, knuckles white on the fabric of her sleeves. She's shaking now, not from fear but from release.

"Where is she, Marjorie?"

Tears pool but don't fall. "She could be anywhere on the property. I don't go in the barn though."

"Why not?"

Her mouth curves in a broken smile. "He told me not to." She shakes her head. "I think that's why the notes came. She's not at rest, and he's not either."

Her words dig under my skin. I've spent half my life fighting ghosts with faces, but this is different.

I take a breath and remind myself, *You catch more liars with sweetness than with anger.* "You say she's not at rest, but I think someone living knows exactly where she is, and they want me to find her." I pause for a beat. "You want me to find her."

Marjorie's gaze hardens. "Then you'd better be ready for what else you dig up."

Silence folds in heavily between us.

I step back toward the door. "I have a call to make. Do me a favor and don't burn anything else while I'm gone."

She doesn't answer. All she does is sink onto the couch, her cardigan wrapped tight, her eyes staring at a place only she can see.

Outside, the wind cuts across the fields.

I call Valdez and ask her to come out to the farm. I need her to babysit Marjorie. I also told her we were on the hunt for a dead body and to bring the team.

My phone buzzes again in my pocket. Another text.

She's still here. Barn. Creek. Ask the brother.

There's no photo. Just words, written like commands.

I look around. Someone is watching me. They know I'm here. They know I'm looking.

Marjorie's silhouette lingers in the window as I climb into my car. She looks smaller than ever. Or maybe the house is just swallowing her whole.

I don't feel sorry for her. She knew and did nothing. That's hard to excuse.

When Valdez arrives, I fill her in. She'll wait for the team and for me to return.

Gravel snaps under my tires as I drive away. I've got a brother to find.

CHAPTER 7: THE BROTHER'S SHADOW

The Benton house is only six miles from the Hale property, but it feels like I've crossed into another world. The Hales' land is neat, manicured out of necessity, like keeping order helps keep Marjorie upright. The Benton place is the opposite — unkempt and sagging, with weeds creeping up the siding and shutters hanging at angles.

I park on the dirt shoulder and kill the engine. The house looms dark even in daylight.

Evan Benton answers the door before I knock. He's in his late forties, his face worn like leather. His eyes are sharp, though, a piercing gray that seems to strip away layers the moment they land on you.

"You're the detective," he says, no question mark at the end.

"I am."

He turns his back and leaves the door open. The message is clear — follow if you dare.

Inside, the living room is crowded with stacks of newspapers, yellowed photos, and coffee mugs that probably haven't been cleaned in years. The air smells of old smoke and damp.

Evan sits heavily in a chair. He gestures to the couch. "If you can find a spot."

I move a pile of clippings — headlines about missing girls, crime sprees, cold cases — and sit.

He lights a cigarette. "So. What lie is Marjorie spinning these days?"

I study him. "You two don't get along."

His laugh is low and humorless. "Did she tell you we did? Hell, I'm surprised she mentioned me at all."

She didn't, but I keep that to myself.

"She lived across from me my whole damn life. We were kids together. Then, Holly went missing, and suddenly, she and Walter were untouchable. Nobody questioned them. Nobody questioned anything."

I lean forward. "Did you?" I can see the answer in his eyes.

His jaw tightens. "'Course I did, but what good did it do? Sheriff at the time was Walter's fishing buddy. Everyone in this county wanted it buried. Holly was just another girl they said probably ran off."

I pull up the photo I'd taken on my phone, the one of Holly at the fair, braces flashing, lamb in her arms. I slide my phone across the table.

Evan stares. His hand shakes as he picks it up. "She was supposed to go to college. First Benton to do it. She didn't even make it to her sixteenth birthday." His voice cracks.

I watch him carefully. "Someone is sending notes and texts using Walter's handwriting." I give it a beat. "Is that someone you?"

Evan's head jerks up. "Handwriting?"

I nod. "Marjorie swears it's him writing from the grave."

He stubs the cigarette out with more force than necessary. "Then you've already got your answer."

Interesting.

"Which is?"

He leans forward, smoke curling between us. "Marjorie. She knew more than she ever said. Maybe she's finally losing her grip. Maybe she wants someone to find what's left."

I'm a little disappointed that's who he's pinning this on.

I shake my head. "No, it's too neat, too obvious. These texts came from an untraceable number, not her phone. One came while I was with her, and I saw firsthand that she's terrified. No, someone else is doing this."

His eyes narrow. "Then it's one of the others."

"Others?" I repeat.

He gets up, walks to a filing cabinet wedged into the corner, and yanks it open. Papers spill, clippings scatter. I grab my phone and place it back in my pocket. He pulls out a folder from the cabinet and tosses it on the table. Inside are photocopies of sheriff reports, hand-scribbled maps, and old Polaroids.

"You think Holly was the only girl?" His voice is sharp and bitter. "This county's been swallowing girls whole for decades. The difference is, my sister mattered to me, so I kept digging."

I flip through the folder. There are at least three other names, and there are dates from the late eighties and early nineties.

"They were never tied to Walter," I say.

"They weren't tied to anybody," Evan snaps. "That's the point. No one wanted them solved."

I pause on a photo of the Hale barn. Handwriting in the margin says, *Boards too new*.

"You searched the barn," I say.

Evan nods once. "Yeah, five years ago. Broke in one night. I obviously didn't find her, but I knew. I knew she'd been there."

I lean back, the weight of it pressing against my chest. "If you knew, why didn't you tell the police?"

He gives me a look like I've asked him if the sky is blue. "You think they'd listen to me? To them, I'm a drunk troublemaker. Say I'm obsessed."

"Are you?"

His lips curl. "Obsession is the only reason she's not forgotten."

The room is silent except for the tick of an old clock.

My phone buzzes in my pocket. Another text.

You're close. Don't trust him.

My gaze flicks up to Evan. He's watching me, his eyes sharp.

I don't let my face shift and slide the phone away without answering.

"Tell me about Walter," I say instead.

Evan exhales slowly. "Walter was a bully with charm. He knew how to make people laugh, how to make them forget, but he had a temper. Everyone knew it. Everyone ignored it including Marjorie."

"And you?"

His jaw works. "I tried to warn Holly. Told her to stay away from him, but she wouldn't listen. Said he was just a blowhard. She thought she could handle him." He finally looks down, his voice dropping. "She couldn't."

The silence stretches. Finally, I stand.

"Where are you going?" he asks.

"To the barn," I say.

He smirks bitterly. "You think you'll find something I couldn't?"

I pause at the door. "Possibly. Maybe you didn't look in the right place." I say softly.

I turn the knob, but before I step out, an envelope sticking half out from the pile on the sideboard catches my eye. The edge is frayed and old. Instinct tells me to look.

"Mind if I . . ." I gesture.

Evan shrugs. "Nothing in there you haven't seen before."

I pull the envelope free. Inside are several photos, black-and-white faded Polaroids. Most are of the Hale farm, but one makes my stomach twist.

A truck cab with its chrome gleaming. Beside it, a man is smiling, his arm slung casually over the open door.

Andy Rawlings.

The name flares in my brain like a match. I've stared at his face for years in my own evidence room, plastered across maps and timelines and endless notes. He's the truck driver who took my sister, the one who vanished into the highways like a ghost with a pulse.

"Where'd you get this?" My voice is sharper than I intend.

Evan squints at it. "That? No idea. Why? You know him?"

I force my expression still, though inside, everything rattles loose. "Maybe. Maybe not. Just . . . looks familiar."

I slide the photo back into the envelope, but the image burns behind my eyes.

Evan leans back, studying me. "You're not telling me everything, Detective."

"No," I say honestly, "but then, that goes both ways, doesn't it?"

Outside, the air cuts sharp in my lungs as I step off his porch. Gravel crunches. My phone buzzes in my pocket again, but I ignore it. My mind is already in my own house, in the locked room where I pin every scrap of Rawlings to the corkboard.

This photo — this single, careless snapshot — doesn't belong here, and yet, somehow, it does.

Holly's disappearance isn't just about Walter Hale anymore.

It might tie to Rawlings.

It might tie to River.

It might tie to me.

CHAPTER 8: THE BARN

The Hale barn squats at the edge of the property, its roof slanted and patched with tin, the red paint more rust than color. In daylight, it looks harmless and ordinary enough, but I've learned barns are never ordinary. They're places where families hide what doesn't belong in polite company — affairs, contraband, and sometimes bodies.

The team still hasn't arrived, but Valdez says they'll be here any minute.

I'm not in the mood to wait.

That photo of Rawlings sits heavy in my jacket pocket like it's waiting to burn through the fabric.

I grip the shiny padlock on the barn door. Someone replaced it recently.

Bolt cutters bite through the shank. The metal drops into the dirt with a sound far too loud for the stillness of the afternoon.

Inside, the air is thick with dust and the sweet rot of hay. Light slants in through the gaps in the boards, striping the floor in gold and shadow.

The barn is divided into two stalls, each with wooden planks rising chest-height. Ropes dangle from hooks like nooses. A workbench runs along the back wall, tools scattered in neat rows. Someone kept this place organized, like they cared.

I move slowly, my boots pressing into straw. The boards in the far corner are discolored. They've been replaced at one point. Evan was right. Fresh wood on an old skeleton.

I kneel and run my hand across the grain. Splinters catch my glove. The boards aren't nailed flush. They were laid fast, like someone covering something in a hurry.

This feels too easy. I can see for myself that the dirt beneath the board is darker than the rest, damp like it's been disturbed.

My chest tightens. I dig with my gloved hands, scooping dirt fast until my fingers hit fabric. Rough. Torn.

The pit in my stomach grows. I clear more soil and reveal denim. A leg. Then a bone, pale against the dark earth.

I sit back hard and swallow bile.

A body.

What's left of one.

The skull is caved in on one side, the jaw twisted. Teen-sized, maybe. Maybe Holly. Maybe another girl Evan listed in his files. Whoever she was, she didn't walk out of here.

I stand and force myself to breathe through the shock. My phone is in my hand before I realize it, flashlight on, photos snapping. Not evidence the way the department would approve, but my kind of evidence. My record.

A sudden vibration shudders through my palm. A new text.

She's not the only one. Keep digging.

I whip around, light slicing across the barn. Shadows jump like startled animals, but no one's here.

My hand trembles as I read the text again.

The sender knows. They know I'm here. They know what I've found.

Who the hell is this person, and where are they?

I see the lights from the team's vehicles flash through the barn. I'll let them finish this, but I can't sit still and wait. Whoever's playing this game wants me to see the truth, but only piece by piece. They're baiting me.

At the workbench, I sift through drawers, every creak loud in the silence. Nails. Wire. Rope. Then, buried beneath all of that is another envelope.

I freeze.

It's worn, smudged with dirt, the edges curled. I snap another photo, then open it carefully. Inside are more Polaroids. Not of the farm this time.

A truck, its chrome gleaming.

The same truck from Evan's envelope.

Different angle. Different day.

In the corner of the frame, blurred but undeniable, is another girl. Could this be my sister? After all this time? It's hard to tell. The face is too blurred, but in my heart, I want to believe it is.

My breath leaves me in a rush. Whoever this girl is — a stranger, my sister — she's smiling like she doesn't know the monster standing two feet away.

Rawlings.

It can't be coincidence — it never is — but what the hell is his picture doing in this barn?

I slide the photo back into the envelope and tuck it deep into my jacket. This one's mine. The department will get the bones. But Rawlings? That stays with me.

Who planted the photo? Was it Evan with his obsession? Marjorie with her silences? Or someone else, the person who's been watching all along?

The barn creaks. A floorboard groans behind me.

I spin, flashlight beam cutting the dark.

No one. Just a rope swaying gently, though I swear I didn't brush against it.

My heart hammers, but I force myself to the door.

Outside, the air is sharper and colder. The sun has lowered.

I wave at the team. It's time. Time to do this right, to give this girl and any others buried here the proper closure they need, but I'm also careful and alert, my mind racing with too many thoughts.

This is now a thread knotted into the same web I've been untangling for twenty years, and I'll be damned if I let anyone pull it loose before me.

CHAPTER 9: THE WIDOW'S SILENCE

Once the team arrives and I answer as many questions as I can, I head to the house, telling the uniforms that I need a few moments with the widow before they walk in.

I don't knock. I push straight into Marjorie Hale's farmhouse, the door creaking wide.

Valdez sees the look on my face, and she stands.

Marjorie's at the kitchen table, her cardigan clutched close like always, tea steaming in a mug. Her calmness rattles me harder than a scream would.

"You didn't waste time," she says, her voice thin but steady.

"You knew." My words cut sharp. "You knew what was under those boards in the barn."

Her lips press so tightly they become colorless. "I told you. Walter buried his mistakes."

"Mistakes?" My voice rises before I can stop it. "That was a girl. A child."

She flinches but doesn't look away. "And what would you have me do, Detective? Call the sheriff? Tell them my husband — the man everyone trusted — killed a girl in his barn? They'd have locked me up too."

I slam a photo down on the table. Not the one with whom I think could be my sister — I keep that one hidden — but the

Polaroid of the truck, the one from Evan's envelope. "And what about this? Why do these keep showing up?"

Her eyes widen, flickering too quickly before she schools her expression. "I don't know. I never took them."

"You expect me to believe that?"

Her hand trembles as she lifts the mug, but she doesn't drink. "Walter had friends. Men who came and went. Drivers, salesmen. I stayed in my lane. I didn't ask questions."

My pulse hammers. Friends. Drivers. Rawlings wasn't just a phantom on the highways. He might've been here, on this land, part of this circle.

"Who sent the notes, Marjorie? Who's sending the texts now?"

Her gaze drops to her lap. "I don't know. Maybe Walter from the grave. Maybe Holly herself."

"Enough." My voice slices through her muttering. "There are no ghosts. Just people. People who hide behind silence. People like you."

Her shoulders fold in, as though she's collapsing under her own weight, but still, she doesn't confess. She doesn't crack.

I lean closer to let her see the fury in my eyes. "Someone's playing a game with me, but when I find out who, I'll make sure you're not the shield they hide behind."

Her knuckles whiten around the mug, but she doesn't answer.

I leave her in the dim kitchen, silence clinging to the walls thicker than the smoke of a burned secret.

CHAPTER 10: EPILOGUE — THE ROOM

I don't turn on the lights when I get home. I don't need them. My feet know the path, every creak in the floorboards.

Everything feels different when I walk straight through without stopping, without pausing in the kitchen or living room. The real heart of this place isn't where I eat or sleep. It's at the end of the hall.

The locked door.

I slide the key from my pocket and feel the familiar weight of the lock turning. The click is quiet, but inside, it always feels like a gunshot.

The door opens.

This is where I truly live. Four walls covered in photographs, newsprint, maps pinned so full of red string they look like veins. Faces that never leave me. Timelines that never end. Notes scrawled in the middle of the night when sleep wouldn't come.

And at the center is Andy Rawlings.

Truck driver. Predator. My sister's shadow.

I tack the new photo beneath his name. My hands are steady, but my chest is tight.

I want to believe that this is my sister. I need it to be her. Of course, I realize it could be anyone, but there's something . . . Maybe it's the blurred smile like she's caught in someone else's story, but I know her. I'd know her anywhere.

This has to be her.

I stare at the photo until my eyes burn.

Why here? Why the Hales' farm? Why now?

Questions I can't answer. Yet.

I step back. The board looks different now. Fuller. The string crosses itself again, another knot in a web I've been untangling for twenty years.

All my rules filter through my head, but it's Rule #5 that echoes the loudest.

If something feels off, it is.

The guilt is mine to carry. Curiosity is mine to burn.

I close the door, lock it, and lean my forehead against the wood. For a long time, I just breathe.

Tomorrow, I'll go back to Holly's case. I'll see what else they find and close the files on as many cases as the earth unburies. I'll file what I can and say what I must, but tonight, it's just me and this room.

And the photo that proves Rawlings was closer than I ever thought.

Closer than I ever wanted.

The End

DEAR READER: A NOTE FROM MERI

Every case leaves something behind. Not just evidence. Not just grief. Something that sticks under my skin and refuses to let go.

This one was about Holly Benton. About a widow who stayed silent, a brother who never stopped digging, and a barn that gave up its dead.

But for me, it was about more than that.

Even here, in someone else's story, Andy Rawlings' name found its way back to me. His face showed up where it shouldn't have been, and he was tied to threads I still don't understand.

That's how it always is. Every missing girl, every buried secret, all pull me back to him. To River. To the promise I made the night she disappeared.

I will never stop looking.

So, if you follow me into the next case, know this — it won't just be about the victim. It will always be about him.

And one day, I'll find him.

—Meri

5.
WHAT THE RIVER TOOK

RULE #5

No one just disappears.

They're always somewhere. The trick is knowing where they don't want you to look.

CHAPTER 1: AFTER THE FLOOD

The thing about this job is I'm always surprised.

Take today, for example. I started my day with coffee and listening to a podcast, and now, I'm here by a river where a body is waiting for me.

The water has dropped two feet, maybe more, since the last time I was here. The banks sport a fresh tattoo of mud, the thick kind that keeps its secrets. Cottonwood fluff drifts over the shallows like puffs of snow. The smell is what it always is after the flood — damp wood, diesel, and something iron.

Deputy Valdez waves me down the slope. "Amber, you're gonna want to see this."

I pick my way around a tangle of branches. The current's slow today, but it still talks to itself in that steady voice, carrying sticks, bottles, even someone's plastic lawn flamingo. The flood took what it wanted. Now, it's returning whatever didn't satisfy.

Three team members are in the water, but right now, I'm watching a man in thigh-high waders in the eddy by the bend, a yellow rope on his belt and a fish net in his hands. He edges a snagged dark bundle away from the roots. "Got it," he calls as the thing slumps into his net with a sound that turns the back of my throat to chalk.

It's a backpack or what's left of one — faded canvas, straps rotted to threads, the zipper covered with rust.

He hauls it up the bank like a catch he doesn't want, water gushing out in sheets.

Valdez glances at me. "You want first look?"

I nod, head down, and kneel on the wet sand. I slip on gloves while all the noises around me soften — the river, the murmurs from the crowd, the distant sound of police sirens somewhere upstream.

The zipper sticks, but eventually gives. I'm not ready for what I see inside. The first thing I find is a compact, the mirror spider-webbed and gray. The next has me retching — a broken jawbone wrapped with clumps of hair. There are more bones, some clean, but not all of them. Phalanges. Metacarpals. A right hand minus the ring finger.

I set the bones on the evidence tray that Valdez slides beside me; one bone is the wet, white curve of what used to be a palm. A beaded bracelet slips out like it was waiting to be found — blue glass, cheap, one cracked bead with the letter "L" pressed into it.

"You seeing what I'm seeing?" Valdez asks.

"I don't know what you're seeing," I say, "but I'm seeing someone who wanted this to stay down." I nod toward the stones in the bag.

Valdez crouches. "We get names for that bracelet?"

"We'll get one." I ease the compact open with the edge of a pen. The powder inside is old, caked, and ashy. In the mirror's splinters, my face stares back in shards, a haunted look in my eyes.

The man in the waders clears his throat and points his chin at the eddy. "There's more caught under the root ball."

"We'll take whatever you can find," I say.

The river's already delivering its next package — a shoe nosing into the shallows like some small animal trying to breathe. Pink canvas, glitter ground to dull, the toe cap scuffed to gray. Not new but not ancient. Child-sized.

I swallow hard, each swallow shredding my throat into ribbons. Valdez radios the ME, the CSU van, and the county dive team. The river gulps, moves a little, belches up a tangle of cord.

"Tell me the story," Valdez says, more to herself than me. "We've got bones, a bracelet with an 'L,' and a weighted backpack. Somebody knew what they were doing and clearly didn't trust the current."

"Nobody should," I say. "Any current is a liar. It makes you think it keeps moving, but it's the eddies that keep the secrets."

A woman in a windbreaker with a city seal on the breast hovers at the lip of the path, her arms wrapped tight around her body. "We got calls from half the neighborhood," she tells me as if I asked. "Soon as the water pulled back, they started seeing . . . things."

"What things?"

"Bits." Her mouth trembles. "Bits of a child."

The word stitches into my sternum as neatly as a needle could. A child. It's always a child.

We mark the site, string tape around the drop to the bank, and log the GPS. People gather on the far side of the river where the path runs — among them are dog walkers, a man in a neon runner's vest, and a teenager with a phone she has the sense not to raise. It's the man in the vest that I'm keeping my eye on. He's watching too closely. His shoulders are already turned toward the bridge. Interesting.

Valdez looks at me. "Anyone come to mind? Any cold cases that match this stretch?"

"Miller Creek Junction's a mile that way." I point downstream. "All of this feeds from it, and the creek feeds the county rumor mill."

"Which bucket of rumors do you like today?"

I take a moment to go through the files in my head. I remember all the names and most of the details. This one doesn't take long for me to pull up. It also helps that I did a quick search through the files after getting called. This was one of the first cases I'd ever worked.

"A fifteen-year-old girl went missing, years ago. Everyone said the river took her. Lacey Quinn." I see the missing poster in my head — her school portrait, her straight hair too, her smile not quite keeping up with her eyes. "They looked for three days then called it at dusk. Found her backpack strap near the spillway. Case closed."

Valdez's jaw flexes. "You worked that?"

"I was new. I carried cones and handed out water. After they called it, I drove home and threw up and told myself that grown-ups knew when to stop looking."

Valdez doesn't say anything. She doesn't have to. The job makes real adults, or it doesn't.

"Why the rocks?" she asks.

That's an easy question to answer. "Control," I say. "They tell themselves it's about mercy and closure, but it's control to keep the story where you put it."

"There's a chain in there," the guy calls. "Heavy gauge like for a bike. It's tangled in the roots."

I stand, and the world sways for a second. I'm running on coffee and little else.

I grab a Halls from my pocket and stick it in my mouth before heading down to the water. We work together, pulling the chain from the dark tangle of submerged wood. There's fabric knotted around one end. A shirt? No, a pillowcase printed with little flowers that held onto their color better than anything else had.

I hold it up. The river turns the cloth into a dull flag.

"You thinking what I'm thinking?" Valdez says, her voice low.

"Thinking I need to see the intake," I say. "There's that old water plant, the one that was decommissioned with the storm overflow. If anything got staged upstream, that's where the river gets told what to do."

She nods. "I'll make the call."

A gull drops low, screaming at us for stealing its macabre buffet. I glance around and notice that the runner in the neon vest has vanished, but the teenager lingers.

I bag the bracelet last. Up close, the cracked bead shows more than an "L." On another bead, a second letter has been rubbed thin, almost gone. It looks like an "A," which would make sense if this is Lacey.

"You okay?" Valdez asks me.

I stare at the water. Sometimes, if I look at people too long, I forget how to talk. "The river didn't take her," I say slowly, "but someone did. The river just found her too heavy to keep."

We move the evidence to high ground where the CSU techs can work.

The ME arrives. She's short and efficient, her mouth already set in the line that means *don't ask me for miracles*. I brief, she nods, and we ritualize our way through the first hour the way we always do — notes, photos, and numbers that will be on forms I'll never sleep without seeing.

When the swarm of lookers thins and the tape flutters on its own breath, I walk upstream alone. Two hundred yards. Three. The flood trimmed the banks raw, and roots now hang like ribs. In some places, you can see the layers where the river has eaten and eaten and still isn't full — sand, clay, rock, a bottle cap, a coin, a rusted nail . . . the history of the town in a cross section that doesn't lie.

There's a culvert under the old service road. The mouth is a perfect black circle. "Come in," the water says in its softest voice.

I crouch and shine my light into the throat. Ten feet in, it curves left, then down into the dark.

"If I were trying to make the river tell my story," I say to the culvert that doesn't care, "this is where I'd start."

I stand, brush mud off my knee, and realize a man is leaning against the far guardrail like he grew there. Early forties. Cap with a local bait shop logo. Clean boots. Cleaner than this bank should allow.

"What a day," he says amiably. "Find anything good?"

I hold my hand over my eyes to block the sun. "We don't use 'good' for what the river gives back."

He tips his chin. "Fair enough. I'm Caleb. I volunteer with the Search and Rescue crew." He points downriver. "Been out here every spring for, well, too many springs. Know this water like my own veins."

He says it the way men say things they want you to write down. I don't.

"You on scene when the backpack came up?" I ask.

"Nah." He stretches casually. "I was down by the railroad bridge this morning checking the snags. You'd be amazed what gets caught there after a flood. Wallets, license plates . . . once a whole set of false teeth." He grins like we're in on the same joke. "You dig up a mystery?"

"We bag what we find," I say.

He nods like we just agreed to something. "If you need a hand mapping how the currents throw, I got time." He taps his cap brim. "Caleb Rusk. Everybody's got my number."

Valdez calls my name from downriver. I turn toward her, and when I look back, Caleb's already walking the service road, easy as a man who knows exactly where the gravel shifts and where it holds. His boots still don't show a lick of mud.

I watch his back for a long beat before I return to Valdez, who's standing with the ME by the taped square of riverbank.

The ME tilts her head toward me. "You get me a name," she says matter-of-factly, "and I'll get you a cause when I can."

"Deal," I say. "Start with Lacey Quinn, and don't stop there."

No one just disappears. Not in this town. Not in any.

The river can keep its stories. I'll write my own.

CHAPTER 2: THE FAMILY THAT STAYED

The Quinn house sits three blocks from the high school, a square white box that looks like it's been bracing against the wind since the day it was built. The curtains in the front window are drawn, but the porch light burns even though it's noon.

Valdez offered to come with me, but some doors don't open for uniforms. Some stories only talk if you strip the badge off and leave it in your pocket.

I knock three raps.

The door creaks open an inch, then another. A woman peers through the crack. She's in her mid-fifties, and her hair is straw blond and brittle. Her eyes are blue but clouded, rimmed red.

"Mrs. Quinn?" I ask.

She hesitates, then lets the screen door ease wider. "You're here because of the river."

"Yes."

Her chin trembles, but she doesn't cry. "I knew it would give her back one day." She steps back and motions me inside.

In the living room, a wall of framed photos stops me. Lacey's face is everywhere — school portraits, softball team shots, a Polaroid of her in a homecoming dress that didn't quite fit in the shoulders. The same eyes stare out year after year, frozen at fifteen.

Mrs. Quinn notices me looking. "I couldn't take them down," she says softly. "If I took them down, it would be like she was gone."

I meet her gaze. "She'll never be gone."

She nods, as if she's been waiting years for someone to say exactly that.

We sit at the table.

She folds her hands, her knuckles white. "They told me she drowned, that she slipped at the spillway. I tried to believe it, Detective, I did, but . . ." Her voice frays. "But I know my daughter. She was afraid of water. Always. She never would've gone near that spillway."

"She didn't," I say. "We pulled a backpack this morning."

I pause, thinking about how much to tell her. If it were me, I'd want the truth.

"It was weighted with rocks, and inside were bones," I add. "Not all but enough."

Her lips part, a small breath escaping. No tears. Just that stunned, silent sound mothers make when truth is freed.

Partially.

So far.

"Do you know if she wore a bracelet with blue beads?" I ask.

Mrs. Quinn blinks then nods quickly. "Her grandmother gave it to her. The beads spelled out her name. She never took it off."

I slide the evidence photo across the table.

She presses a hand to her mouth, then drags it down. "That's hers."

Her certainty pins the case down like a nail through wood.

"Who was she with that day?" I ask.

Her eyes flicker. "Her friend. Abby Stroud. They were joined at the hip. Abby said she left Lacey at the corner by the park and went home. That's what she told the police."

"Did you believe her?"

"No." Her voice is sharp now, hard with years. "Because Abby never came by after. Never called, never brought flowers, never asked. It was like they were strangers."

I write Abby's name in my notebook.

"Do you know where she is now?" I ask.

"California. Married. Two kids. I saw it on Facebook before I stopped looking." Mrs. Quinn grips the table edge. "She knows something. I've always believed that."

"She might."

The kitchen clock ticks, slow and heavy.

"Mrs. Quinn," I say, "did Lacey ever talk about anyone new in her life? Someone older?"

Her face shutters. "You mean a man."

"Yes."

Her voice drops. "There was one. A volunteer. He helped with the softball team. Said he was with Search and Rescue and that he knew the river better than anyone. He gave her rides sometimes."

My pen stills. "Name?"

"Caleb."

The way she says his name stops me. There's a history with this name.

The man at the culvert. The man with clean boots. Caleb Rusk.

"Did you ever tell the police?" I ask.

Her eyes flash anger. "Of course, but they said he was helping and that he was respected. They told me not to go around accusing people because I was 'emotional.'"

I bite back the curse burning my tongue.

Mrs. Quinn leans closer, her voice fierce. "If you find him, you ask him what he did with her because I swear, Detective, the river didn't take my girl. That man did."

I thank her, promise updates, and leave her at the table like a broken doll.

The air outside is sharp, wet earth still breathing from the flood. Instead of getting into my car, I walk the block. A neighbor waters her front flowers with the hose running too strongly, her eyes fixed on me over the spray. A man with a leaf blower pauses to watch me pass, the machine roaring silently in his hands. Everyone knows why I'm here. Everyone's wondering if their secrets are next.

Back inside my car, I jot notes.

Abby Stroud — reinterview.
Caleb Rusk — front and center.

I drive away, Mrs. Quinn's words heavy in my head. "The river didn't take my girl. That man did."

And men leave trails.

No one just disappears.

CHAPTER 3: THE PACT THAT WASN'T

The records room is never warm. The radiator ticks and clanks, but the air is always damp, a basement chill that lingers in the skin. I've spent enough hours here to know which drawers stick and which ones give you the wrong case on purpose.

Lacey Quinn's file is thin enough to get lost between thicker failures. I lay it out on the table like a puzzle I already know is missing pieces.

Fifteen years old. Last seen by her best friend, Abby Stroud, walking toward the park on a Saturday in April. She was supposed to be home for dinner at six, according to her mother, except she never made it.

The search lasted for three days. The river was high that spring, and the banks were muddy. I remember that, for sure. Everyone said the same thing — *She slipped. The river took her.*

I flip the report to the back. There was no recovered body and no confirmed sighting past Abby. Just a backpack strap snagged at the spillway and a conclusion dressed up as evidence.

Except no one just disappears.

Those words repeat in my head, steady as a metronome.

I scan the witness statements again. Something in Mrs. Quinn's voice when she said *she knows something* won't leave me alone.

Abby's interview jumps out even though I've read it before. *"We walked together from the feed store. She said she needed air. I turned off at the corner of Birch and went home. She was headed toward the park. I never saw her again."*

Air. Headed toward the park. Alone.

Too neat.

Teenage girls don't peel off like that unless something's already pulling them, and if Abby really "never saw her again," then why didn't she call the Quinns later? Why didn't she show up for vigils?

Because silence is its own pact.

Next, I pull the supplemental notes Detective Keller scribbled in the margins.

Abby solid. Parents vouch. Nothing further.

Solid. That's one way to describe a wall.

I push back from the table, stand, and pace the aisle between cabinets. Keller's handwriting follows me. It's too curt and per-functory. It reminds me a lot of the other cases I've gone through — the same early dismissals, the same habits of doors closing too soon.

I return to the table, snap a photo of Abby's statement with my phone, and drop the file into the return bin harder than necessary.

Back in my car, I dial Valdez.

"You get anything good?" she asks.

"Depends on your definition of good," I say. "Abby's statement reads like it was rehearsed."

"She was a kid."

"Kids trip up." I shrug. "They contradict themselves. They don't sound like transcripts."

Valdez exhales. "You want me to dig her up online?"

"No, I already know where she is. California. Married. Two kids."

"You looked on her socials?" She snorts, knowing the answer before I say it.

"No, I talked to Mrs. Quinn. She's been watching her for years."

"You gonna fly across the country to knock on a PTA mom's door?"

"Not yet. First, I want to know what she said off the record."

Valdez pauses. "Meaning?"

"Meaning Keller. He worked the case."

I doubt he's going to enjoy another call from me again. In fact, I'll be surprised if he even answers.

Valdez whistles low. "You gonna poke that bear again?"

"I'm going to do more than poke."

* * *

I could have called, but I had a feeling he wouldn't have answered, so instead I head out there. Keller's place is a one-story ranch with a sagging porch and a flag faded almost to gray. He's on the porch already in a lawn chair, a beer sweating in his hand.

"Detective Amber," he says, squinting like the sun's too much for him. "You still dragging skeletons out of the river?"

"Someone has to." I climb the stairs, but I don't take a seat.

He smirks. "Water takes what it wants."

"No," I correct him. "People take. Water just spits it back when it's tired of holding it."

His smirk fades. "You didn't come here to philosophize."

He's right. I didn't.

I hold up my phone, Abby's statement glowing on the screen. "What did she really say?"

He shrugs. "It's all in the file."

"No. That's what you wrote. I want to know what she said, what you didn't put in."

He leans back and sips his beer. "Girls her age, they say a lot. You learn to filter."

Is he kidding me?

"You filtered the wrong way."

His eyes narrow. He's not liking either my comment or my attitude. "You accusing me of negligence?"

"I'm accusing you of convenience. You liked things tidy." I glance around at the saggy porch. It's like he's past caring. "According to you, the river takes a girl, case closed, no threads to pull. When did you give up?"

He laughs, short and bitter. "Give up? Look at you, a detective with a heart. You think we had resources back then? You think we could chase every whisper? We barely had gas for the cruisers."

I ignore the sarcasm. "She mentioned air," I say. "Said she needed air, except that's not what a girl says when she's just walking home. That's what a girl says when she's suffocating."

He looks away toward the yard gone to seed. "She said something else," he admits finally, not looking at me. "Said Lacey told her she was meeting someone."

And that wasn't in the file?

"Who was she meeting?"

He puts his beer down. "She didn't say, just someone from the team."

"What team?"

"You don't think I asked? She wouldn't answer, so I wrote down the clean version and saved her from herself."

"Or saved someone else."

He doesn't answer, not that I'm surprised.

I tuck my phone away and stare out toward my car. "You know who it was," I say.

It's not a question. Definitely an accusation.

He shakes his head. "I know better than to say."

I step closer, the porch boards groaning. "It was Caleb Rusk, wasn't it?"

His jaw tightens. He doesn't confirm, but he doesn't deny, and that's all I need.

I turn to leave.

"Amber," he calls after me, "you keep digging, you'll find more than you want."

I don't look back. "That's the job, or did you forget?"

* * *

The drive home is long enough for my mind to circle the same drain. Abby knew Lacey was meeting someone, and Keller buried it. Caleb's name keeps resurfacing like driftwood.

I pull into my driveway and cut the engine, but I don't go inside. Instead, I sit in the quiet, my phone in my lap.

I close my eyes. The river hums in my head, endless and patient.

Rule #5 presses against my ribs like a heartbeat. *No one just disappears.*

If Caleb thinks otherwise, he's about to learn what the river already knows.

Secrets float.

CHAPTER 4: CLEAN BOOTS

I find Caleb Rusk where I knew I would, on the service road by the river, leaning against his truck with a cocky attitude. Same bait shop cap, same pressed flannel, boots still spotless. The river's mud doesn't touch him.

He smiles when he sees me. "Detective. Or is it just Meri? I overheard one of the officers talking to you the other day."

"Detective's fine," I answer. "You volunteering today?"

"Always." He gestures to the bed of his truck — ropes, waders, and two tackle boxes stacked neatly. "Flood season keeps a man busy. Things get loose and drift places they shouldn't. Somebody's got to haul it all back."

"Some things don't drift." I step closer, my eyes on those unnaturally clean boots. "Some things get put in the water on purpose."

He chuckles low. "You saying the river's got help deciding what to keep?"

"I'm saying no one just disappears."

His smile fades. "That what her mother told you?"

"That's what the evidence told me."

He watches me for a long beat, then pushes off the truck and takes a slow step forward. He smells like cedar soap and engine oil, a combination that says *I work with my hands* without admitting what those hands have done.

"Funny thing about evidence," he says. "It can wash away. Erode. By the time someone like you shows up, all you've got left are scraps, and scraps don't tell the whole story."

"Then tell me the whole story."

His eyes flick to the river behind me, the current sliding lazily now that the flood's passed. "I told the police back then she wasn't in the water. They didn't listen. Suits never do. They want quick closures and tidy endings."

"Where was she, Caleb?"

He leans in close enough that his breath grazes my ear. "Not where you're looking."

I hold my ground. "Where then?"

He straightens, grinning again. "I'll let the river decide if you're ready."

That grin reminds me of Rawlings. Men like this smile when they know the rest of us are playing catch-up.

"Did you know Abby Stroud?" I ask, keeping my tone level.

"Everyone knew Abby. Sweet kid. Nervous type. Always following Lacey around like a shadow." He shrugs. "Some shadows don't survive when the light shifts."

"Was she there the night Lacey disappeared?"

Caleb pauses just long enough to answer me without words. Then, he says, "She didn't tell you? Guess that means she still knows how to keep her mouth shut."

My phone buzzes in my pocket. I don't look. My eyes stay on him.

"You volunteered for Search and Rescue back then," I press. "That gave you access. To Lacey. To Abby. To the scene."

"That gave me a purpose," he says flatly. "The river takes things. I bring some back. That's what I do. Been doing it longer than you've been playing detective."

I take a step closer. "But you didn't bring Lacey back."

Something flickers in his eyes. Anger, maybe, that or memory, but it's gone before I can pin it down.

He pulls his truck door open and leans against the frame. "You keep poking, Detective, you're gonna find out the river's not the only thing that swallows people."

"That a threat?"

He shakes his head, his smile back in place. "It's a fact. No one just disappears, right? That's what you said. Maybe start applying it to yourself."

He climbs in, the engine roaring to life, gravel spitting from his tires as he pulls away.

I stand there, my pulse hammering.

My phone buzzes again in my pocket. There's a new text from the same untraceable number.

Careful. Caleb isn't the only one who knows. Abby was there too.

I hate being watched. I especially hate feeling like I'm a puppet and someone else is in control.

The river gurgles beside me, pretending it isn't a crime scene.

I pocket the phone and look at the water. "No one just disappears," I tell it, "and I'll prove it."

CHAPTER 5: INTAKE

The old water plant sits at the end of a service road, its brick walls mottled with moss, its windows bricked up decades ago. The county fenced it off when they built the new facility upstream, but the chain-link gate hangs half open, the padlock cut and dangling.

I step through the gap. The ground squelches under my boots. Hmm. The grass has been flattened by recent tires. Someone's been here.

The intake mouth yawns at the far side of the plant, a concrete throat dark with algae. The culvert I scouted earlier feeds into this. Floodwater would have rushed through here, carrying whatever the river decided to claim — or whatever someone decided to give it.

I crouch by the edge, my flashlight cutting across the slick concrete. Rusted grates are half-bent. One bar is missing in the middle. It should be big enough for a backpack. Maybe even a small body.

My flashlight beam catches on something wedged in the grate. It's a strip of fabric, pale against the dark slime. I slip on gloves and reach with my pen to tease it free. It's cotton, patterned with tiny blue flowers, torn along one edge. A shirt or a pillowcase.

Behind me, gravel crunches. I straighten fast, swinging my light wide.

No one's there, just the fence creaking in the wind, the weeds bending.

But there are fresh tracks with deep grooves leading from the service road down toward the intake. Maybe a heavy truck with tires wider than county vehicles.

I kneel, snapping photos, and measure the treads with my notebook for scale.

I know three things.

One, they don't match Valdez's SUV.

Two, they don't match my sedan.

Three, they do match Caleb's truck.

I follow the grooves. They veer off toward a dirt clearing behind the plant. The grass is pressed flat, a square patch like something sat here for hours. I crouch, my gloved fingertips grazing the ground. Ahead of me, there's a dark stain, faint but visible against the dirt. I bring the flashlight closer. It's not oil.

It's blood.

The river murmurs behind me, reminding me it's waiting.

I snap photos of the stain, bag a sample of the stained soil, and stand, every muscle humming.

I might not be able to prove it, but I'm certain Caleb's been using this intake as his dumping ground for years.

The question is how many girls he's fed to it and why Abby Stroud kept her silence.

The air shifts, now cool against my neck. I spin again, my light catching only weeds and chain-link. No one is there, yet I'm being watched. I know it.

I return to the intake and crouch for a better look. The missing grate bar is bent outward, not inward. Someone pried it open to shove something in, not to pull it free. The river didn't choose its offerings. A hand did.

"No one just disappears," I whisper out loud to steady myself.

The words echo against concrete, low and sure.

I go back and take one last sweep of the site and head back to the gate. My car waits where I left it, untouched, but I still check the backseat before I get in. It's an old habit, but it's kept me alive so far.

The sun's dropping as I drive back toward town, the river flashing orange through the trees.

My phone buzzes again in the cup holder. I let it sit for a mile before I check out the text.

She's ready to talk but only to you.

No name. No number traceable.

Just an address.

I slow as the GPS pinpoints it. San Luis Obispo. Abby Stroud's house.

The timing isn't a coincidence. Nothing ever is.

I grip the wheel tighter, the Rawlings photo flashing in my mind. Him with his truck, River blurred in the corner. Caleb with his spotless boots. Abby with her silence.

Three pieces of the same puzzle.

If Abby's finally ready to talk, I'm going to make damn sure she tells me everything because no one just disappears. Not Lacey. Not Abby. Not River.

Not even the truth.

CHAPTER 6: ABBY BREAKS

I don't book the flight until I've stared at the wall for a full minute with the anonymous text open. *She's ready to talk but only to you.* I book the flight and can hear Valdez in my head telling me to loop her in, to file travel, to do this clean. I also hear the river, patient and low, and Mrs. Quinn whispering, "The river didn't take my girl. That man did."

There's a line between procedure and truth, and it isn't always where the handbook says.

I text Valdez anyway. *Off-grid interview. I'll brief when I land.*

Her bubble pops up. *Don't get dead.*

Working on it.

By late afternoon, I'm in a rental sedan rolling past lemon trees and tidy medians, the ocean in the distance. The address takes me to a cul-de-sac where every driveway holds a skateboard and a basketball hoop. I park one house shy and kill the engine. Once the AC shuts off, the heat inside the car presses against my skin. My heart thuds once, hard, and then finds a steadier pace.

Abby opens the door at my knock. Her shoulders drop a fraction, relief and dread braided together. Ah, so she recognizes me. That's a surprise, considering I never spoke with her, but if it means this will go easier, I'll take it.

"Meri Amber," she says, like saying my name settles the rules for what comes next. "You came."

She steps back to let me in. The house smells like coffee and vanilla. There's a cluster of school pictures on a table — two kids, a boy and a girl, gap-toothed, hair perfect in a way no child's hair is naturally.

Abby has the look of a woman who makes lists and actually completes them. Her hair is cut into a careful bob. There's a yoga mat rolled up in the corner, and a calendar on the wall with *Fun Run* circled in pink.

She locks the door behind us. That small sound is louder than it has any right to be.

"Is there anyone else home?" I ask.

"No, it's just us. My husband is at work, and the kids are playing with the neighbors." Her voice is steady. "I can only talk for an hour."

An hour is better than nothing.

"That'll do."

She leads me to a kitchen that could be in a magazine with its white counters, a fruit bowl full of oranges, and knives in a block arranged by size. I take a seat at the table. She doesn't. She grips the back of the opposite chair.

"I saw the news," she says. "About the river. About the . . . backpack." She struggles with the word. "It's all over my feeds."

All over her feeds? Either she was looking, or people were sending her articles.

"We found a beaded bracelet," I say. "There was a round blue glass with the letter *L*. It was cracked."

Abby's face folds without tears, her lips quiver with unsaid words, her eyes redden with withheld emotions. "She loved that thing. Said it made her feel like somebody noticed she existed."

"She existed," I say. "She exists."

Neither one of us says anything. I wait to see if she'll break first. She doesn't.

"I need you to tell me what happened the night Lacey went missing," I say. "Not the version you gave the police. The real one."

She heads to the counter, where she grabs a dishcloth and wipes an already clean area. "I've told myself I didn't know. I've told myself that lie for fifteen years, that if I didn't see what happened, then it wasn't real. But that's not true." She finally raises her gaze. "I knew enough."

Finally.

"How did it start?" I ask.

"It started with the Search and Rescue practice," she says. "He — Caleb — he called it *familiarization.* He showed up at the high school one afternoon with flyers about being 'water safe.' I remember him saying that girls needed to know rescues take teamwork. Lacey liked that. She liked being useful." She purses her lips. "He made her feel seen."

I bet he did.

"Did he touch her?" I ask.

Abby flinches. "He put his hands on our shoulders to 'position' us for throwing ropes. He adjusted our life vests like he needed to be the one to do it. Nothing you could point at and say *bad.* Just . . . too much." She looks off into the distance. "He had a way of making rules sound like invitations."

And there it is.

"When did you meet him alone?"

She hesitates like she doesn't want to answer, like she hasn't already admitted it happened. "The second Saturday in April." She drops the cloth in the sink and turns on the tap. "Lacey said she was suffocating. Home was . . . hard." She pauses and grabs two glasses from the cupboard behind her. "There were a lot of money issues. Her mom was always yelling at her, and then her mom's new boyfriend started sleeping over." She brings the glasses over and places one in front of me. "Caleb said if we wanted to practice for real, he could show us the intake tunnel and how water moves. He said he could teach us where to stand so we'd never get pulled in. Honestly, he sounded like a hero."

I'm sure he did.

"He told you specifically to come to the park?"

She shakes her head. "He told Lacey. I told her not to go, but she said it was important for us to know and that we'd go together. I made her promise that we'd leave the second it felt wrong." She swallows, and her fingers clutch the chair again. "We walked from the feed store, but at the corner, I changed my mind. I told her that and said we should go home. She looked at me like . . ." She swallows and takes a second before continuing, "Well, like I'd betrayed her. So I said I'd wait at the bench by the culvert, and if she wasn't back in fifteen minutes, I'd call the police."

My jaw clenches. "You waited."

"I waited for the fifteen minutes. Then I got a text from him but from a different number." She closes her eyes as if she can still see the message. "*You can come too if you want,* it said. I didn't. I told myself it was because I didn't want to be alone with him, that I knew something was off with him."

"But?"

She lets out a sigh. "But the truth is . . ." She meets my eyes. "I was jealous, okay? He noticed her more. I wanted him to notice me too, and when he didn't, I wanted her to feel a little scared."

The ugliness of that confession sits between us. She doesn't look away.

"What happened next?" I ask quietly.

"The truck drove past the bench. He waved. Lacey was in the passenger seat. She looked . . . excited. Like she was finally doing something that mattered." Abby's fingers whiten. "I got mad at myself for being petty. He turned down the service road to the old plant. I ran to follow. I caught up just in time to see them walk toward the intake. He was showing her something about the grate. He crouched. She crouched. He put his hand on the back of her neck like he was steadying her so she wouldn't slip." Abby's voice thins. "And then he pushed."

The room tilts, but I force my breath to remain even. "You saw him push her."

"Yes." The word is a thread about to snap. "She grabbed the grate. He pulled her back up by her jacket. She was laughing and mad at the same time, hitting his arm. Like it was a joke that went too far." Abby closes her eyes. "I almost left. I told myself I'd overreacted, but then he took something from his pocket. A strip of cloth. He put it over her mouth. I don't know if he meant to choke her or shut her up. She fought. He . . . he hit her head on the concrete. It made a sound I still hear when I'm trying to sleep."

For a beat, the only sound in the room is the sound of both of us breathing.

"You called no one," I say. Not accusation. Fact.

"I ran." Her voice is full of shame. "I ran until my lungs tore. I told myself if I didn't see the rest, it wouldn't be true. I showered. I went to bed with the lights on. In the morning, when the town started searching, I showed up and cried and said I didn't know anything because I thought if I said it enough, it would become true. People hugged me and said I was brave."

"Did he contact you?"

"Two days later from a blocked number. He wrote: *River took her. If you say otherwise, the river will take you next.*" Abby's mouth trembles. "I believed him. I still believe he could have."

"Did you ever tell Keller? The detective?"

She shakes her head. "He didn't ask the right questions. He asked if Lacey ran away. If she liked attention. I said no."

A car horn sounds, startling us both. I realize my hands are fists on my knees. I unclench them.

"The cloth, did it look familiar?" I'm reaching, but if I don't know the right questions to ask, I need to at least ask the wrong ones.

Abby nods, her eyes far away. "His truck always smelled like laundry. He kept a pillowcase in the back under the seat. Said it was to cover 'delicate evidence' if he found any while volunteering. I think he used it for whatever he wanted. I think that's what he used to cover her mouth."

"Why now?" I ask. "Why text me your address? Why talk?"

Abby lets go of the chair and finally sits. She looks smaller, younger, closer to the girl at the bench. "Because the river gave you something. Because of the news and because I realized if I don't say it out loud now, I'm going to be saying it in my head when I'm eighty and can't change a thing. Because my daughter is the age Lacey was. Because last week, Caleb sent me a friend request from a new account with a picture of the service road as his banner."

My chest goes cold. "He's still watching you."

"He's always been watching. I moved states. I changed numbers. I got married and had kids and joined the PTA and learned to make casseroles that freeze well, and every spring, I hear water in the gutters and I'm a teenager again and running."

No one just disappears.

"You're going to give a statement," I say. "Recorded. Under oath. You're going to tell me everything you told me now and everything you remember when you think you're done."

She nods, quick. "Will he—"

"He will not touch you," I say, a promise edged with iron. "We'll coordinate with the local PD. You'll have protection, and he won't see you first. I will."

Abby presses her palms flat on the table and leans forward like the motion might empty her of everything that hurts. "Mrs. Quinn," she whispers. "You have to tell her. Tell her that she didn't go to the river. Tell her someone took her there."

"I will," I say.

"And tell her I'm sorry," Abby adds. "I know it won't fix anything, but I need someone to hear me say it who isn't me."

I let a long breath out. "It matters. It doesn't fix things, but it matters."

She nods, her entire body shaking. "What happens now?"

"Now I go home," I say. "I arrange for someone to come get your statement while I get a warrant and pull Caleb's records. We'll seize his truck. We'll tear up the intake, and we'll dig until the river runs clear." I make sure to add confidence to my voice. It's not something I have to force. It comes naturally because I know we'll get him.

He's too cocky, and he'll think he's a step ahead. He'll be wrong.

"And if it never runs clear?" she asks.

"It will," I say. "The river can keep its silt, but it can't keep a secret."

Her laugh is a gasp that doesn't quite survive.

She walks me to the door. Her hand pauses on the deadbolt. "Detective?"

"Meri."

She swallows. "Thank you for coming yourself and for not sending . . ." She stops, then starts again. "I remember you from the river. You smiled at me. No one else that day did. I knew if there was a chance for anyone to believe me, it would be you. I was hoping, anyway."

I try to remember seeing her, but I don't. I was new. I did crowd control, and that was it.

"I didn't come to believe," I tell her. "I came because no one just disappears."

She closes her eyes like it's a prayer. When she opens them, she nods once and works the lock.

Outside, the light is bright, the day ordinary with children shouting, sprinklers spraying, and a dog barking.

I sit in my rental and type the notes with thumbs that don't miss keys. This matters too much. At the end, I add one line in caps. ABBY SAW HIM. Then, I add another beneath it.

On the flight back, I watch the coastline peel away under the wing, the ocean folding and unfolding. I close my eyes and see the intake grate, the missing bar bent outward, the strip of blue flowers in my evidence bag. I see Abby at the bench, Lacey laughing, Caleb's hand on the back of a girl's neck like he owns her.

When the wheels thump onto the runway, my phone lights up with a voicemail from Valdez and a text from an unknown number.

The text is short.

He's waiting for you. Be ready.

I don't reply. I don't need to.

CHAPTER 7: THE ARREST

We don't go in with sirens because we don't need to. Men like Caleb Rusk aren't taken down in noise. They're taken down in silence, when the ground under their boots shifts and they realize the river isn't on their side anymore.

Valdez drives. She doesn't talk, just clenches the wheel tight enough to leave dents in the leather. I've briefed her, and she knows all about Abby's confession, Keller's omission, and even the evidence at the intake. All of it, especially with Abby's confession, was enough for the warrant. It might not be enough for a conviction, but it's enough to drag Caleb into a room where the walls are smaller than the river, and his smile won't fit.

I'll get what I need for the conviction. I have no doubt about that.

We park two houses down from his place. The yard is neat with the hedges squared off, the porch swept, and the blinds perfectly even.

I can smell bleach before we even step onto the driveway.

"Guy's got a type," Valdez mutters. "Clean boots. Clean house. Dirty hands."

We climb the steps together. Caleb opens the door. He's smiling, of course, looking like he's been expecting us.

I know Valdez would love to wipe that smile off his face. I would too.

"Afternoon, Detective Amber," he says, completely ignoring Officer Valdez. "Come to see the trophies?"

Valdez's voice is steel. "Caleb Rusk, you're under arrest for obstruction of justice and suspicion of homicide in the case of Lacey Quinn."

He doesn't flinch. "Suspicion," he repeats like it's a game. "That's a nice word. Vague. Slippery."

"No one just disappears," I say. I don't care how many times I have to repeat myself. Eventually, he'll hear me. This time, he does. "Not Lacey. Not Abby. Not the girls you thought the river would keep quiet."

For the first time, his smile falters. It's just a flicker, but I catch it.

We step inside. The smell of bleach is stronger here, undercut with something sour, like damp wood left too long in the dark.

On the mantel are three framed photos, Search and Rescue team shots with Caleb front and center. The girls in the background are younger, their shoulders stiff, smiles uncertain. Lacey is in one of them. My stomach knots.

Valdez cuffs him while I move through the room. The closet door near the kitchen is ajar. Inside there's a set of waders — spotless, of course — rope coiled in perfect loops, and a stack of pillowcases, all patterned with flowers.

"Transport van's on the way," Valdez says over her shoulder.

Caleb doesn't resist. He looks at me instead. "You think you've got her back? You think a bracelet and some bones make her whole? You don't get her, Detective. You get pieces."

I step close, so close the cuffs rattle when he shifts. "You don't own her. You never did, and now she's the reason you're done."

His eyes narrow and harden. "You're making a mistake."

"No, you did."

Valdez hauls him out the door. He doesn't fight. He doesn't plead. He walks like a man who still believes he's untouchable.

But I've seen that walk before. They all break in the end.

* * *

The CSU team combs the house while we stand outside. The sun's dropping, shadows stretching long. Neighbors gather in twos and threes on the sidewalk, whispering. Some shake their heads. Others cross themselves. Everyone watches.

A tech emerges with a box of evidence. Inside is a cracked compact, matching the one in Lacey's backpack.

Another tech follows, holding a stack of Polaroids sealed in plastic. I catch a glimpse — girls, riverbanks, culverts. Some faces I recognize from old files. Others I don't.

The river kept pieces. Caleb kept the rest. It's crazy he didn't destroy these. He had to know we were coming, that I'd caught him.

Valdez leans against the cruiser where Caleb sits cuffed in the back, still smiling faintly. "He's gonna lawyer up," she says.

"Let him," I answer. "He can't lawyer his way out of this one."

She studies me. "Are you okay?"

I look at Caleb through the glass, his smirk reflected back at him in the cruiser window. Then, I look at the Polaroids, the blue bead, the flowered pillowcases.

"I'm fine," I say. "He thought she disappeared. Now he knows better."

* * *

Back at the station, I find Mrs. Quinn waiting for me. She looks older, more tired.

"Lacey didn't drown," I tell her. "She didn't slip. She didn't just vanish. A man put her in that river, and now he's in custody."

Her tears come then, sharp and sudden. She takes a seat and drops her head into her hands, whispering something I don't need to hear. I doubt it's for me. It's for her daughter.

I step out of the room, leaving her with her grief.

In the hallway, Valdez falls into step beside me. "Case closed?"

"Not yet," I say. "We've only found pieces, and I have a feeling the river's not done talking."

She doesn't argue. She never does.

CHAPTER 8: THE ROOM

The house is quiet when I get home. I don't bother with the kitchen, and I don't turn on the living room light. My feet carry me straight down the hall to the locked door.

The key is warm in my hand. The lock clicks, a sound I feel more than hear.

Inside, the air is cool, still, and familiar. My evidence room. My true home.

The walls stare back at me — maps, clippings, photographs, notes written in the middle of too many nights. Every pin has a thread, and every thread leads to the same face.

Andy Rawlings.

At the center is River. My sister.

I tack up the newest piece — a photocopy of truck logs from April, the week Lacey Quinn disappeared. Rawlings' route passes through Miller Creek, right where the search parties swarmed, right where the police said the river claimed another girl.

I step back and look at the line stretching across the map. One more overlap. One more knot in the net I've been building for twenty years.

I press my palm flat against the corkboard to ground myself.

Caleb Rusk is behind bars. Mrs. Quinn has answers. Abby has spoken at last.

But Rawlings is still out there. Still smiling in grainy photographs. Still driving. Still hunting.

The river took Lacey, but it gave her back. Caleb thought he could make her vanish, but he was wrong.

Rawlings will be wrong, too, because I know the truth.

Rule #5 — No one just disappears.

Not Lacey. Not River. Not the men who think they can hide them.

I close the door, lock it, and lean my forehead against the wood for a long moment. The house is quiet, but the room behind me hums with voices that will never fade.

Tomorrow, I'll chase a new case. Another missing girl. Another family left behind.

The End

DEAR READER: A NOTE FROM MERI

Some cases don't begin with blood or screams. Some begin with a smile. You'd think that would be the least dangerous thing in the world, but I've learned smiles can hide bruises deeper than skin, and secrets can be heavier than bones.

The girl I'm about to tell you about, Luce, was mute when I found her. But that didn't mean she couldn't communicate — she just couldn't use her mouth the way she wanted to. She'd been forced to use her mouth to hold up a mask someone else forced on her. Don't worry if you don't understand now; you soon will.

Sometimes we're told to smile when we want to scream.

I wish Luce had screamed.

She reminded me of myself when silence was the only way I could survive after River disappeared.

You'll hear pieces of Luce's story, and in them, you'll hear echoes of mine. This isn't about fairy-tale rescues. I couldn't fix her. I couldn't undo what had been done, but I could listen hard enough that her silence began to make sense.

Before you read further, remember that sometimes, survival looks like defiance. Sometimes, it looks like not smiling when you're told to. And sometimes, if you listen closely enough, it sounds like a single word whispered through the cracks.

"Persist."

—Meri

6.
THE GIRL WITH A BROKEN SMILE

RULE #6

The eyes never lie.

Even when the mouth does.

CHAPTER 1: THE BROKEN SMILE

The call comes at 2:13 a.m., just as the tinnitus in my right ear finally quiets enough for sleep to look me in the face and bargain. I let it ring twice, stare at the ceiling where the neighbor's porch light leaks through the curtains into a crooked trapezoid, and answer anyway.

"Detective Amber?" the dispatcher says, her voice apologetic. "Patrol's requesting you at Mercy Bridge. Juvenile female, possible amnesia. EMS says she won't talk."

"Won't or can't?" There's a difference, and it'll determine how I act with the victim.

A pause. "Hard to tell, but she keeps smiling."

"I'm sorry. Can you repeat that please?"

"She keeps smiling for some reason."

The drive out to Mercy Bridge is a long black ribbon with no shoulder and way too many deer. The river runs beneath it, dark and mysterious. The bridge itself isn't much — steel bones and rivets, flaking gray paint — but at night, it gathers every echo into its ribs and hums with them. By the time I pull up, there are two cruisers angled nose out, lights rotating, slow and tired. An ambulance idles, its engine ticking like a nervous metronome.

Patrolman Keating meets me at the tape. He's new enough to still iron the creases hard into his sleeves. "She was walking

"

the center line," he said, leading me past the ambulance doors. "Barefoot. No ID. No visible injuries."

"And the smile?"

"You . . . should just see it."

He isn't wrong. The girl sits on the low stone wall, her legs tucked under her, a blanket around her shoulders, steam breathing out of her like she's a cup of hot coffee. She's thirteen, maybe, fifteen if you count by the bruised moons under her eyes. Her hair is dripping wet. And her mouth . . . her mouth keeps trying to be a smile and failing, as if the muscles learned a different choreography and refuse to perform. The corners pull, tremble, and then set again. It isn't grotesque. It's so much worse.

"Hey," I say, careful with my tone. "I'm Meri."

The girl looks at me directly, and I see the first crack in the case — no scatter, no drug fog, no performative vacancy. She's alert, tracking everyone and assessing everything.

The broken smile holds like a mask she's been ordered to wear.

"Can you tell me your name?" I ask.

She doesn't answer, but the blanket falls open an inch. On her lap lies a folded photograph, the white edges worn into fur. She notices me noticing and refolds it into the pocket of the blanket like a magician palming a coin.

"Any injuries?" I ask the EMT, a woman with a braid so tight it makes my scalp ache.

"Vitals normal. No obvious trauma. Throat looks irritated, like she's had a cough or screamed herself raw. She hasn't made a sound since we got here."

"You try writing?"

The EMT holds out a pen and a torn scrap of run sheet. "Sure have."

On the sheet, in all capital letters, is what I assume is her name. *LUCE.*

"Where'd you find her exactly?" I ask Keating.

"Right about the center of the bridge," he says. "Facing east."

"Toward the old factory district," I say.

"Yeah."

I crouch so I can be level with the girl. Up close, her pupils are equal and reactive. Her fingernails are clean and cut short, not the ragged, chewed kind you see on most runaways.

"I'm going to ask you to come with me to the hospital," I say. "We'll keep you warm, run a few tests, and make sure everything's okay. You don't have to talk if you can't."

Her eyelids flutter. The almost-smile holds. She reaches up and very precisely touches the right side of her jaw with two fingers once, as if pressing an invisible bruise. Then she slides off the wall, blanket still around her, and stands. Her bare feet on the cold stone don't make her flinch.

Not even a little.

"Okay," I say softly. "Okay."

We load her and leave without lights and no siren. I ride in the back and watch the river retreat through the rear windows in a long obsidian smear.

Halfway to County General, the girl takes the photograph out again and unfolds it on her knees. She glances at me, then turns the photo so I can see. Consent or perhaps a test.

A man in his forties stands with an arm around a younger version of the girl with brighter hair, braces, and the kind of shy pride you see in kids who have been told this is a good moment and they're trying to live up to it. Behind them is a chain-link fence and a modular building with white siding. In the corner of the photo is a partial logo of a crescent moon cradling a small house. The edges of the moon are razor-thin, like a smile sliced into paper.

"Is that you?" I ask. The girl nods once. "That your dad?"

Her eyes flick to mine, then away, and then back to the man's face. She places her finger on his cheek in the photograph and holds it there until the ambulance bumps and the pen line of her finger blurs on the glossy surface. Then she takes her finger away and taps the dark space behind the fence.

"Inside?" I say.

She nods again. Then, carefully, she folds the photo and tucks it away.

At the hospital, I hand her to a burly night charge nurse who has a face like a disappointed saint and a heart like a city bus.

"We'll get a sexual assault nurse," the nurse murmurs in my ear, already steering the girl toward a room, "and a social worker. You staying?"

"Yeah."

I take the waiting chair outside her door and text my partner, Deputy Valdez. *Found girl on Mercy Bridge. Won't speak. Smiles like a broken hinge. Photo with a crescent-house logo. You recognize it?*

She responds. *Maybe. Moon House Recovery? Pastor Ed's thing? The one out by the old switchyard.*

Moon House. I've heard about it. A "recovery home" for wayward teens — church-affiliated, donor-sustained, volunteer-staffed, beloved at pancake breakfasts, rumored to be a place where rules come down hard and fall harder. I have no proof of anything, just the way a girl in Intake once flinched at the word "quiet time" like it was a synonym for punishment.

I stand, stretch my back until it makes a noise like cracking ice, and walk to the hallway phone to request a SANE nurse officially, then to the vending machine to feed it a dollar for a coffee that tastes like old slate. When I come back, the girl is perched on the edge of the hospital bed, the blanket neatly folded beside her. Her bare feet dangle, one heel making small, desultory taps against the metal rail. Tap. Pause. Tap-tap. Tap. A code only she knows.

"Can I sit?" I ask, and when she doesn't refuse, I pull the visitor chair close enough to share the stale warmth of the room. "I recognize the moon on your photo. It might be a place called Moon House. Is that right?"

The girl's broken smile flickers like a bad fluorescent light. She lifts a hand, traces a crescent in the air — yes — and then presses two fingers to her own lips, sliding downward into her throat — no. It takes me a second. Yes, Moon House. No . . . voice?

I keep my face calm and my breath slow. I want to ask too many things at once. Who took your voice? How long has your smile been broken? Where is the man in your photo now? But even though questions pile up like stones, I've learned not to build walls that the victim then has to climb.

"Okay," I say. "We'll go slow. I'll talk, and you correct me when I get it wrong." I pull my notebook and flip to a clean sheet. "Your name is—"

She lifts her hand and flattens it, palm out. Stop. Then she reaches for the pen and writes slowly and painstakingly, left-handed, *LUCE*. The E wavers like it has tremors.

"Luce? Or Lucy?" I ask, letting the name be a small light between us.

She holds up one finger.

"Hi, Luce."

Her face doesn't change except for the tiniest easing at the corners of that broken not-smile. She taps the notebook and adds another word beneath her name. *DAD*. Then she draws a little square within a square, like a window with blinds, and a dot in the middle. I don't get it until she presses her finger gently to the right side of her jaw again — the same place as on the bridge — and pushes, making her mouth skew. Then she opens her hand and closes it, open and close, a shape like a door becoming a fist.

Door. Window. Dot like a peephole. Jaw pressure.

"Someone watched you through a door," I say. "Someone made you . . . smile."

Her throat works once, and the not-smile holds.

The SANE nurse arrives then, a woman with silver hair and a directness I trust. We go through the script — consent, explanation, options. Luce listens like a good student and shakes her head at the kit. Not now. Maybe later. She lets the nurse draw blood and look at the back of her throat with a penlight.

"No tearing," the nurse murmurs to me, professional and neutral and furious all at once, the way we get. "There are small abrasions on the buccal mucosa like . . . pressure from inside the cheek. Repetitive."

"Like pushing her fingers there?" I ask.

The nurse nods grimly.

I step out to call Valdez because saying it in the hall feels safer than saying it in front of Luce. "We need a warrant for Moon House, specifically the intake logs, visitor logs, and staff rosters. And I want to know who runs it now."

"Pastor Ed died last year," she says. "Heart attack. At least that's what was in the press. His wife took over. Marian. Everyone calls her Sister Marian even though she's never been a nun."

"Get me everything," I say, "and see if we have any missing persons that match Luce in the last . . . six months."

"On it."

When I head back in, Luce has arranged the blanket just so, hospital corners neat and tight. Is that from habit or training?

I pull my chair closer again and sit by her side, making sure not to look at her directly. Sometimes, that's too much.

We listen to the hallway cart squeak and a distant cough, the world trying to pretend it's normal.

"Luce," I say finally, "if I show you a few photos — of buildings, of logos — will you point if you recognize the place you came from?"

She nods once.

I pull up my phone and search my case notes for the Moon House pamphlets we seized two years ago but never made stick. The crescent-house logo smiles up at us from the screen.

Luce touches it, then pulls her hand back like it's burned.

"Okay. Tomorrow, we go there." I wait, and when she doesn't flinch, I add, "I don't know what they told you about people like me, but my job isn't to get you to talk. It's to listen hard enough that your silence makes sense."

For the first time, the not-smile falters in the other direction downward, the muscles failing their old choreography, and something raw shows through. Not tears and definitely not fear.

Relief, maybe?

"Can I tell you something I live by?" I ask. She looks at me steadily, and I know she'll remember. "Just once. Then I won't repeat it." I hold her gaze and, not much louder than a breath, offer the rule that has saved me more times than I can count, "*Rule Seven — the eyes never lie even when the mouth does.*"

Luce blinks slowly. The corners of her mouth twitch, not up, not down. Just a tremor, an unlearning.

She lifts the photo from her lap and slides it across to me. On the back, in a different hand than the one she used to write her name, is a date from nine months ago and three words. "Moon House Family."

"Okay," I say again. Sometimes that's the only word big enough to hold what needs to be done. "We'll start there."

Her heel gives one more absent tap against the bed rail. Tap. Tap. Then she tucks her feet up, turns on her side facing the wall, and, without any noise at all, finally falls asleep.

I stay in the plastic chair with the photograph in my hand and let the night lay its weight on my shoulders. Mercy Bridge hums in my mind, steel holding echoes. Somewhere between the river and the moon, a place wears a smile like a blade.

Tomorrow, I will make it show its teeth.

CHAPTER 2: MOON HOUSE SHADOWS

By morning, Luce is transferred to Pediatrics under a protective hold. The hospital staff whispers about her smile in the hallway, some with pity, some with unease, as if trauma can be contagious.

I stay long enough to watch her eat half a cup of applesauce. When she's done, she folds the napkin into a tight square and tucks it under the plastic tray. Another ritual.

Valdez texts. *Meet me at the switchyard. Bring coffee. This place gives me hives.*

Moon House sits on county land, half hidden by tall weeds and the skeletons of train cars rusting in their graves. The siding on the main building is newer than the trailers it replaced, pale vinyl scrubbed clean of graffiti, but the logo remains — a crescent moon cradling a square house, painted above the door in fading navy.

It looks innocent enough, the way most traps do.

Valdez leans against the hood of her sedan and takes the coffee I hold out for her. "Pastor Ed's widow still runs it," she says, squinting at the building. "She's got three volunteers, no licensed counselors on record, and a board made up of retired church folk who love potlucks more than background checks."

"Any state funding?" I ask.

"None, which means they fly under licensing. It's all donations and 'faith-based healing.'"

I walk the perimeter first. The yard smells faintly of bleach and freshly cut grass, a combination that makes my teeth ache. The narrow windows have been reinforced with interior bars that someone has tried to disguise with lace curtains. There are two doors, one in the front and one at the back. Both are locked.

Valdez trails behind me, muttering, "If this were a kennel, Animal Control would've shut it down ten years ago."

"Did you pull their intake?" I ask.

"Working on it. Marian's a zealot about privacy. Claims she's protecting the kids from sin creeping back in. Records are probably on paper in some locked drawer next to a Bible."

We stop at the back corner, where the siding doesn't quite line up. A thin crack runs from the foundation to the eaves. I press close, my ear to the wall. Faint voices filter through, a sing-song cadence, and then a woman's voice, loud and clear, reaches me. "Say it after me — obedience, silence, purity."

Valdez shakes her head. "Cult-lite."

"No. Cult-practical," I say. "Cheaper than therapy, easier than accountability."

We circle back to the front. Marian appears, framed in the doorway like she's been waiting for us. She's in her late fifties, her hair pinned tight. Her smile is wide enough to show every tooth, but her eyes don't match the smile, and once you see that kind of fracture, you can't unsee it.

"Detectives." Her voice is honeyed and sharp. "What an unexpected blessing."

I flip my badge. "Detective Amber, county. This is Officer Valdez. We're looking into a juvenile found on Mercy Bridge last night. We believe she may have ties to Moon House."

Marian's smile tightens but never falters. "Our doors are always open to those who need redemption. However, I can't discuss the children under our care without proper authorization. Privacy is sacred."

Valdez snorts into her coffee. "So's not dumping traumatized girls barefoot on bridges."

I shoot her a look, but Marian's eyes flick over her like she's a fly against her window. Then, she focuses on me, weighing, measuring. "If you want to speak with me further, you'll need a warrant. Until then, I suggest you pray for her recovery. We do."

The door closes with a finality that feels more like a slap.

We stand there a moment, listening to the lock click into place, the crows overhead restless.

"Warrant will take days. Judge Harper eats out of Marian's hand at church socials," Valdez says.

"Then we find another way in."

I remove Luce's photograph from my pocket. On the back, her father's handwriting glares up at me. *Moon House Family.* His smile in the photo looks genuine and protective, the kind of smile you believe in, yet he's gone, erased from Marian's version of truth.

I fold the photo again and slip it back into my coat. Marian's smile haunts me more than Luce's broken one. At least Luce's is honest in its fracture. Marian's is a mask, seamless and practiced, a smile that hides teeth sharpened on scripture.

And behind those walls, I still hear the chant, "Obedience, silence, purity."

CHAPTER 3: ECHOES IN DAYLIGHT

By nine, I carry a Styrofoam cup of hospital coffee that smells like it has already lived another darker life and toss it into a waiting garbage can.

"Morning, Detective," the charge nurse says. "Your girl's awake. She ate toast. Two pieces."

"Victory," I say, grinning. Food is a pact with the body that says it's worth staying.

I pause at the doorway to Pediatrics. Luce sits upright, cross-legged over the blanket. Her hair is frizzed in a halo from sleep. She's arranged the plastic cup of water, the apple juice, and the packet of crackers into a straight line. The edge of the photo peeks out from beneath her pillow like a talisman that she daren't keep in plain sight.

"Hey," I say softly.

She flicks her gaze to me and then to the triangular slice of daylight on the floor where the blinds don't quite meet. The smile — the not-smile — makes an appearance and hangs there, a stage cue she can't skip.

I take the chair. "Any more words today?" I ask, touching the notebook.

She reaches for the pen and prints carefully, as if the letters are a test. *NO.*

"Okay," I say. One small loss among small wins — like eating toast, sitting up, and letting me in the room again. "I'm going to check some things. I'll be back before lunch. A social worker will come by. Is there anything specific you want me to bring?"

She considers that like I've offered a riddle. Then she writes in smaller letters, *HAIR TIE* and draws a circle that has two rabbit ears that could also be a smile if you wanted to see it that way.

"I can manage a hair tie," I tell her. I can manage two, three, a whole fistful.

As I rise, she reaches out and taps the bed rail twice, pauses, and then taps it one more time. I find myself matching my breath to it without meaning to. Tap. Tap. Tap.

In another life, in another room, there had been other tapping — not mine, not hers — a television no one watched, and a shoe heel on linoleum while a big man in a trucker cap pretended to choose beef jerky from a rack but watched the corner mirror instead. My reflection, thirteen, trying to make my mouth do something it didn't want to because that's what the man wanted to see — a nice smile from a nice girl. My mother had been in the restroom with a migraine packet she never left home without. I'd been sent to fetch water.

That's what I remember now — the way my face felt like my enemy, the way a smile could be evidence used against you, the way the mirror held me without mercy. I had no clue who he was or even what his name was, not then at least. I had no idea that my failure to be chosen that day would later feel like a kind of survivor's guilt.

I knocked the water cup against the counter loudly, and the man moved on to the lottery tickets and then out the door into the afternoon glare.

I rub the heel of my hand over my right jaw until the old ache flares and then subsides. When I look back at Luce, she's watching not my mouth but my hands, like she recognizes something. I nod to her, the silent promise sitting between us like a simple thing. "I will go. I will come back. I will not leave you in the hands of smiles."

Valdez meets me in the lobby with a box of hair ties in her hand, like she raided an entire aisle at the drugstore. She hands them over. "I texted the judge's clerk twice, which means we'll get that warrant around Hannukah," she says. "Until then, I've got you a workaround. County filings."

"Hit me."

"Moon House is technically a faith outreach of Morningstar Community Church. They filed their new articles when the widow took over after Ed died. State says they have a 'residential discipleship program' and a 'family reunification wing.'"

"Family reunification," I repeat. The phrase tastes like ammonia. "You pull any permits for construction? Fences? Locks?"

"Nothing."

We step out into daylight. Hospitals all look the same from the outside, no matter the city, with glass intended to signify transparency and landscaping intended to signify care. A groundskeeper pushes a rake through leaves that makes a sound like someone shushing a rowdy classroom.

"Before I head to Moon House, I want to find Luce's father," I say. "If he was alive nine months ago, someone wrote him out of the story. Paper leaves a trail. Love leaves one too."

"Name?"

"Don't have it, but we've got a date on the back of that photo and the church. Maybe the church's bulletin does our work for us."

Valdez frowns. "You mean we get to do the thing I hate most — talk to cheerful people."

* * *

Morningstar Community Church sits on the edge of a strip mall between a Pilates studio and a vape shop. Honestly, that's what God looks like in our county these days — whatever fits next to vacant square footage. The congregation has done its best to make the exterior welcoming with pastel chalk on the sidewalk and a verse about joy. Someone even tied a yellow ribbon around a planter. The door stands propped open. Music drifts out, three chords and a chorus you could sing with your eyes closed.

We arrive between services. The lobby smells like free coffee and the overwhelming plume of perfume from the volunteers.

A woman at the welcome table beams, thrusting a program at me. "First time? We're so glad you're here."

"Detective Amber, county," I say, showing my badge in the sandwich-space between gentle and firm. "We've got a juvenile who may be tied to Moon House. We're trying to locate her father. The photo we have looks like it was taken here."

The woman's smile falters. "Oh," she says, stretching the vowel. "That would be . . . Sister Marian has been running Moon House since Pastor Ed's Homegoing. I can fetch her. She's here."

"We've spoken," I say. "I was hoping there might be a bulletin board with photos."

The woman's shoulders ease. "Our Family Wall!" she says with a relief you could stack books on. "Right over here."

She leads us to a series of corkboards framed in whitewashed wood. There are smiling faces, babies with bows bigger than their heads, and men in flannel holding fish next to verses about being fishers of men. There, on the third row, two over, is Luce, the sun in her hair, her braces flashing. The same man stands behind her with his arm around her shoulders, his thumbs awkward as if he didn't know where to put his hands when told to hold onto joy.

"Can I photograph this?" I ask.

"Of course," the woman says, and then her eyes soften. "They were only with us a short time."

"Name?" I ask.

She hesitates. "I probably shouldn't—"

I wait, and silence does what it does when used well — it makes space where resistance swells.

"Gabe," she says finally. "Gabe Landry. He came for three Wednesdays. People from Moon House brought him and the girl. Marian asked us to be extra friendly. He seemed nice. Quiet. Asked where the bathrooms were a lot," she added, like she's ashamed of offering nothing.

"Does Gabe attend now?"

Her face closes. "I haven't seen him in months."

"Did they announce anything? Baptism? Decision?"

"We don't do public decisions," she says, and for the first time, something unpracticed goes through her smile. Irritation, maybe. "We do life groups. Sister Marian doesn't think that kind of emotionalism sticks."

"Do you have contact information for Gabe?" Valdez asks. She turns up her sincerity. "Even a small detail could help."

The woman's eyes flick to the door that leads backstage. "I can ask the administrator if we have a card, but I really should—"

"We'll wait," I say.

She slips away, and we stand with the faces on the Family Wall looking back like they'd been told to freeze.

Valdez leans close to a set of photos in the corner. "They blurred the girls' last names on their 'testimonies' before printing," she says softly. "They're not idiots."

"They're not saints either."

I'm not going to lie. I'm struggling with this.

A different woman emerges from the door with a sense of forced calm. "Detectives," she says, holding out her hand. "I'm Andrea, the administrator for Moon House. I hear you are looking for some contact information on one of our families? Unfortunately, while we do keep a database for follow-up, we only have the contact listed as Moon House."

"Families?"

She flushes. "Participants," she corrects herself. "Sister Marian will be available after the second service if you—"

"We've met," I interrupt. "What about Pastor Ed's funeral bulletin? An obituary? Sometimes families sign the guestbook."

Andrea's relief is almost funny. "Oh! Yes. We keep those in the office."

She disappears and returns with a stack of programs bound in twine. While she fans them out, a name jumps like a fish.

Thanks to those who served alongside Pastor Ed — Marian, the Board, and community partners, including Gabe Landry.

"May I photograph this?" I ask again. She nods. "Do you happen to have a last known for Mr. Landry?" I'm hoping that if I ask this in a different way, I'll get a different answer.

Her mouth works, but nothing comes out. "We—" she begins and then stops. "I'm so sorry. I don't think so."

It's enough. People leave footprints they don't intend to. You just have to know how to harvest the print.

I thank her and take a program for myself, and we leave before Marian can come sweeping out to call us wolves.

Back in the car, Valdez has the county database up before her seat belt clicks. "Landry, Landry," she says like a litany. "We've got three. One's eighty-nine, one's in jail, one's — ah. Gabriel Landry, forty-four. Former mechanic, now unemployed. Former address is Maple Court, unit C. Left about four months ago."

"Before or after the date on the photo?" I ask.

"After," she says. "Billing address switched to a PO Box in the next county. He got a fine for trespassing behind a rail yard two months back, but it was dismissed."

CHAPTER 4: THE BRIDGE

We drive to Maple Court even though we know he's not there. It's a U-shaped stack of apartments on the affordable end of broke. Two kids play soccer with a milk jug. A woman smokes on the second-floor landing in a robe the color of old snow. Unit C still bears the tape X of a landlord who thinks that makes a lock. Inside, all of the furniture is gone, and there's a mark on the wall paler than the paint around it where a cross had hung.

"A unit like this, you'd think would be rented by now."

I walk through with the kind of step used in graveyards — respectful and invisible, knowing it doesn't matter but knowing it does in its own way. In the kitchen junk drawer — because there's always one — I find rubber bands that have lost their elasticity, a novelty pen with a mechanic's logo, and a takeout menu from a pizza place that boasts *We Deliver to the Switchyard!* On the back of the menu is a note in blocky, careful handwriting. *Wed 7 p.m. — Church w/ L.* The *L* has a tiny loop at the end, like a smile trying not to happen.

"Let's check with the superintendent," Valdez said. "If Gabe was trying to reunify, he must've asked for an extension before eviction."

The super is a man who has seen too much too early and now sees nothing too late. He recognizes Gabe's name. "Nice enough guy. Kept to himself. The girl came around sometimes. Quiet.

Didn't run with the other kids. He had a van. Blue. An old Ford. He asked about moving to a place with a backyard." The super's eyes shift toward the closed office door where a radio drones with the weather. "He said something about needing a place with a fence. I told him the waiting list is long, and next I know, he's gone."

"Not evicted?" I ask.

The super raises his palms. "Just gone."

"Any idea where he worked before unemployment?"

"Sunrise Auto," he says.

Sunrise Auto sits on a side road. A single man works the front, his beard catching the light like a net. He remembers Gabe. "Good with transmissions," he says, "but bad with people." He shrugs like it's normal. "I liked him. He'd bring that girl of his sometimes. She'd sit in the office and do homework. He was trying, you know?"

"What happened?" I ask. So far, Gabe doesn't sound like a bad father.

The man shrugs. "Pastor Ed happened. And whatever the wife calls herself now. They told him she needed 'structure,' and he needed 'covering,' and then he stopped bringing her around. I told him not to listen to them, that he was doing a good job raising that girl, but he changed after that. Got real quiet."

"Did he say he felt watched?" Valdez asks.

The mechanic makes a face. "Watched? Hell, he wouldn't take a leak if he thought God had stepped out of the room and somebody else had stepped in."

"Did he ever mention Mercy Bridge?"

The man's mouth pulls downward like he means to spit but thinks better of it. "There's a rumor, Detective. You want it?"

"Rumors are threads," I say. "I knit."

"Kids from Moon House — girls mostly — they get 'walks' if they do well. Walks are treats. Sometimes, they walk to the bridge and stand at the ledge in pairs. Stand and smile and pray."

"Pairs?" I ask. "Ever see Luce with someone?"

He shakes his head. "Didn't see her out there. Only time I ever saw her was when she was with him, Gabe."

We thank him and leave.

I call the hospital from the car and ask the social worker to sit with Luce if she can.

"She's knitting," Ingrid says. "Someone brought yarn. She's making a square with holes where the needles got confused. It's perfect."

The bridge in daylight surprises me. In the night, its steel is like a rib cage. In the day, it's a spine. The river below moves with patience. If you live long enough or work in my line of work long enough, you recognize patient things like water, grief, and places that wait for you to come back.

A yellow bouquet leans against the stone. Tucked in the ribbon is a tract from Morningstar about second chances. "Love is not a prison," it reads in block print. "Love is a path." The paper had gotten wet and dried again, causing the letters to bleed.

Valdez peers over the railing. "No cameras," she says. "Also no witnesses from last night. If they use this bridge as a test, it's been going on long enough to get boring."

"And long enough that the locals don't blink twice anymore," I say, getting really tired of all of this. "That's when it gets dangerous."

On the center line, baked into the asphalt by the sun, are two pale shoeprints or, rather, footprints. They look off, wrong, but I can't put my finger on it.

"Bleach," Valdez says behind me, bending and sniffing. "It's faint, but there's enough of a trace. I wonder if they noticed this?" She pulls out her phone and takes photographs. "They cleaned something here."

I stand there, the air in my chest like a held note, and turn slowly, taking in the geometry of it — the point of the bridge where the view bends, the angles for cars, and the place a pair would stand for photographs if they were building a collage of obedience. A rake of rail marks punctures the curb where a van might have overcorrected once and left a message made of scraped paint.

"Let's not wait on the judge," I say, frustrated with where all of this is leading, if it's leading at all.

"We can't just break in," Valdez says, but she says it like she's reading from a script.

"No," I say, "but we can talk to their neighbors."

Neighbors, in places like this, include anyone with a porch and an opinion. Two houses down from the bridge, an old woman in a sweatshirt with a Christmas reindeer on it is sitting on a swing that creaks on the forward motion and holds its breath on the back. She introduces herself as Mavis.

"You cops finally remember the bridge exists?" she asks without malice. "I ever tell you about the time someone found a goat right there with a ribbon 'round its neck? Halloween. I told my daughter not to take the ribbon, that it was probably cursed. She took it anyway. Nothing happened. It made me feel left out."

It takes me a few moments to process that. "Do you see kids standing here?" I ask. "Kids from the church out by the yard?"

She snorts. "The Moon House? Yeah, they walk like they're trying not to step on their own shadows. Always in twos. Always hands folded. Smiles like pageant girls. Sometimes, there's a woman with hair like a helmet." She pauses and scratches her head. "Sometimes there's a man with a clipboard who does. That one worries me."

"Have you seen this girl?" I show her a screenshot of Luce.

Mavis nods slowly. "That one keeps her eyes on the water," she says, tapping the photo. "She had a daddy with her once. He didn't come back. The woman with the helmet told another lady that he decided drugs were more important than his daughter." Mavis tsks. "He didn't look like a drugs man to me. He looked like a man who didn't know how to argue past his own throat."

"Did you ever see her at night?" I ask. "Alone?"

Mavis goes quiet, the swing creaking. "Last week," she says eventually. "Just her. Barefoot. Saw her from my window. Thought I dreamed it."

"Did anyone pick her up?"

It takes her a moment. "A van, I think," she says. "Blue."

Blue van. The story is starting to braid together.

I thank Mavis, and we drive to where the rail yard falls away to parking lots and then to weeds. A blue van sits in the lot adjacent to Moon House, the paint oxidized to the color of old denim, the rear bumper bruised. The van has a magnetic placard on the door of a crescent moon cradling a house. The magnetic corners curled.

"Plate's registered to Morningstar," Valdez says, staring at her phone. "No priors. No tickets. Nothing."

"We could wait to see who drives it," I suggest, "but I don't feel like playing lifeguard while people drown three feet from the edge."

I stare at the Moon House building, at its fake lace and real locks. I think of Luce's heel tap and the way she pressed her jaw to make the smile behave.

"What are you thinking?" Valdez asks.

"That we can be devout too," I say slowly. "To paperwork. To sunlight. To the kind of inconvenience that makes bad people sweat." I pull my phone and dial CPS. I use the words that make bureaucracies wake mid-nap — *imminent harm, unlicensed residential, pattern of coercion, and witness under protective hold*. I mention the hospital and the bridge. I mention the patrol report. What I don't mention are the rumors, but I let their shadow sit heavy in my tone.

When I hang up, Valdez whistles. "You just rang the bell."

"Now let's see who answers."

We stand in the parking lot. A car pulls out of the church lot. My phone buzzes with a text from the social worker. *She asked for the hair ties. She braided her own hair. It's lopsided and perfect.*

"We need to head back to the hospital," I tell Valdez. "I need to see her before we push any harder."

She drives without commentary, and on the way, we pass the strip of pawn shops and payday lenders that tumors around the hospital like opportunists. In the window of one shop, a frame displays a silver bracelet engraved with *HOPE*. It looks like a dare.

Luce sits with her back to the door when I come in, her knees pulled up tight. A square of pink yarn lies in her lap, and a hair tie bands her braid. She turns at the sound of my shoes. That smile of hers tries to come but fails. Good. Failure means the muscles are loosening, and the mask is losing its glue.

I sit. "We found your father's name. Gabe. Does that sound right?"

She stares at my throat as if words are physically visible there. Then she nods.

I wait a beat and then add, "We're going to find him, and if he can't come, we'll find why."

Her heel begins its rhythm. Tap. Pause. Tap-tap. I match my breath, like stepping into a dance that only one of us can hear. The photo waits under her pillow. After a moment, she slides it out and hands it to me. I turn it over in my palm and feel the date imprinted there like a brand. Nine months ago. Long enough to grow a thing, long enough to lose it, long enough to pretend the clock was your friend.

"I went to your church," I mention. "They keep a wall with pictures. You're there. It's not a secret anymore."

I watch her eyes and catch her flinching at the word *secret*. I take a breath that hurts my ribs and say the thing I don't want to because saying it makes it a direction. "They don't get to keep you."

For a second, the room holds still. Then her hand, the same one that drew a window within a window, moves. She places it in the air between us, not touching, just hovering, as if confirming the distance. Then she lowers it to her lap, picks up the yarn again, and puts the needle through one loop and then the next, and though she made another hole where the loop should be, she keeps going, unembarrassed by the imperfection.

I watch Luce's hands, steady now. I think of how a smile can be a door, and a door can be a mouth, and a mouth can be a wound, and a wound can be a map. I think of how yesterday I promised a girl who didn't trust words that I would listen until her silence made sense. She's giving me sentences now, one loop at a time.

"I'll be back," I say finally. "If someone comes from the church, you don't have to see them. You don't have to hear them. You get to choose whose eyes you meet."

Her eyes meet mine then, and between us passes something I can't name without breaking it. A benediction that doesn't require belief. An agreement that doesn't need a handshake. She nods once, like she's signaled a train with her heel and finally hears it, faint, but it's coming.

I stand and leave the hair ties on the windowsill in a rainbow, all elastic and practical and ordinary.

In the hall, I text Valdez. *CPS on the move?*

She sends back a single word. *Yes.*

Good. Let them come with clipboards and bad coffee and the weight of the state. Let them inventory the rooms and count the locks and ask Marian to produce signatures for all the silences she keeps. Let them learn what I know from bridges, that what looks sturdy often isn't, what looks cold can carry you, and the middle space between banks is where the echoes teach you what was said on either side.

I head back to Luce's room. Stories like this don't unspool without a witness, and I've made a career of being the person who stays when other people's smiles begin to crack.

CHAPTER 5: THE VANISHED FATHER

The records office at County Hall smells of dust, toner, and the kind of paper that remembers too much. Valdez grumbles while the clerk fetches boxes for us. I flip through folders with the mechanical calm of someone who knows that buried under bad handwriting and coffee rings is the evidence that changes everything.

Gabe Landry isn't a ghost, at least not officially. We find a birth certificate for Luce, listing him as the father. There's a restraining order filed five years ago against Luce's mother, who has since vanished from the grid, a fine for trespassing, and then nothing.

The clerk hands me a final envelope. "This one's recent," she says, her voice lowered. "It came through last month. Death certificate."

The paper inside has my hands sweating despite the air conditioning. *Gabriel Thomas Landry. Cause: accidental overdose. Location: abandoned rail yard shed.* Signed by the county coroner. No next of kin listed.

Valdez swears as she reads the paper. "They buried him."

"Not just buried," I say. "They erased him."

Because everything I've seen of Gabe, every thread I've tugged, points to a man clawing for his daughter's safety, not a man who'd fold in on himself with a needle. Not a man who'd die alone in a shed with no one to find him.

I drive out to the rail yard myself and find the shed where Mr. Landry apparently died. It's nothing more than a rusted tin shed leaning on habit. There's no padlock, and when I open the door, all I find inside is a dirt floor covered in cigarette butts and a flattened sleeping bag. The air smells of bleach, sharp and wrong, too clean for a place that should have been dirty.

I crouch. There are no needles. No spoons. Just absence. Manufactured absence.

I think about Luce, her finger pressing to her jaw, and her broken smile. Her father's hand on her shoulder in that photo. His smile was not fractured, not forced. If he's been erased, then she's been taught to pretend he never existed.

That is worse than killing him because it's killing her piece by piece.

* * *

Back at the hospital, I find her knitting again. The square is larger now, the holes more frequent. She glances up when I enter, her eyes sharp and measuring.

I place the folded copy of the death certificate on the bed where she can see the county seal, but I don't show her the words yet. "I went looking for your dad," I say softly. "The county says he died." I pause. "By overdose."

Her hands freeze around the yarn. Then she shoves the square aside and snatches the paper. Her eyes track the lines, once, twice. The not-smile appears, grotesque in its steadiness, and then, finally, she shakes her head. Hard.

"No?" I ask.

She grabs the pen and scrawls over the margin. *LIE.*

The word stabbed through the page.

"All right," I say. "Then we prove it."

Her eyes meet mine, burning. For the first time, her lips twitch not in obedience but in defiance. The broken smile cracks, showing the jagged edges beneath.

I recognize it. That is a smile that survives.

Valdez leans against the doorframe, watching us. "So," she says, "what's the play?"

"The play," I answer, folding the copy of the certificate and slipping it back into my coat, "is to make Moon House show us its lies and then burn every smile they've taught into ashes."

Luce's heel taps against the bedrail. Tap. Tap. Tap. This time, I tap back, and in that unspoken rhythm, I hear the echo of her father's fight.

And mine.

CHAPTER 6: INSIDE MOON HOUSE

CPS doesn't move like cavalry. Instead, they move like clerks with clipboards in hand, their ties crooked, trying to look invisible until the moment they have to be noticed. Sometimes, they do it right, and sometimes invisibility is a weapon. Bureaucracy carries a peculiar weight. When wielded right, it crushes faster than fists.

I drive behind their van, Valdez beside me, and my chest tightens as Moon House appears at the end of the gravel lane. The front door is propped open wide, like a host pretending nothing is wrong.

Sister Marian stands framed in the doorway, her hair helmet-smooth, her smile locked in place. Her arms are folded — not welcoming, not open. "Good morning," she calls, her voice syrup poured over knives. "What a surprise."

The lead CPS worker, a tall man named Harris, shows his badge. "We've received a report of potential endangerment to minors in residence. We're conducting a site inspection. You'll need to grant us access immediately."

Her smile doesn't flicker. "Our children are safe. They are in prayer right now. We do not open our sanctuary to outsiders without a warrant."

"You'll want to reconsider that." Harris is as polite as a sermon, as firm as a gavel. "Failure to comply escalates quickly."

Behind her, I glimpse a shadow with small shoulders and a bowed head. A child. I hear the echo of chanting, "Obedience, silence, purity."

I step forward. "Sister Marian," I say, "we can stand here all day, or you can let us in and show us the truth."

Her eyes narrow at me. "You're the detective — the one who found our lost lamb on the bridge. She should never have been out there alone. She broke covenant. We were correcting her."

The words punch through me. Covenant. Correcting. My fists want to close, but I hold them open.

"Correction doesn't involve leaving a girl barefoot on asphalt at midnight. Correction doesn't erase a father."

Something flickers in her gaze at that, quick and defensive. "Gabe Landry was weak. He chose the world over his daughter."

"No," I say. "He chose her, and you erased him."

Valdez leans close to Harris. "That's obstruction dressed in scripture. Time to push."

Harris nods. "We're entering."

The CPS team moves forward in practiced formation, two by the door, one circling back.

Marian steps aside, finally, her jaw clenched, her smile frozen. "May God forgive you when you see what you're trying to destroy," she hisses.

In the entry hall, photos line the walls — girls with identical smiles and stiff postures.

A cluster of children sits cross-legged in the main room. They sing in low tones, the words thick with forced sweetness. A volunteer hovers nearby, a clipboard in hand. The moment he sees our badges, the color drains from his face.

"Inspection," Harris says, his voice even. "Please separate the children by dormitory. We'll be speaking with them individually."

The volunteer looks to Marian.

She gives a tight nod. "Cooperate," she says, her voice brittle.

I follow the group down a corridor. The rooms are bare, with bunk beds lined like soldiers and sheets tucked tight enough to bounce a coin. A single Bible rests on each pillow. There are no personal belongings, no posters, no stuffed animals.

Their childhood has been scrubbed out.

One girl, twelve maybe, peeks up at me. Her mouth is fixed in the same not-smile Luce wore, and my stomach twists.

I crouch. "What's your name?"

Her lips press tighter. She flicks her eyes toward the ceiling, then back to me. Silent, rehearsed.

"She won't answer you," Marian says behind me, her voice sharp. "Our girls don't speak to strangers."

I rise and turn to her. "You mean they don't speak to anyone who might hear the truth."

Marian's smile thins. "They are pure. They are safe."

"Safe doesn't look like this," I say, barely keeping my anger in check. "Safe doesn't wear a mask."

* * *

In the office, we find the files. The binders are locked in a cabinet, names written in neat block letters. Intake forms have been signed only by "guardians," most of them Marian herself. Records of "discipline" are marked with dates and scriptures instead of explanations. A lot have pages missing.

Tucked between them is a ledger with handwritten notes of donations and expenses. A line item jumps out. *Special Care —* *G.L.* Listed beside it is a date, almost a month before Gabe's death.

I take a photo, my heart pounding.

When we leave, CPS carts out the files, photocopies, and even two of the children for immediate protective hold. Marian stands on the porch, her arms rigid, her eyes blazing with something beyond fury — conviction.

"You will regret this," she says, her voice low enough that only I can hear. "The world needs covenant. Without it, girls like her will break. You can't save them all."

I lean close, my voice just for her. "Maybe not, but I'll save the ones you taught to smile."

She flinches, and for the first time since this began, I know she's afraid.

CHAPTER 7: PAPER LIES

The files smell of ink and mildew, a scent you can't scrub out no matter how hard you try. Valdez spreads them across the diner table between us, next to my untouched coffee. The waitress has topped it off three times, and it still tastes like burnt pennies.

"Look at this," she says, jabbing a finger at one of the ledgers. "Five hundred dollars then another thousand the next month, right before the coroner says Gabe overdosed."

"Special care," I repeat. "Not food, not housing, not program supplies."

"Which means hush money. Or disposal money. Either way, not the kind of care you advertise at pancake breakfasts."

She flips another page. "And here, disciplinary notes. Half the entries are redacted, like someone censored their own journal, but this one's clear." She pushes it toward me.

Child resisted correction. Smiles not consistent. Needs reinforcement.

My stomach twists. "They trained them."

"Worse," Valdez says. "They documented it."

I stare at the handwriting, neat and upright, the kind of script that belongs to someone who believes every word they write is gospel. I look away, and my reflection stares back in the diner's window, pale in the morning light, my jaw clenched. I remember

Luce tapping her heel, knitting holes into her yarn square, and pressing her finger against her jaw until her face betrays her.

"Paper lies," I say quietly. "But she doesn't. She hasn't."

* * *

Luce is sitting cross-legged on her bed when I return, the yarn square spread across her knees like a flag of some fragile country. She looks up at me, her eyes sharp. Her braid has slipped loose, a few strands curling against her cheek. The not-smile hovers but doesn't stick.

I pull the chair close and place the folder on my lap. "We found some papers from Moon House," I say. "Records. Do you want to see?"

She hesitates, then gives one small nod.

I open the ledger first, turning the folder so she can read the neat columns of dates and numbers. I tap the line, *Special Care — G.L.*

Her eyes widen, and her finger traces the initials, once, twice, like she's afraid they might vanish if she doesn't hold them down. Then she snatches the pen and scrawls on my notebook: *DAD.* Underlined. Hard.

"Yes," I say. "That's him. That's Gabe."

Her hand trembles as she writes again. *NOT DEAD.*

I swallow. "The county says he overdosed. They filed a death certificate."

Her head shakes violently. She presses the pen so hard that the tip tears the page. *LIE.*

I slide another document toward her, the disciplinary notes.

She reads these, her lips tightening, and then she presses her hand against her jaw, dragging down the way I've seen before. Her not-smile warps into something raw and painful. She writes: *THEY MADE.*

I put my hand flat on the folder, covering the words. "You don't have to carry their lies anymore. Not with me. You can show me what's true, and we'll make it louder than anything they put on paper."

Her eyes fill, but the tears don't spill. She flips to a blank page and draws a rectangle with bars, a stick figure inside, and another figure outside holding something like a clipboard. Then she adds a third, taller figure standing between them, blocking the way. Over the taller figure's head, she draws a circle — her father.

He isn't gone. He's been shut out.

I breathe carefully, steadily, the way you do when holding a live wire. "They told you he was dead, but you saw him."

She nods once. Fierce.

"When?"

She writes, *3 MONTHS. CAME. SAW. THEY STOPPED.*

Stopped. They stopped him? Stopped her? Stopped the truth?

I want to rage, to tear the folder into pieces, to march back to Moon House and drag every secret out by the roots. Instead, I keep my voice soft. "Okay. Then we don't stop. We find him. We prove it. Together."

Her hand tightens on the pen. She writes one last word slowly and deliberately. *PROMISE.*

I look at her, at the jagged holes in her knitting, at the strength in her silence, and say, "I promise."

Her heel taps the rail. Tap. Pause. Tap-tap. For the first time, it feels like a heartbeat instead of a code.

* * *

When I step back into the hall, Valdez is waiting. "Do you believe her?"

"She saw him," I say, "three months ago. Alive."

Valdez exhales. "So the death certificate—"

"Another lie. Someone else." I shrug. "So now we find the truth and figure out why they buried it."

I close the folder, feeling the weight of its false words, and think of Luce's square of yarn. It's flawed and full of holes, but still holding together. Just like Luce.

CHAPTER 8: UNLEARNING THE SMILE

By the afternoon, volunteers roll carts of books past the door and offer stickers with crooked stars. A toddler down the hall wails, and a teenager laughs too loudly. Hospitals are large machines built to remind you that you are both singular and nothing special. It helps, and it doesn't.

I bring Luce the good hair ties this time, the kind that don't snap, as well as a soft-bristled brush with a blue handle. I set them on the tray and pull the chair close. She has her square of yarn again. The holes are lining up into accidental patterns. She glances at the brush, then at me, measuring. Trust is not a river. It's a series of cups you hand back and forth without spilling.

"May I?" I ask, lifting the brush an inch off the tray and holding it in midair so the question sits there, visible.

She considers it for a moment, then turns on the bed, her knees folded beneath her, and lets the loose braid fall down her back.

Permission.

I stand behind her and work through her hair. I work from the bottom patiently, listening to the faint rasp of bristles through curls. In the mirror across the room, I can see us — my hand slow, her neck tense, the small tilt of her chin when a tangle pulls, and I pause without being asked.

"This is going to sound like a question about hair," I say, "but it's not. Is the braid something you chose? Or something someone told you to wear?"

She lifts a shoulder and lets it fall, then reaches for the notebook. *CHOSE*. She pauses, then adds, smaller, *then told*.

"Chose then told," I repeat. "They let you choose it once so they could call it your choice forever." I keep my voice even. Anger is a luxury the person with control gets to use.

Her shoulders shift. Not quite agreement, not quite relief, but something in between that I recognize like a song from a radio left on overnight.

I gather three bands between my fingers and separate the hair into sections. "Can I show you something?" I ask. "You can say no."

She reaches up without looking and touches the back of my wrist with one brief, precise tap. Yes.

I braid deliberately loose this time, leaving air between the crosses. At the base, I use two ties, not one, room to adjust without starting over. When I'm done, I set the brush down and step back so she can see in the mirror.

Her head tilts right, then left. She lifts one hand to the braid and rubs the elastic, testing its give. Then she writes *NOT TIGHT*.

"Not tight," I repeat.

She looks into the mirror again and doesn't look away from her own eyes. The smile — the trained one — flickers but fails to launch.

There's a knock on the doorframe. The social worker, Ingrid, leans in, her hair escaping its clip, a file tucked under her arm like a shield. "Got a few things, Detective," she says quietly, "and a heads-up."

I turn the chair and keep a hand on the back, a tether. "Tell me."

"CPS is on-site at Moon House still," she says. "They've separated minors by dorms and started interviews. Sister Marian is

. . . performing cooperation. It will hold until it doesn't. Also, there's a woman from the church downstairs. She happened to be visiting a parishioner and asked if she could drop off a prayer blanket for Luce."

I watch Luce's face at the word *blanket*. Nothing moves except her fingers — one, two — into the yarn, through the hole where a stitch slipped.

"What's the woman's name?" I ask.

"Didn't say, just said she's 'in Sister Marian's circle,' which I think is like the Mafia but with casseroles." Ingrid's mouth twists. "Your call. If we deny access outright, we tip our hand. If we allow a minute, we control it and see what they try to plant."

I weigh the options the way you decide whether to pull a splinter now or later. I look at Luce. "You can choose," I say to her. "See her for two minutes with me in the room or not at all. Your decision."

She doesn't blink. The pen moves. *NO*.

"Understood," I say. "Thank you, Ingrid. Tell the front desk she's not to have contact. If she leaves anything, it goes to evidence, not to this room."

Ingrid nods and vanishes.

Luce's shoulders loosen just a fraction. She taps the braid then the yarn square on her lap, a little joke I don't fully understand but want to, the way you want to learn the slang of a new city so you can belong.

"I also brought something," I say. "Only if you want it."

I hold out the photocopy of the ledger page with *Special Care — G.L.* and, separately, a still from the Family Wall I printed, so seeing her father's name and seeing his face won't have to happen in the same breath.

She takes the photo of the wall first. She presses her thumb to her own image as if applying a seal. Then she touches the line where her father's arm crosses her shoulder. The skin above her own shoulder reddens under her touch, a ghost of pressure. She moves that same thumb to the ledger copy and sets it on the initials like she's stamping an affidavit.

"Do you want . . ." I begin, then stop because I have to ask the right question. "Do you remember the last time you saw him?"

Her throat moved. She writes: *BACK DOOR. TALL MAN SAID PRAY. DAD SAID PLEASE.* She stops and squeezes the pen until the plastic creaks. When she writes again, the letters are smaller. *I didn't smile.*

I have the urge to say *good,* but I don't. "What happened when you didn't?"

She draws a rectangle with a dot. The door with a peephole, the same symbol she used before. She adds a little square inside the rectangle — window within the door — and scribbles a dark patch where a latch would be. She presses two fingers to her jaw and pushes until the right corner of her mouth drags downward and up again, the muscle flinching under her skin.

"Reinforcement," I say. The word tastes like rust. "How long?"

Her pen hovers. *DAYS/WEEKS.* A slash. The honest notation of somebody who knows time is a liar in rooms without windows.

I take a breath and let it out slowly. "Okay."

Outside the door, a cart's wheel squeaks twice in rhythm, remarkably like her heel tap — squeak, squeak, pause, squeak-squeak. She flinches half an inch, then sets her jaw until the muscle jumps.

Before her body can translate the squeak back into orders, I ask, "Want to learn something that helped me?"

She doesn't move. That is still a yes.

"When I was younger," I say, "someone wanted me to be the kind of girl who smiles when told. I wasn't very good at it, which is the only time I'm glad to have been bad at something. A counselor taught me a trick. She called it 'uncoupling.' You teach your body to separate one thing from another so the old chain of command breaks." I lean forward until my elbows almost meet my knees. "You hear a squeak? Your heel doesn't have to answer. You feel your jaw? Your mouth doesn't have to follow. Sound can mean sound. Pressure can mean pressure. Not orders."

Luce listens with the kind of attention that is work. She makes no expression at all, and it's perfect. A blank face is not an absence. Sometimes, it's a shield being forged.

I set my phone on the tray and pull up a metronome app I used once to steady my breath on a long night when I needed to take time with a child who needed the time taken. I dial the tempo down until each click has room around it.

"May I?" I ask.

She nods.

I set the metronome to a slow pace and hold the phone so she can see the little pendulum swing and hear the soft click. I click it off then on again, letting the sound exist without meaning. After three intervals, I say, "Tap your heel on the offbeat. Not when it clicks. Between. Your choice, not the metronome's."

She watches the pendulum with a focus that makes the air in the room feel thinner and more necessary. Click. Her heel stays still. Between clicks, it taps once. Click. Pause. Tap. Click. Pause. Tap.

Her eyes flick to mine cautiously.

I let my face be the thing it is best at — plain. "Good," I say softly. "Again."

She taps. The rhythm changes. Not their rhythm. Hers.

We go on like that for a while, a minute, five, I can't tell. Hospitals float time like balloons you can't pop. Outside the door, someone laughs. Someone cries. Nurses' shoes whisper like conspirators. Click. Pause. Tap.

When I finally turn the metronome off, the room feels wider. She exhales. Only then do I realize she's been holding her breath in the smallest way since we began, the way a body learns to become smaller just in case.

"You did that," I say. "Not me."

Her fingers wrap around her braid gently, as if confirming that softness can stay.

Ingrid knocks and steps back in, a file now open in her hands. "Two things," she says. "One, your church lady left a prayer blanket, and security intercepted it and bagged it as requested. Two, CPS found a locked basement storage at Moon House labeled 'Laundry.' Inside, they found carpet cleaner, a ledger of chores, a mirror hung at child-height, and no laundry." She swallows, her voice thinning with fury. "The mirror faces a chair."

Luce's shoulders spike.

I hold up a hand, not to stop her, not to hush her, but to put the boundary around the information. "You don't have to hear this now."

She shakes her head — *no, tell* — and sets the pen flat.

"They used the mirror," I say, and it feels like I'm reading her bones, not telling her a fact, "to make girls practice being good by their definition and to see if the smile is 'consistent.'"

Ingrid looks from me to Luce, her jaw working. "We're moving for immediate removal of remaining residents pending emergency hearing. The judge can stall us in a hundred small ways, but Harris is good. He knows which ones to bulldoze. And . . ." She glances at me. "He found a maintenance log with entries in two hands. One is Marian's. The other . . . might be the same as the note on the back of Luce's photo."

"Gabe's?"

"Maybe," she says. "There's a notation three months ago. 'Back door hinge fixed. Father persists. Escorted away.'"

The skin along my forearms tightens. "Escorted by whom?"

"Names omitted," Ingrid says. "Of course."

Luce is already writing. *HIS SHOES. BLACK.* She draws two rectangles side by side with little square toes and a line where the leather would crease. She frowns at her drawing and adds three little wavy lines above them. She's trying to say they smelled.

"Black shoes," I say. "Clipboard man?"

She shakes her head and writes *OTHER*, underlining it twice. Not the volunteer. Someone else.

"Security?" I ask. "Or the person who wants to be mistaken for it? Either way, we'll find him."

She taps the page where she's written *DAD PERSISTS* in Ingrid's paraphrase and underlines *PERSISTS*. She sets the pen down and closes her eyes for a count of two, three. When she opens them, they are not wetter, not harder, just steadier.

"Do you want to try something else?" I ask.

You always ask before you carry someone across a distance they didn't choose.

She nods, but the nod isn't small anymore. It holds weight.

"Okay," I say. "You tell me what you want your face to do."

She stares at the mirror for a long breath and then writes the smallest word yet — two letters — like she's practicing with a pencil for the first day of school. *No.*

"No face," I say. "Neutral. Your version."

She sets the pen down and lets everything go. Not slack. Present. The mouth unhitched. The corners neither drag nor lift. The eyes unhook from the guard posts they've been tied to. The face she turns toward me looks like a sky on a day when you know storms might come.

"There you are," I say, not out loud or maybe yes, barely. "There you are."

The door opens without a knock, and a nurse I don't know starts to wheel in a vitals cart.

I hold up a hand and say gently, but firmly, "Two minutes."

The nurse blinks, catches up, and reverses. The cart squeaks two notes offbeat, and she retreats. Luce doesn't flinch. Not because she's hardened but because she's chosen.

"Hungry?" I ask after we let the quiet be itself. "I can raid the good vending machine."

She raises a finger, holds it up in a patience sign, and then reaches for the pen. *CAN I GO WITH?*

My mouth answers before my cautious brain can raise a procedural hand. "We'll ask Ingrid," I say. "If she says yes, we go with a security escort. If she says no, I bring the world to you."

Ingrid says yes, but there's a system. First, we need an orderly for the chair — hospital policy — me on one side, Ingrid on the other, a guard in gray walking behind us. We take the slow route past the mural of a forest where the bunnies look like they've been warned about wolves, past a radiator that gurgles like a tired brook, and past a waiting room where a set of grandparents hold hands without speaking. Every turn we take, I name. Naming a place maps it and makes it belong to the person who hears you.

"That's the fish tank," I say as we round a corner. "Everybody watches the yellow one because it looks like a highlighter with fins."

Luce leans toward the glass. The yellow fish eyeballs us. Luce's mouth does nothing. Her eyes take in everything.

At the vending machines, I let her see the choices, not just the names. Salt, sweet, something that pretends to be fruit. She points to a bag of pretzels as if it knows a secret, then to a chocolate bar.

"Both," I say.

We commit the crime of vending together. The machine dispenses with a cough. The guard pretends not to judge us. Ingrid takes out a dollar to feed the next parent who looks like they've forgotten their wallet.

On the way back, a woman in a cardigan comes around the corner, stops, and smiles. I recognize the brand of kindness that requires witnesses. "Oh," she says. "Sweet girl. You are so brave. God sees you."

Luce goes absolutely still. Her jaw moves — faint, automatic — like a hand reaching for a light switch in a room you don't live in anymore. The old reflex.

I step forward like a person stepping between a match and tinder and look at the woman, at her cardigan, at her mouth that wants to be congratulated for saying a benediction she would go home and repeat for herself. "We're good," I say evenly. "Her bravery doesn't need an audience."

The woman blinks, steps back, and offers a tiny, chastened bob. "Of course. Bless you." She drifts away like a dandelion puff that failed to land.

I turn back to Luce. Her face is still neutral — her neutral. Her heel tap is click, pause, tap. Not the woman's rhythm. Not Moon House's. Hers.

Back in the room, she climbs onto the bed under her own steam. I hand her the pretzels. She eats three. Then she sets the chocolate bar on the tray and aligns it next to the brush and the hair ties, three objects that have nothing to do with one another and everything to do with the day.

"Do you want to try a sound?" I ask. "Any sound. Doesn't have to be a word."

She doesn't answer with a pen. She presses her palm to her sternum and breathes. When she lets the breath out, it makes a small, unremarkable vibration in her throat. Not a hum. Not yet. The lowest note a body makes by existing.

"Again," I say.

This time, I don't have to show her a metronome. She makes the sound on an offbeat of her choosing. It reaches no one outside the room, sets off no alarms, changes nothing measurable, but it still feels like a sign.

Ingrid looks at the ceiling for a moment, as if she's telling somebody up there to pay attention. The guard in gray stares at his shoes. I watch Luce and let my hands stay open on my knees.

The square of yarn slides onto the sheet beside her. Without looking down, she pulls it close and puts the needle through a loop as if her fingers remember a direction they haven't been given. The hole she makes isn't a mistake this time. It's a pattern.

My phone buzzes with a message from Valdez. *Judge signed emergency order. Removal begins now. Also, Sunrise Auto owner says city tow yard impounded a blue Ford van two weeks ago near the switchyard. Wants to meet. You in?*

Give me thirty. Then yes.

"Good news?" Ingrid asks.

"Movement," I say. "The kind that knocks on locked doors."

Luce's eyes go from my phone to my face. She lifts her chin, not a question, not a plea, more like an acknowledgment.

I nod. "We're going to look for your father next," I say. "We'll start with his van. We'll go to the tow yard and ask for the form with the signature. If it's his, we'll have a line. If it's not, we'll have a thief."

She takes the pen and writes a single letter. *G* Then she sits with it a moment before she adds *A* then *B* then *E*. She underlines the name twice and places the pen down deliberately.

"Gabe," I say. "Yes."

She reaches for the chocolate bar and peels the corner of the wrapper back carefully. She breaks off a square and sets it on the tray. Then she breaks another square and places it in the space between us, halfway, like a marker on a board.

I pick up the square of chocolate and let it thaw on my tongue, bitter first and then not. "I'll come back after the tow yard," I say. "Do you want anything besides the truth?"

She taps her braid, then lifts one of the hair ties and flips it around her wrist like a bracelet. She writes, *MORE TIME* and then, as if hearing a phrase she likes the sound of, writes it again, smaller. *more time*.

"You have it," I tell her. "You're allowed as much as you need."

She makes the small sound again, slightly higher this time, somewhat longer. Then she breathes, and she doesn't smile.

That's progress.

I stand and tuck the photocopies back into the folder. On impulse, I reach for the extra hair tie and loop it around my own wrist.

"Back soon."

Her heel taps click, pause, tap — the rhythm of a promise being kept. The rhythm of a bridge at noon. The rhythm of a girl teaching her body a new negotiation, one small beat at a time.

Downstairs, the woman in the church cardigan is gone. A different volunteer has set a stack of blankets on a chair — plain, clean, not perfumed, not prayed over. One has a label safety-pinned to the corner, *Laundry — Okay to Use*. The mundanity of it comforts me, the way the right word in the right place makes a map.

I palm the elevator button and catch my reflection in the stainless steel — hair tie on my wrist, folder in my hand, jaw unhitched. Time to find a man who persists.

CHAPTER 9: THE VAN THAT WAITED

The tow yard is a graveyard for machines that outlived their usefulness or have been caught where they shouldn't be. Rows of cars sit with dust on their windshields and citations tucked under wipers like headstones with the wrong names. Valdez leans on the chain-link gate while the attendant unlocks it. The man has oil ground so deeply into his cuticles that his hands look bruised.

"You're here for the Ford?" he asks. "Been sittin' two weeks. City wanted it cleared from the switchyard. Abandoned."

"Blue van," Valdez confirms. "Ford. Plate matches Morningstar Church."

The man nods and leads us down a lane where rows of vehicles slouch against one another. The van sits near the end, oxidized paint dulled to denim, the bumper bent. The magnetic placard still clings to the door, the crescent moon cradling the little house.

I touch the handle. Cold. Stiff. When I pull, the door gives with a cough of rust and the smell of mildew. Inside, there are two bucket seats, a rear bench, and floor mats warped from heat. No trash, no fast-food wrappers, no soda cans. It's clean. Too clean.

Valdez leans in, a flashlight in hand. "No tools, no spare. No dust ring where a toolbox should've been. Somebody stripped this before they left it."

I climb in and run my hand over the dashboard. My fingers find a nick in the plastic. A shape pressed into it, letters carved deliberately. I angle the light.

G.L.

I trace it. Not graffiti. Not random. A signature. A mark left by a man who knew he was being erased and wanted someone, someday, to prove he'd been here.

Valdez whistles low. "That's him. Gabe Landry."

In the glove compartment, we find a stack of pamphlets from Moon House, their edges curled with moisture. Between them is a scrap of paper torn from a ledger sheet, a single line written in the same blocky hand as the note on Luce's photo.

Back soon. Tell her I persist.

I sit back hard against the seat, my heart hammering. Gabe hasn't just survived past the county's false death. He's leaving messages, carving his name into the world where he hopes his daughter might one day see.

Valdez looks at me grimly. "So he's alive. Or was. Question is, where is he now?"

* * *

Back at the hospital, I slip into Luce's room with the scrap of paper placed in an evidence bag. She looks up, her eyes sharp, her braid falling loose around her shoulders.

I lay the paper on her tray beside her square of knitting. "We found your father's van," I say. "He left this."

Her hand shoots out, trembling but steady enough to flatten the paper under her palm. She reads the words twice, then presses her knuckles to her mouth. Not a smile, more like a shield against something larger — hope, maybe, or the cost of believing it.

"Persist," I say softly. "He used the same word you did."

Her heel taps the bedrail. Tap. Pause. Tap-tap. This time, the rhythm feels different.

Valdez leans against the wall, her arms crossed. "We'll keep pulling the line. If he's out there, we'll find him. If they've got him . . ." Her voice trails off, but the promise hangs.

Luce slides the paper under her knitting square. When she glances up, her eyes are clear and steady. She doesn't need to write the word again. I see it there already.

"Persist."

CHAPTER 10: THE LOCK BREAKS

With the rest of the children transferred by CPS to alternative housing, the building now stands hollow, the lace curtains still hanging, smiles still painted over its face.

Valdez and I stand outside. "Ready?" she asks.

We head to the basement door labeled *Laundry*. A single light-bulb swings overhead, throwing shadows against cinderblock walls.

Against one wall is a chair bolted to the floor. Opposite it is a mirror at child-height, the corners flecked with fingerprints, and on the wall beside it, scratched so faintly you have to angle the light just right, *G.L. persists*.

"Jesus," Valdez mutters.

"He was here," I say. "He left her a trail."

In the corner, a toolbox sits half open. Inside is a torn, grease-stained work glove with initials written in block letters on the inside cuff. *G.L.* again.

Valdez pulls out her phone and snaps photos. "We've got enough now to bury Marian under a mountain of her own lies."

But I'm not thinking about Marian anymore. I'm thinking about Gabe — alive, resisting, leaving breadcrumbs in a forest designed to swallow children whole.

Back at the hospital, I show Luce the photo of the glove. She presses her fingers to the screen and traces the initials. Then she picks up her knitting square and, with deliberate slowness, loops a new stitch. No hole this time, no mistake. Her mouth doesn't try to smile. It stays still, her still.

"You'll see him again," I say. "We'll bring him back to you."

I know I shouldn't promise this, but I can't help it. I can feel that he's alive, that he wouldn't leave her. If it takes me a lifetime, I will keep this promise.

Her eyes lock on mine fiercely. For the first time, she makes a sound that isn't just breath. It's a low hum, fragile but steady. A voice. Her voice.

CHAPTER 11: THE GIRL WITHOUT THE SMILE

Two months later, Marian is indicted on counts that will keep her behind walls tighter than the ones she built. The "volunteers" from Moon House don't even stand behind her, every single one of them denying knowledge and trading information for lighter charges. The CPS turns Moon House into evidence with every room cataloged and every lie inventoried.

Unfortunately, we don't find Gabe in time for the trial, but I know he's out there. Somewhere, Luce's father is alive.

Luce is in county care, but I visit her often. She doesn't smile anymore, not the broken smile or even the practiced one, but I don't blame her. She's letting her face rest. When she wants to show happiness, she taps her heel against the rail, the rhythm her own. When she tries to speak, she hums, each note longer, braver.

On our last visit, she held up her knitting square for me to see. She stitched the holes into a pattern now, a deliberate design. She handed it to me with one word scrawled on the edge in uneven letters — Persist.

I keep it in my desk under the case files. Sometimes, survival doesn't look like a smile. Sometimes, it looks like a girl refusing to wear one.

And that, more than anything, is the truth worth listening to.

The End

7.
THE APARTMENT

RULE #7

There are no coincidences.

Patterns don't lie. People do.

CHAPTER 1: VACANCY

I notice the apartment block hunkering in the winter-shaded margin of Main Street, four stories of battered brick and soot-stained limestone, built in an era when function outlasted beauty. Its windows are all slit eyes, glowing the sickly yellow of mismatched bulbs and the dingy gray of interior neglect. A metal fire escape, streaked with rust and city grime, clings to the north side like a skeletal hand, each platform slick with November drizzle.

I park just outside the tow zone, and watch the wind tease at a tangle of yellow tape someone draped over the fire hydrant. The only streetlamp close by flickers, more off than on, which suits the building perfectly. Nothing here looks designed for scrutiny.

The inside is a rectangle of dim lighting and worn linoleum. Every footstep echoes as if the building itself is hollow. Just inside, a woman stands with her hands buried in the pockets of an oversized parka. Naomi, according to the dispatch, though the nervous dart in her eyes suggests she would prefer to remain anonymous. Her hair is braided so tightly against her scalp that it looks painful. Her lips pinch into a question, and her eyes are raw from lack of sleep.

"You're Detective Amber." She doesn't wait for confirmation. Instead, she thrusts her phone at me, holding it like a badge, or a cross, or possibly a grenade. "Listen to this," she says, tapping play before the phone even hits my palm.

The recording begins with a hiss of static, a click, and then a pause long enough to expect disappointment. Then I hear it — heavy footsteps, slow and uneven, and the unmistakable scrape of a heel across tired floorboards. At first, I think it's a loop, until a dry, stifled sob cuts through. A child's voice, maybe eight or nine, is muffled by distance and something darker — fear or a closed door. Maybe both. The keening rises and then snaps off, as though someone clamped a hand over her mouth.

Naomi watches my face, desperate for a flicker of recognition or alarm. "That was just after midnight," she says, "but it started before eleven. It goes on and on. Sometimes, she cries. Sometimes, she laughs, like, a lot." She hesitates, hunting for the right word. "It's not . . . happy laughter. It's like it's forced."

I hand back her phone. "You're sure it's the unit above you?"

She nods, the braid swinging. "3B. It's right over my bedroom. You can hear every step." She bites her lip. "I called the manager, but he says it's empty. He keeps blowing me off, saying I'm just being . . ." She trails off, panic and resentment playing across her face.

I don't need to ask how many times she's called before someone sent me. There's a tone in voices like hers — the exhaustion of not being believed.

"Any chance you've seen someone go in or out?" I ask.

She shakes her head. "Never. Not even a delivery. The last tenant moved out six months ago. They taped the door, but . . ." Her voice cracks. "I know what I hear."

"They taped the door? Is that normal?"

She shakes her head. "Units don't sit empty for long."

"Show me."

She leads the way to the stairwell. Her footsteps groan on the steps, though she can't weigh more than a hundred pounds. On the third landing, Naomi pauses and presses her ear against the wall. I hear nothing but the whistle of the draft and the slow heart-beat of the building, the radiator clicking on and off.

"It's always louder at night," she whispers, pointing down the hallway. "Like it's waiting for me to go to bed first."

The hall carpet, a threadbare runner of maroon and gold, is worn through to the mesh in the center. Each door along the corridor is a different shade of dirt and age. Apartment 3B's brass numbers are nailed on at a drunken tilt. Across the seam, official city tape, stapled at both ends, reads *VACANT UNIT: NO ENTRY*. Dust rests on the doorknob, undisturbed, and the dead-bolt appears new.

I crouch to inspect the jamb and lock. No pry marks, no scratches, but the air hums with a tension I've learned never to ignore.

"Last night," Naomi whispers, "it sounded like someone was dragging furniture for hours then pacing over and over."

I press my palm against the door. It's cold and unyielding, but the faintest vibration shivers up my arm. Maybe old wood settling, maybe something else. I lean in, breathing shallow. For a moment, I think I hear a footfall echo, or maybe it's my heart mirroring the rhythm. Then, nothing.

I straighten and meet Naomi's eyes. "I believe you heard something."

She relaxes only slightly, as though bracing for ridicule. "Thank you. The last guy who came up here never got past the stairs. He said maybe I was picking up pipes rattling or a stray cat in the crawl space."

I let silence hang. The absence of sound can be more damning than a confession. The tape is intact. The lock is unpicked, but nightmares don't repeat unless something real is fueling them.

"We'll need to talk to the manager," I tell her. "He should have a key or at least an access log. I'll file for a warrant if necessary."

Naomi nods, lips trembling. "He's downstairs. He never leaves."

We descend to his "office," the door propped open with a metal wedge even at this hour. The tang of bleach and burnt coffee fills the air. The manager sits behind a table, wearing a golf shirt embroidered with the building's name in drooping script. His round, waxy face holds a permanent frown of inconvenience as if every request is a personal affront.

He doesn't stand when I show my badge and ID. "You're here about the noise complaint?" He flicks the words like they're a spent cigarette.

"Yes," I say evenly. "Apartment 3B. When was it last occupied?"

He squints at his screen, then shrugs. "Nine months since the last lease. City came out for mold remediation and taped it up. Not allowed to rent till inspection. Not my rule."

"Any service calls up there? Maintenance contractors, anyone accessing the unit?"

He shakes his head. "Nope. Nobody's got a key except me and the owner. I keep it locked tight." He sets down his mug and glares at Naomi. "Some people just got thin walls, is all."

I ignore his tone. "I'll need to look inside now if possible."

He rolls his eyes, fishes a master key set from his drawer, and mutters, "You're not gonna find anything. It's just old pipes and creaky floors. The place is a hundred years old."

I take the keys. "Then it should be quick."

He trails us up the stairwell, making a show of every step. Naomi hangs back by the elevator, her arms folded tight.

On the third floor, the manager peels away the city tape, then unlocks the door with a flourish and swings it open.

The unit is bare, just as he'd promised. Pale rectangles on the walls mark where pictures once hung, and the only furniture is a broken lamp in the corner, its shade cocked like a lopsided hat.

But the air tastes faintly of sweat and mildew, undercut with a sickly sweet tang I've smelled too often in sealed places.

I step inside, my shoes squeaking on the floorboards, and scan the perimeter. The windows are latched. The closet in the bedroom stands open, empty. There's no bedding, no toys, no sign of recent life, yet I can see how sound would carry here, how bare boards and space might amplify every footstep and sigh.

I kneel by the baseboard beneath the window and notice a faint trail marking the surface, as if something rubbed against it.

"Satisfied?" the manager calls from the hallway, his voice dripping with sarcasm.

I stand and turn. "Not at all. Keep the key handy, will you?"

The manager locks the door with a hollow click.

CHAPTER 2: CEILING VOICES

Naomi's apartment door swings open on squeaky hinges, and I step into a space so small it feels like a coffin. A single lamp in the corner guts the darkness in a cone. Past its edge, shadowed walls loom, ready to pounce.

Naomi's eyes burn with exhaustion. "You don't believe me," she snaps, wrapping her arms tight. "I called the cops before. They told me to turn on a fan." She laughs, sharp and brittle. "A *fan*."

My jaw clenches. "I'm here now," I say, forcing a soft smile to ease her.

She grips that promise like a life preserver and glances at her watch. "It'll start soon, just after ten. Sometimes later. Sometimes, it drags on until sunrise."

I check my watch. "Then we'll wait."

Killing the lamp, the room shrinks back into shape, raw and restless. Streetlights slam prison bars across the wall, and the radiator's tick is continual. Naomi's breath rattles in the hush.

I slip through the gloom, my phone's beam grazing the ceiling. Fresh paint covers a water-stain repair, but the color was applied hastily and never matched, resulting in an angry pink rim against faded white — a hairline crack snakes along the plaster seam. Above the stove, the vent cover sits crooked, the screws forced at an angle.

"Any smells?" I ask, my voice barely more than a rasp. "Bleach? Old carpet? Dust?"

She inhales sharply. "Dust. Cheap perfume." Her whisper trembles.

In the hallway, the ceiling sags.

Naomi stays glued to my back. "When it starts," she admits, "I hide under my pillow, but I still hear . . . something dragging."

I edge into the bedroom. Shadows pool in the corners. The glass bowl fixture hangs from the ceiling, its frosted surface glinting, a layer of gray-brown dust covering the top. I perch on the bedframe's edge, the metal springs groaning beneath my weight, and reach up with outstretched fingers. Naomi's eyes flare wide, her pupils dilated to black moons. She wants to stop me, but fear pins her lips shut.

My index finger traces through the dust, leaving a clean whorled print. "See this ring pattern? Bulb's been unscrewed and reseated from above."

"How . . ." Her voice catches.

"Ever have any light issues? Flickering or just going off?"

She nods. "I keep replacing the blurb but…"

"More than likely, you share a junction box," I tell her, anger coiling in my gut. "Old buildings leak power like secrets. Someone reaches in from the apartment above, cuts your light, and watches you squirm in the darkness like a bug under glass."

Naomi's mouth opens then closes on a choked sob that rattles in her throat. "Why would—"

"To terrify you," I spit through clenched teeth.

I drop off the bed, landing with a soft thud on the worn carpet.

She curls into herself on the mattress, her knees drawn to her chest, her fingers clutching at the collar of her shirt.

We wait in the thickening silence. Pipes groan like arthritic joints, a distant laugh stabs the quiet, and a siren moans past. Minutes stretch, elastic and thin.

Around eleven, the ceiling ribs creak, a weary, living sigh, and then I hear it. A drag . . . pause . . . drag again. There's a soft thud, like a boot heel planting dread, each impact sending microscopic plaster dust spiraling down in the beam of my flashlight.

Then I hear the cry. It's muffled through layers of plaster, but it's undeniably a girl's voice, a broken plea strangled mid-word, high-pitched and desperate as a wounded animal.

Rage floods my throat, hot as molten metal.

Something is wrong with the voice, though. I hear it again and realize the issue. It's flat, mechanical, the same pattern, the same pitch, the same cutoff point.

It's a looped recording. I clamp my jaw until my molars ache.

"You hear it," Naomi breathes, her words barely disturbing the air between us.

"I hear it," I answer, "but it's a recording, someone's sick prank."

Her relief cuts through her panic. "Why?"

"To break you. To cover real footsteps." I watch her face. She's haunted by betrayal. "You've been sleepless for way too many months."

She bites her lip. "I thought I was losing my mind."

I head to the hallway and kneel by the slump, tapping the dip with my knuckles. It's hollow behind the plaster, a soffit built to lie. I trace its edge. Painter's caulk has sealed a secret.

"Flour?" I ask.

Her eyes blur. "Flour?"

"Or anything that falls slow."

She scrambles to the kitchen and returns with a paper bag. I sprinkle fine white dust along the seam. Three tiny puffs dance, sharing the draft points.

"The gap's small," I say. "Just enough for air and sound."

The dragging vanishes. A new heartbeat starts — tap-tap-tap, pause, tap-tap-tap. Like Morse code from hell.

I kill the flashlight. Darkness binds the room tightly. I tap twice on the wall three feet below the flour line. Tap-tap. Silence.

Then two taps answer. Tap — tap.

"Someone's up there," Naomi whispers.

I tap again — three single blows — the ceiling shifts, a wooden shuffle, knees against joists, and then two taps in reply.

"Manager won't let anyone up," Naomi says, her voice trembling. "He claims the floor's unsafe."

"Unsafe floors get condemned," I growl, "not ignored."

I creep to the fridge and slide it aside. A sealed dumb waiter door glares from the wall.

Naomi's sob cracks her composure. "No one told me—"

"Shh." I press my ear to the wood.

There's a faint, stifled sound.

I whisper, "We're here."

No answer.

Naomi swallows. "What now?"

"We go back up," I say, "and we find what we missed."

Her eyes track the ceiling as if it might speak. "I thought I was going crazy. No one believed me."

I place a hand on her shoulder. "You did right. Wolves are real. They just wear better masks."

Her exhale is a broken shudder that feels like hope. I flip the lamp back on. The room shrinks, secrets choking in the glare.

In the stairwell, the banister quivers under my palm. On the landing, a framed notice lists emergency contacts with wrong extensions. I snap a photo.

At the bottom, the manager's office sits dark, but beyond the window, I see a muted TV flickering behind blinds. I knock twice. Blinds shudder. Then, there's stillness. I take a pen and write a note on my card before slipping it under the door. *URGENT — Tenant Safety.*

Outside, the brick facade glows under the streetlamp like a liar in makeup. I text Valdez. *312 Main. Lock tools, camera, your meanest smile. Manager is ignoring me.*

On my way, she shoots back.

Good.

CHAPTER 3: THE KEEPER OF KEYS

The manager finally opens his door, and I wrinkle my nose at the stench of body odor and mildew. His desk is a battleship of oak scarred by coffee rings and the faint burns of cigarettes put out in the wrong place. A single lamp casts everything in a jaundiced light. On the walls hang yellowed, outdated inspection notices, curling at the edges, and a photograph of him as a younger man in front of this building, standing taller and prouder. Now, he looks worn down, his cardigan sagging at the elbows, his hair thinning in stubborn wisps.

"You again," he says when Valdez and I step inside. His voice is flat. He gestures vaguely toward the chair opposite his desk. "Tenant already filed another complaint. Told her the same thing I'll tell you. Apartment 3B is vacant and has been for months."

I push back my chair, the legs screeching on the floor. "Vacant apartments don't drag furniture at midnight," I say, my voice low and hard.

He quirks a savage smile. "Old pipes groan. Beams settle. This place is a hundred years old. It talks."

"Funny. That's not what I heard."

His eyes sharpen, but I don't flinch.

Valdez fills the doorway, her arms crossed, her silhouette lethal. "You got ghosts on payroll or tenants you forgot to mention?"

He flicks a glance at her, then back at me. "Detectives see monsters in every shadow. Gotta justify those badges."

I tap my card, which he left on his desk. "I saw more than monsters in the shadows." I flip open my notepad. "Fresh caulk on a soffit. A dumb waiter sealed with new screws. A ceiling light tampered from above. Sounds crawling in walls, not pipes. Someone's been moving up there."

He tugs his cardigan tighter as if bracing for a storm. "Lonely tenants imagine things."

Valdez steps forward, and her voice cuts like glass. "You mean women like Naomi, who's been begging you for months to look into this?"

He spits. "She's late on rent half the time like most of this building. Everyone's looking for drama."

I lean over the desk. "I heard a cry. Not a pipe. A girl's voice."

His jaw twitches. Silence fills the room, thick as smoke.

"What are you hiding up there?" I ask.

He exhales, his eyes drifting to the faded photograph on the wall — when he had been two decades younger and far more hopeful. Now, his face is carved with regret. "I don't ask questions I don't want answers to."

Valdez laughs bitterly. "Like we've never heard that before."

He doesn't flinch. He yanks open the drawer and fumbles among papers. "Inspectors don't check what doesn't profit them. Cops walk in, see dust, and walk out. Who cares about ghosts in walls? I keep the lights on. That's my job."

"No," I say, my voice tighter than a noose. "Your job is to keep people safe. You failed."

His gaze snaps to me, sudden and lethal. "You think you're a hero? You're just another pawn in a system that devours you. Look away, and you live. Get curious, and they bury you."

The room tilts, but I steady my breath. "Curiosity saves people. Complicity hides their graves."

Valdez strides up, her voice low and dangerous. "Key. Now."

He freezes, haunted. He glances at the crumbling notices, the file cabinet, and the smiling photo, and then sinks. His fingers close around a heavy ring of keys. They clink of bitter betrayal. One brass key, its teeth worn smooth, lands on the desk with a final thud.

"You're gonna get me in trouble," he mutters.

Valdez snatches it, her lips curling. "Whose fault is that?"

We rise. At the door, I pause before the photo and look at a man who once believed in something. Now, he's a mere ghost in his own building.

"You always had a choice," I whisper.

He doesn't look up. "Choices get you killed."

His words hang as we step into the dark hallway and climb the stairwell. Each step echoes, reverberating off the walls.

At the top, outside 3B, the resealed city tape stretches across the frame.

I slide the key into the lock. The tumblers turn with a sigh. I peel the tape aside, open the door, and step into the silence that is waiting for us.

CHAPTER 4: VACANT AIR

For an apartment that is supposed to be vacant, this place shows signs saying otherwise.

There should be layers of dust everywhere, from the floor to the countertops, the floorboards, and the lights. Instead, faint tracks mar the surface, the tracks too deliberate for rodents and too heavy for drafts.

The first thing that hits me is the air. It's stale, yes, but not abandoned. Vacant rooms smell like plaster, dust, and time. These smells are layered, like bleach buried beneath mildew, perfume half faded, something metallic that raises the hairs along my arms.

Valdez closes the door behind us, and the sound is louder than it should be, a slam swallowed into silence.

"Anything changed from when you were up here?" she asks.

I point to the marks on the floor, the ones that don't match my boot prints. She just nods.

"Vacant, my ass," Valdez mutters, crouching near the wall. Her flashlight beam catches smears of dust where furniture once sat, a perfect square against the wall. "Someone's been staging this place like a set."

She has a good eye. I hadn't noticed that earlier.

I move toward the kitchenette. The sink is dry, and the faucet gleams in a way no other metal fixture in the building probably does. The counter, though, when I bend close, has grooves, the kind a serrated knife leaves when dragged too hard.

The cabinets are bare, the doors open as if in surrender, but one shelf carries a faint residue of something grainy. Salt, maybe, or plaster dust shaken loose from above. I touch it and rub it against my thumb. It feels wrong against my glove, gritty and off.

The air conditioner unit under the window rattles once, then falls silent. The noise echoes longer than expected for such a small machine.

In the hallway, the ceiling sags by an inch, as if the building has grown tired. I reach up and press my palm against the plaster. It's cool but not solid.

Valdez follows, running her hand along the baseboard. "You see this?"

The wood trim isn't flush. A sliver of darkness yawns where wall and floor should meet, a seam someone tried to hide with paint.

"This was cut."

We push deeper into the unit.

The bedroom is worse, namely because the carpet's stain is a dark blot that resembles blood or wine. The walls are empty, and the closet door hangs open. Inside, a single wire shelf stretches bare across from wall to wall, but the drywall bears hand-shaped smudges repeating in vertical streaks. Someone pressed their palms here time and again.

At a child's height.

Valdez's jaw tightens. "Ghosts don't leave fingerprints."

The bathroom draws my attention next. Dust streaks the mirror's surface in a thick layer of film. At the center, someone has wiped a circle clean, big enough for a face. I lean closer. Light halos my reflection, but for a heartbeat, I swear I see another face — a child's, wide-eyed, lips pressed shut. Then, the bulb overhead flickers, and I see only myself.

I turn away, my heart in my throat, my resolve tougher than nails.

We regroup in the hall. For a long moment, neither of us speaks. We don't need to. We've done this scene before and been in places like this before. We know what's coming next. It's always inevitable.

The silence in the apartment isn't empty. It's taut, stretched thin like a wire waiting to snap.

And when the snap comes, it's in the form of a drag, slow and deliberate. Wood scraping against wood.

Valdez's hand hovers near her weapon. "You hear that?"

"I hear it."

The dragging pauses. Then, there's a cry, faint and low. It's muffled, a girl's voice pressed through layers of plaster. The same pitch and the same choke I'd heard in Naomi's recording.

Valdez swears under her breath. "Hell."

I force myself still, my ears straining. The cry comes again. Too perfect this time, the same inflection, the same cutoff. A loop, just like before.

The air in my lungs deflates. "It's just a recording," I say. "Someone planted it."

"Why?"

I shake my head. There are too many reasons to list, but I can think of two right now. "To make her doubt herself or to cover something real."

She closes her eyes for a split second. "Or both."

I nod.

The dragging resumes, closer this time. My flashlight beam sweeps the ceiling. In the corner above the stove, the vent cover sits crooked. Not loose but not flush either.

I cross the kitchen, climb onto the counter, and press my fingers to the vent. A faint vibration hums through the metal, mechanical and rhythmic, like a tape spool turning.

I look back at Valdez. "Someone's wired this place to bleed sound."

She shakes her head. "A whole damn puppet show."

The dragging stops. The silence swells again, heavy and oppressive.

"He says this place is vacant," I murmur. "That's the biggest lie this room tells."

Valdez tilts her head. "Well, no one lives here, so what can it be then? What's going on?"

I sweep my light across the room one final time. Every corner vibrates with absence that isn't really absent.

"It's a mask," I tell her, "and masks mean there's something worth hiding."

CHAPTER 5: THE HOLLOW
BETWEEN WALLS

The first board splinters with a sound too loud for the midnight hour. Valdez freezes, her crowbar braced mid-swing, both of us listening for footsteps in the hall, for the indignant slam of a neighbor's door, for a voice calling down the stairwell to mind the hour.

Nothing. The building keeps its counsel the way places do when they've practiced secrecy longer than the tenants have practiced sleep.

She pries again, slower this time. The nails come free with a long squeal of old metal resisting change. A strip of baseboard lifts, revealing a dark slit where the wall should have met the floor. Dust puffs outward, dry and chalky, the scent of old plaster and something else.

Valdez angles her flashlight into the gap. The beam slides along rough plaster and vanishes. She whistles under her breath. "That's no mouse run."

I crouch beside her. Inside the slit, dust has been disturbed in smudged ellipses, a repeated pattern of pressure and release. No paw prints, no tails dragged. Not a rat. The heel of a hand.

"Someone's been crawling through here," Valdez says.

We trace the seam down the hall, our steps a soft rasp over the carpet. Valdez slips the crowbar under the edge and leverages gently.

The board gives, but the wood fibers complain. The opening yawns wider, large enough for me to lay my hand flat against the inner wall.

The plaster is cool. Beneath the cool is a warmth that isn't air but something alive moving somewhere in the building's ribs.

We make our way to the bedroom. The closet's drywall bears similar hand smudges I noticed earlier, the prints layered like ghostly high fives, low on the wall at the height of a child trying to stand upright in a space that didn't want them to. The idea tightens something under my ribs. I press my own palm to the marks, matching the size too easily.

Valdez looks at me, almost like she's asking me if I'm ready. I'm not, but that's never stopped us before.

I give a single nod, and she sets the crowbar just above the base plate and drives it forward. The plaster cracks in a jagged starburst. Dust plumes. She strikes again, then again, until the wall folds inward and a dark mouth opens, the room's clean edges torn wide enough to swallow a body.

We lean in with our lights.

A crawl space spans the width of the apartment, a deliberately carved hollow between studs, the floor joists bridged and boxed to create a hidden space. Plywood lines one side, stained and smoothed where hands and knees have worn paths. Someone laid down a strip of cheap indoor-outdoor carpet in the middle, the kind that mimics grass. It's flattened into two distinct tracks, a traffic pattern indicating this route has been used repeatedly.

Along the far wall, milk crates sit in a row, their plastic stained gray with dust. Inside each is a cassette player or a small digital speaker, the wires coiled and labeled. A multi-outlet strip snakes through a drilled hole to a hidden socket. The labels are written in neat black block letters on masking tape — *Weeping 2, Weeping 3, Laughter 1, Laughter 2, Pacing A, Pacing B, Prayer — Female, Prayer — Male, Music — Hymn,* and *Furniture Drag 1.*

A library. Not of books but of sounds.

What the actual . . .

My stomach tightens into a fist. I grab a set of gloves from my pocket and put them on before reaching in and lifting one of the players carefully, with two fingers, as if handling a venomous thing. The tape inside has been rewound to the beginning. The clear plastic spools reflect my light in jittery halos. I click the lid and read the little white sticker. *Loop 4.* The same designation as the strip we found earlier. I slide the player back and take out my phone to take photos, quick and steady, catching labels, wire paths, and the order of crates.

Valdez crouches, her shoulders filling the opening, her flashlight sweeping slowly. "Jesus, Meri," she says, voice low. "This is all planned, but why?"

I'm not sure I trust my voice yet, so I only shrug.

Next to the crates lies a scattered heap of objects, things like a single pink sneaker scuffed at the toe and missing its lace; a hairbrush with three teeth snapped, a braid of hair still caught in the spine like an afterthought; a once-white stuffed rabbit, one ear resewn with thick, clumsy stitches; a plastic bead bracelet in neon colors, knotted tight, the knot fuzzed by worried fingers; and a laminated library card with a cartoon dinosaur on it, worn nearly blank at the name.

I pick up the bracelet. The threads are stiff.

A speaker crackles to life to my left, and we both jerk. The cassette player's spools turn, a faint electric whir. A breath, a hiccup, and then the sound Naomi first heard — a girl's cry, muffled and urgent. "*No.*" A hand over a mouth. The tape clicks as it loops and feeds again to itself.

I reach over and yank the power cord. Silence falls, sudden and thick.

Valdez exhales through her nose. "They timed them," she said. "Why? What's the goal here? Do they need the tenant below to leave? Are they trying to cover any noise they make? But why a child crying? Why something that draws attention?"

All good questions. None that I have answers to. Yet.

A different device hums, the smallest speaker tucked deeper in the hollow. This one isn't a tape. It's a digital box with a red LED and a smudged touchpad. The LED blinks twice, pauses, and blinks twice again like a heartbeat. I slide my light across it and notice greasy fingerprints in a pattern that suggests repetition. Someone touched this pad over and over with the same two fingers, always tapping the same places.

Maybe we'll get lucky. I'm not counting on it, though.

I trace the wire to the ceiling. The hole it passes through has been chewed open with a dull bit. Splinters stick out around the edge, smudged with what looks like grime rubbed into the wood from repeated handling. Behind me, in the larger room, the apartment holds its breath.

"Look." Valdez moves the light left. "Some kind of hatch."

At the far end of the crawl space, not much taller than my shin, a panel has been cut into the plywood. The hinges at the top are new, bright metal against old wood. A string hangs from the bottom, frayed at the end. The area around the panel is scuffed darker than the rest, the way a doorframe gets when a busy house has children.

I belly-crawl forward, ignoring the way my knees complain, and lift the panel with two fingers. The hinge clicks, and cold air kisses my face. On the other side is another void much narrower than what I just crawled through. I ease the light in and catch the edge of a metal duct. Taped to it with blue painter's tape is a small envelope. On the front, in blocky letters, is *FOR HER*. The edges are grimy. The tape is slightly loose.

"What is it?" Valdez asks.

"An envelope." I hold it out, and we both stare at it. The flap has been sealed and then resealed. "You don't think . . ." I don't finish the question because I read the answer on her face.

The envelope makes me think of a girl I'd once found on a bridge, mute, alone. We bonded in the hospital, where I promised I'd find her father, who had gone missing. Since then, I've found a few envelopes from him, messages he'd left for his daughter, almost as if he knew I was looking for him. Valdez believes he stays hidden to protect his daughter, that he's involved in something more dangerous than he expected.

I wouldn't be surprised if she's right.

I glance at Valdez and wait for her nod. This is evidence, but it's also more than that. I stay cautious when I open the envelope, and my chest tightens when I see what's inside.

It's a small Polaroid. The frame shows the kitchen of a different apartment — old linoleum, a dented pot on the stove, and the corner of a broken clock. In the foreground, a hand holds up a scrap of paper with four letters and two numbers written in thick marker. *BL-6 / 112*. On the back, in the same blocky hand as the looping labels, are two words. *I persist.*

My heart thumps hard in my chest. I know those words. They're the same words carved into the inside of a van's dashboard, a father sending breadcrumbs into a maze he couldn't solve alone.

A father searching for his daughter.

Luce.

"Could it be coordinates?" Valdez asks, leaning close.

"Maybe." I don't think so, though. "Building level 6? Or block 6. Unit 112. Or a locker. Or a storage room." I take a photo before I slide the Polaroid back into the envelope and write the time and location across the back. My hands shake only a little.

"How is she, by the way?" Valdez asks.

I give her a smile. "She's living."

A shadow covers Luce, and it will probably always be there, considering what she lived through, but now we're one step closer to her father. One step closer to finding healing.

One step closer to me keeping my promise.

The air shifts, and I still.

A sound comes from the farthest dark corner beyond the crates and cardboard propped against the stud wall like a makeshift screen. The cardboard moves once, twice.

"Hello," I say softly, keeping my light angled away so it won't blast straight into whoever is hiding. "We're here. It's safe to come out."

CHAPTER 6: THE GHOST

Two wide eyes peek over the edge of a ragged piece of cardboard. The pupils are dilated, eyes rimmed with dirt, and the skin beneath is a blur of mud streaks and shadows. Strands of messy hair fall over narrow shoulders, each thread hanging onto dust.

Valdez stands frozen beside me, tense. We're both aware that any small movement could cause the girl to slip back into the darkness of the crawl space.

"My name is Meri," I whisper, letting the words settle. "I'm a detective. You don't have to come out. You don't have to say a thing. Stay right here until you feel safe."

Her eyes flit from my face to my hand resting, palm down, on my thigh. I keep my gestures slow and deliberate. I recognize that breath pattern — hold, release, hold, release — as if her lungs can't decide whether oxygen is friend or threat.

Behind us, a speaker crackles to life, unleashing the same muted plea Naomi recorded. The sudden sound is like ice against her ears. Her shoulders hunch, and her eyes squeeze shut. I don't turn fully, but I reach behind me, my fingertips grazing the cold plug, and I yank it free. The cry cuts off mid-note, leaving an echo of desperation.

"You're safe," I murmur.

Her lids part, and those enormous eyes find mine again. She doesn't nod, but something in her gaze sharpens, like a manual lens click bringing an image into focus.

Through her shoulder mic, Valdez voices a calm chain of code — our building number, coordinates, and a gentle plea for medics, CPS, and additional units. She does not raise her voice. She remains locked on that narrow sliver of cardboard hole, steady as a negotiator on a rooftop.

"Would you like some water?" I ask, my tone soft. "There's no hurry."

Her cracked lips part, and I see a tremor of a tongue within. She glances toward the stacked wooden crates, their labels blurred by grime, then back to me.

I nod. "Okay," I say. "I'll set a bottle right here. You can drink whenever you want."

I inch back, each movement slight, and lean to reach the beige canvas bag tucked by the closet wall. I always carry sealed bottles. Years ago, a child wouldn't touch anything an adult had drunk from. I unscrew the cap of a bottle and lift it into her line of sight. She watches the water ripple inside. Then I set it at the edge of the dim pool of light, two feet from her hiding spot.

Silence settles like dust. Overhead, the building's HVAC system hums, a vibration that travels through the joists. Outside, a patrol car siren wails, its pitch warping with distance.

Her shoulders shudder.

I shake my head and keep my voice soft. "They're here for you, good people to keep you safe."

Her gaze slides to the clear plastic bottle, then returns to me. The frayed blanket around her shoulders tightens in her grip. She leans forward millimeter by millimeter but halts. One bare heel, gray with dust, taps once against the rough plywood. No Morse code, just life reminding itself it still belongs.

That tap echoes in my memory. Luce tapped when we found her. A civilized sound in a room weaponized for cruelty.

I sweep my light across the crawl space's interior. Milk crates with stamped words, metal shelves, a cassette deck with dangling cords, and smudged fingerprints pressed into the play button. A script of suffering on dusty surfaces. Kneeling here, cycling through recorded pleas as one might test lightbulbs, turns my mouth to iron.

This was done on purpose. The why is a fingerprint I intend to find.

Valdez exhales, and I know we're in silent agreement that we're going to burn this place down." Not with kerosene tonight but with subpoenas and indictments, the legal fire that makes predators quake.

The girl inches forward, her blanket slipping in small waves. She doesn't seize the bottle but touches it, then recoils.

"It's okay," I say. "Take your time."

My light drifts upward to the joist above the closet hatch. There, letters are gouged into the wood with rough depressions. *G L P E R S I S T S.* The spacing is uneven, the line jagged, as if carved blindly. My throat tightens. Gabe, Luce's father, pressed these marks here. Why? Did he think Luce would end up like this, too? This all has to be connected somehow.

"Help's coming," Valdez whispers.

Heavy boots strike the hallway floor. A radio chatters in static. "Unit on scene."

After a firm knock, an officer in a navy uniform peers in. "Everything okay in here?" he asks, his voice clipped.

I nod and gesture him back. He drops a med bag, then retreats with caution written in his posture.

The girl startles.

My knees ache as I shift, the edge of my phone pressing cold into me. The small envelope labeled *FOR HER* crinkles against my thigh like a heartbeat.

I meet the girl's eyes. "There's going to be a lot of noise for a minute," I say. "When it's loud, you can look at me or at your blanket, or at the bottle. Whatever helps."

Her gaze flits among those three anchors. Then, in an act of small rebellion, she slides the bottle nearer by half an inch. Not a yes, not a no. Her claim.

Paramedics crouch at the opening, two women in scrubs. Their faces are calm masks.

One leans forward, her voice gentle enough to cradle. "Hey there. I'm Tasha. We'll slide a small board under you so you don't have to crawl. We'll go slow. You can look at me, or your detective friend, or close your eyes. Breathe with me."

The girl's eyes shift to Tasha, then sideways like a wild creature scanning a clearing. She pivots a knee, the blanket bunched tight. Just above the ankle of her exposed foot, I notice faint scrawl, black lines that could be letters or numbers drawn with a dry marker. A name not to be forgotten.

On silent pads, the paramedics slide a pediatric spine board beneath her. Tasha gives a soft nod to me, then waits for the girl's hand on the smooth plastic before she moves. Inch by inch, we all move, the blanket never leaving the girl's grip. Her eyes remain pinned to me, a lifeline.

"Good," I whisper, the word a broad shelter — *You are safe. You did well.*

We guide her through the jagged closet mouth into the stale expanse of the room beyond.

She flinches, maybe from the glare of the overhead bulb. Valdez flicks the switch, and we operate in our own beams again, sharp cones of determined light.

As they wrap her in a fresh, warm blanket, I glance back. The crates stand in mute rows, the scratched words glittering where my beam catches them. On one crate is labeled *B L 6*. The letters overlap. My heart knocks.

"Got her," Tasha says, relief softening her tone. "Pulse racing, dehydrated, no major injuries except scrapes and bruises."

"Thank you," I say, though the words feel too small.

She nods, clearly understanding.

We move as a silent procession — Valdez shielding the door, the medics steering the board, and me going backward so the girl's triangle of safety remains intact.

In the hallway, Naomi waits barefoot, her hair in loose waves, her knuckles white on the banister. When she sees the girl, her face splits into a hopeful grin, as if she might run forward and cradle her, but she halts at the yellow tape's edge.

"She's real," Naomi breathes with relief. "She's real."

"You saved her."

Passing the manager's office, I glimpse the TV blinking silently and blue, a chair rocking back as if recently abandoned. The coffee cup on the desk carries an acrid hint of something sweet gone bad. He may think he's escaped, but he won't have gone far.

In the lobby, the glass front doors show our reflections — the girl snug on the board, the paramedics with practiced gentleness, Valdez's jaw set, my wrist inked with notes.

Naomi stands behind us.

Outside in the chill, the ambulance idles with low amber lights. The girl's breath puffs once in the air. She flinches, probably at a distant siren unrelated to our rescue.

I hold her gaze while the medics lift the board into the open doors. For a moment, her fingers release the blanket with a subtle tremor. I lift my hand in response, and she lets me see a ghost of a smile before the doors click shut.

I return upstairs, where 3B's closet gapes like a wound. The makeshift cassette players lie silent, their cords dangling. My palm cradles the envelope, warmth seeping through my glove. My light finds the carved message one last time. *G L P E R S I S T S.* I whisper a prayer that persistence is a legacy.

Valdez steps beside me, follows my gaze, and nods. "We'll bag everything," she says, "each tape, every screw, every scrap. We'll log the wiring and trace the purchase receipts for that much masking tape and cassette deck."

"And we find BL-6, 112," I reply, my voice firm. "Whatever it is."

She gives a tight-lipped smile. "Could be a basement level. A storage locker. A parking stall. For all we know, a breadcrumb trail for wolves."

Left by whom? That's what I'm determined to find out.

CHAPTER 7: THE KEEPER'S SILENCE

The manager is brought down in handcuffs. Stupid men always think they can get away with everything. He doesn't protest, just shuffles his feet as the officers guide him forward, his shoulders bent, his cardigan sagging.

Neighbors line the stairwell and lean out of doorways, drawn by the noise. A few whisper. One old man crosses himself. A teenage boy records on his phone until an officer barks at him to cut it out.

I'm impressed the kid listens.

I step into the manager's path. "You knew," I say. "All you had to do was say something. Save someone."

His watery blue eyes flick upward and look tired. His mouth shapes into something like a smile, but it's thin. "All I do is collect the rent. What they do with the unit? Not my problem."

My stomach turns. "So you're okay with your building being used as a prison?"

He rolls a shoulder. "This block's full of rot. You pick which kind you live with. I picked the kind that kept the lights on. I need to live too, you know."

Valdez barks a bitter laugh. "I hope the rest of your life is full of nightmares."

The manager doesn't blink. "You think anyone would've cared if I told? You think inspectors don't take envelopes? Cops don't look away? People don't see what they need to? I keep my head down. That's how you survive."

His words sit like grease on water — thin, floating, and refusing to mix with anything clean.

"You may call that survival," I tell him, "but you'll soon find out it's complicity."

He looks at me then, long and slow. "Complicity keeps you alive longer than curiosity, Detective. You of all people should know that."

The officers pull him forward. His shoes drag, and the neighbors part. For a moment, the whole building seems to exhale.

Valdez mutters under her breath, "Caretaker of the damned."

"Caretaker of the lost," I correct softly.

Naomi turns to me then, her voice breaking. "Will she be okay? The girl you found?"

"She's alive," I say. "That's where okay begins."

Her chin trembles. "I thought I was going crazy."

"You weren't," I tell her. "You were listening when no one else did. That's why she's alive tonight."

Her eyes fill, tears slipping unchecked. She reaches for my hand, just briefly, her fingers cold and damp. "Thank you."

I press my card into her palm. "If you hear another sound, call me. Don't ever let anyone tell you it's just pipes again."

She nods, clutching the card as if it might burn.

Valdez and I step into the night air, and I glance over my shoulder. The building looms above, its brick dark and blank, but I can feel the weight of its memories pressing outward. Walls remember. They don't forget, no matter how many coats of paint you slap over the truth.

"Manager is just a pawn," Valdez says as we cross the lot. "You know that."

"Yeah, but pawns keep lists. Someone told him when to look away and who to let in. He'll talk, or his files will."

Valdez shoves her hands in her pockets. "And if he doesn't?"

"Then we go higher," I say. "There's always someone higher."

The night presses cold against my teeth. Somewhere above me, a window shade stirs. How many more secrets are still caught in the bones of this place?

We walk toward the cruiser lights, red and blue cutting the dark into pieces.

The End

DEAR READER: A NOTE FROM MERI

Some nights, I can still hear the sound of that apartment door closing behind me — the soft click of a lock meant to keep things out, not in. I tell myself I left nothing behind, that I walked away clean. But silence has a way of following you home, doesn't it? It seeps through the cracks, lingers in the corners of your thoughts, and waits until you're alone to whisper what you've tried to forget.

They call people like me "relentless." As if it's a compliment. As if being unable to let go of the dead, the missing, the broken is something admirable. But I know better. I chase ghosts because they feel more honest than the living. They don't lie to protect themselves. They just wait to be found.

The case in the apartment should've been another file closed, another name checked off a list. Instead, all I'd done was pull a thread to a much larger web, one that hasn't been fully taken apart yet.

Sadly, sometimes that happens. Someone else has the case now. Someone else is untangling that web, and I'm trying to let it go. It's hard to do, though. I've been told that obsession can make you blind. Maybe that's true. Or maybe it sharpens your vision until you see too much — until you wish you could unsee what's been done.

—Meri

8.
THE PACT

RULE #8

Truth is rarely buried deep.

It's just covered in shame.

CHAPTER 1: THE DISCOVERY

Some days, I love my job. I love the challenge the Missing Persons department gives me. I love the feeling when I'm able to close a file knowing our victim was found and brought home, and I love when families are able to find closure one way or another. But other days, I hate this job and wonder if life would be easier owning a coffee shop.

I haven't decided how I feel about today yet.

The rain hasn't stopped all night. It's coming down in sheets, hammering against the cracked windows of the old house like it's trying to wash away the past. The air is thick and heavy, like it's full of secrets.

"Detective Amber . . ." The coroner stops and rolls his shoulders. "We're all done here."

I thank him before I turn to look at the house. The porch I'm standing on is sagging, the wooden railing flaking away at my touch. I'm sure this house was charming back in its heyday, when the neighborhood was new, and the streets were busy with bikes and hopscotch chalk instead of the cracked pavement and overgrown hedges that surround me now.

Behind me, the coroner's team loads the stretcher into the van, the bright yellow tarp glowing beneath the emergency lights. One technician pauses and glances back at me, his face unreadable. Then, he closes the doors with a heavy *thunk*.

Just like that, Ella Shaw is gone.

They are calling it suicide.

I don't buy it.

I step into the house, duck under the rusted doorframe, and slip on a pair of latex gloves. The floor moans beneath my boots, the wood warped from years of neglect and now soaked through from the storm. Inside, it smells like mold, cheap air freshener, and dried blood.

It's definitely a scent I won't forget for a long time.

The living room is dim. A single lamp on a side table flickers, still plugged in, still warm. I take it all in the way I need to — cataloging details, filing them into mental drawers marked *immediate* and *wait and see*. Something tells me I'll be opening all those drawers before this case is over.

On the wall across from me hangs a photo of two teenage girls, arms slung around each other, looking at something outside the frame.

"Looks like they were inseparable," comes a voice from behind me.

Officer Lou Garland stands in the hallway, his wet uniform clinging to him like an afterthought. He looks tired, more so than usual.

"Tell me about them."

"Ella Shaw," Lou says, pointing to the girl with dark hair that's been pulled into a high ponytail. "That's her best friend, Jade." He glances down at his notebook. "Jade Harris."

Jade looks like a shadow compared to Ella. Where one girl carries a bright and joyful smile, the other is softer, her lips barely breaking in a grin.

A girl who carries too many secrets.

"Do we know where Jade is?" I ask.

Lou is grim. "Jade hasn't been seen since last night. Parents said she left the house around eleven. No note, no text, no calls. Her phone's off."

I glance back at the photo. "This town sure loves its ghosts," I say softly.

Lou steps closer. "There's more. I found this upstairs."

He holds out a small, leather-bound notebook. The cover is torn at the edges, but I recognize the type — cheap, spiral-less, the kind you buy in a pack for a discount. When I open it, the pages are full of slanted handwriting, words crammed into margins. Poetry. Lyrics. Confessions.

One page is dog-eared. I flip to it.

We made a pact. One secret. Three girls. Forever.
NO ONE GETS OUT UNLESS WE ALL DO.

I close the book slowly. "How many people were in this house last night?" I ask.

"Just Ella and Jade," Lou tells me. "Parents were out of town, and the girls were having a sleepover. They got home this morning and found the bathroom door locked. Kicked it in. Ella was already gone."

"And Jade?"

He shrugs. "She wasn't here when they left." He glances down at the notebook he's carrying. "According to her mother, she was in a weird mood and needed some time to herself before the sleepover. She overheard the girls on the phone. Said Jade promised to text Ella when she was on her way."

"Did we find those messages?"

He shakes his head. "We only have Ella's phone, and it's been wiped clean. Texts, call log, social media . . . gone."

I exhale through my nose. Wiping a phone? That's intentional.

"And no one has heard from Jade, correct?"

"Correct."

"Is there a basement?" I ask almost absently as my gaze drifts toward a crooked doorway near the kitchen.

Lou hesitates. "Yeah. It's locked. Looks like it hasn't been opened in years."

Another intentional act?

"Get someone down here to open it," I demand.

"You think there's something down there?"

"I think there's always something in the basement."

I crouch and notice a reddish-brown smear along the floorboards, a drag mark partially cleaned. My flashlight flickers over what looks like a handprint, faint but unmistakable, etched into the dust like a message.

Ella's death isn't a suicide. It's a warning.

Or maybe a confession.

I rise to my feet, brushing my hands on my pants, and survey the room again. On the wall beneath the photo of the girls is a torn piece of paper.

Lou sees it at the same time, and he picks it up, opening it carefully. He whistles low and slow before handing it to me so I can read it myself.

I wasn't supposed to leave her.

A chill skates up my spine.

I turn to Lou. "We need to treat this as a homicide until we can prove otherwise. Jade Harris isn't missing. She's either running, or she's been taken."

Lou's jaw tightens, but he nods.

As he radios the team, I walk through the house slowly, taking in the details — the scattered nail polish bottles on the vanity, the music playlist frozen mid-song, and the broken charm bracelet on the bathroom floor.

Two girls made a blood pact.

One's dead.

The other's gone.

I've worked a case like this before, in what feels like a lifetime ago, a case that never sat right, even after it was closed. A missing girl. A sealed-up basement. A system that failed the victim.

I won't let that happen again.

CHAPTER 2: MOTHER KNOWS SOMETHING

The Harrises live only five streets over from the crime scene, but the drive feels like a long one. The rain has slowed, now only tap dancing across my windshield instead of pounding fists against the glass like earlier.

The house is a tidy split-level home with blue shutters. The soft tinkle of wind chimes in the breeze greets me as I open my door. On the surface, it looks normal and safe, like an open book, with its potted plants, landscaped yard, and welcome sign at the front door.

Looks are always deceiving.

I knock once before stepping back.

A woman opens the door, her makeup smeared, eyes puffy and red-rimmed.

"You're the detective?" she asks, her voice brittle as an old newspaper.

"Yes. Detective Meri Amber." I flash my badge. "Are you Diana Harris?" I wait for her nod. "I'd like to talk about your daughter. May I come in?"

Diana hesitates before stepping aside. "We've told the other officers everything."

"I understand you," I say, softening my voice. "There's been a development, however, and I believe Jade might be in danger. I need to understand exactly what happened."

She leads me into a too-quiet living room with a too-white couch. I'm almost afraid to sit on it. A half-finished cup of tea sits forgotten on the coffee table.

My gaze lands on a framed photo on the table, as if it has just been set down. Jade looks to be around ten or twelve, flanked by Ella and a third girl. Blond, a little thinner, her body hunched like she's trying not to be seen.

"Who is this other girl?" I ask, gesturing to the photo.

Diana pales. "That's just an old neighbor. Lila."

I wait.

"She moved away a few years ago," Diana says too quickly. "The whole family left town suddenly, but it has nothing to do with this." Her voice trembles just enough to show doubt.

"You're sure?"

Diana looks as if she wants to crawl out of her skin. "I don't know what you think is going on, but my daughter is a good girl. She's quiet and keeps to herself. After what happened to her and Ella back then . . . she just . . . changed."

Interesting. I gingerly sit on the edge of the couch cushion. "What happened back then?"

Diana's mouth clamps shut. "You should ask Jade."

"I would if I knew where she was."

Silence.

Then Diana whispers, "They never got over it. The three of them. Whatever they saw that day . . . whatever they did . . . it stuck to them."

I'm not sure if it's her words or the way she says them, but a chill runs along my spine. "What do you mean?"

"They made a pact," Diana says, her one hand waving dismissively. "Some childish thing. I thought it was harmless. They used to whisper about it all the time. 'No one gets out unless we all do.' That's what they'd say. But then Lila disappeared, and no one ever talked about her again."

Disappeared.

The *thump-thump-thump* of my heart picks up speed. "How long ago was that?"

"I don't remember exactly how long now," Diana whispers.

My phone buzzes with a message from Lou, who is still at the crime scene.

Basement door is open. You need to see this.

That's all I need to hear.

"That door is open," I whisper to myself.

Diana stares at me with wide eyes.

"Thank you, Mrs. Harris," I say, standing. "Please, if Jade reaches out, call me immediately."

Diana grabs my wrist as I turn to go. "What door?" Her grip is weak but desperate. When I don't answer, she shakes my arm. "If you go down there," she continues, her voice trembling, "don't go alone."

CHAPTER 3: BENEATH THE FLOORBOARDS

The basement door yawns open like a wound, its edges jagged from where the forensics team pried it loose. The scent that wafts up isn't just mildew or the stale breath of old spaces. It's heavier, saturated with time, dust, and something far more wrong.

I pause on the threshold, breathing through my mouth.

I hate when I'm right.

The stairwell descends into darkness, steep and narrow. I click on my flashlight and run the light over the walls, looking for a light switch, but I find none. With slow, careful steps, I make my way down, the wood groaning beneath my weight.

The walls are unfinished, consisting of gray, cold concrete lined with what appears to be old paneling in some spots. Torn wallpaper peels down in long, sagging strips, revealing ancient water stains shaped like distorted faces.

Halfway down, the air changes, colder now and more still. I shudder as I carefully take the final steps.

My flashlight cuts a wide arc through the shadows. The space is long and narrow, cluttered with forgotten relics — rusted metal shelves, crates stacked high with molding books and newspapers, and a broken tricycle in the far corner. On the left wall sits a stained mattress, its springs coiled through the torn fabric like ribs.

Beside the mattress is a plastic bowl — red, cracked, coated with grime. A second bowl sits beside it, empty. A stack of children's books, warped from the damp room, rests just beside it. And beside those . . .

Handprints.

Dozens of them. Tiny, faint impressions smeared with dirt across the concrete. Some are pressed flat, others dragged down like whoever made them had been slipping, reaching, clawing.

My stomach churns as I pray I'm wrong. I want to be wrong. In cases like this, I never want to be right.

I kneel and run a gloved finger near the markings. The wall is colder here. Damp. And yet . . .

These aren't old. Bile rushes up from my stomach, and I swallow it down, forcing myself to remain professional and give whoever was down here my full attention.

I'll throw up later.

"They kept someone down here," I whisper. My voice sounds too loud in the stillness. "This isn't just a hiding place. It's a cell."

I rise, turning slowly and letting the flashlight skim every surface.

Near the ceiling, barely visible, are etchings, scratches made with something dull. Numbers. Dates. Names.

Lila. Lila. Lila. Lila. Lila. Lila. One name carved six times in a line and beneath it, a single word repeated over and over in a child's shaky hand.

Stay.

I turn away, blinking hard, forcing the cacophony of emotions bombarding me into a box and locking it shut.

My phone buzzes in my pocket, the vibration harsh in the silence. I reach for the phone, but I don't answer it yet. There's a low humming noise somewhere to my right.

I move toward it, past an old washer and dryer coated in rust. Tucked behind them, nearly invisible, is a simple piece of wood paneling covering a section of the wall. No latch. No knob.

A hiding place.

I press my ear against it. Nothing. Then, there's a soft scuffle.

I immediately step back. "If someone's in there, I'm not here to hurt you," I say, raising my voice while keeping my tone calm yet firm. "My name is Detective Meri Amber. I can help you."

No response.

"There's a crawl space," a familiar voice calls.

I turn to find Lou silhouetted at the top of the stairs.

"Behind the water heater," he says, his voice tight. "Looks recent. We found signs of movement. Bedding. Trash. Someone's been here."

I glance around carefully. If someone's been here, maybe they still are.

"Did you see them?" I ask.

He shakes his head. "It's too dark. I looked for more lights but all I found are these flashlights," he grumbles as he climbs down the stairs. "The air, though . . . Something's . . . not right, Meri."

I see what he's talking about as soon as I reach the water heater. The panel behind it has been pulled back just slightly, enough to suggest either a hasty entry or retreat.

I crouch and shine my light inside.

The crawl space is narrow, barely tall enough for a child to sit upright. The walls are unfinished with insulation hanging in drooping clumps like decaying flesh. In the back, almost hidden behind a curtain of black garbage bags, I see it.

A nest.

Bedding made from old clothes. A teddy bear missing its head. A pile of wrappers and scraps of food.

In the middle of the makeshift bed is a notebook that looks like it was tossed to the side. It lies open on a page scrawled with looping, frantic handwriting. On the far wall is another message written in red: *She said we all had to stay.*

Something twists inside me as that phrase sinks in. I've seen this phrase before, not on a wall but written in pen all over a girl's arm. It was years ago in a small town two hours from here, where a young girl had vanished.

The name of the girl I'd interviewed had been Lila. It was her arm that had been covered in pen.

And the girl who vanished? Avery Shaw. Another possible runaway since no body had ever been recovered.

Is this the same girl from then? Lila. Her name is carved in the wall over and over.

My heart wants to say it's not, that it's someone different, but my head knows the truth.

Behind me, there's a creaking sound.

I whirl around, but no one is there.

I take some quick photos with my phone, then duck back out of the crawl space, and stand, my chest rising and falling.

Lou is waiting for me at the bottom of the stairs. "We didn't find anyone outside. No tracks. Nothing fresh."

"She's still here," I say, my voice low.

Lou's brow furrows. "Who?"

"Lila. Or someone who thinks they're her."

He's skeptical. I see it in his eyes and the slight shake of his head. He doesn't get it. He doesn't know the backstory like I do.

He waits a quick moment before he dips his head in a nod, letting me know he'll follow my lead on this.

I turn back to the crawl space, my jaw tight. "Jade didn't run," I add. "She came back."

"For who?"

I glance toward the wall with the handprints. "For the one who never left."

CHAPTER 4: THE NOTEBOOK

While Lou takes photos, I stand off to the side, holding the recovered notebook in hand. I want to go through it before it gets thrown into an evidence bag and needs to be processed, but first, I need to prepare myself. Nothing good ever comes from notebooks found like this.

It's a school journal, one of those wide-ruled kinds with a sparkly unicorn sticker still clinging to the cover, now aged, its corners curling at the edges.

I remember when I used to cover everything with stickers. My favorites were the scratch-and-sniff ones.

The first few pages are water-damaged, the ink bleeding like bruises across the lines. Beyond that, the words are sharp with erratic loops. Sentences that start and stop mid-thought.

> *She screams at night. No one hears. We are shadows in the floor.*
> *Ella forgot the rules. Jade forgot too. But I REMEMBER.*
> *And I STAYED.*
> *The pact keeps us safe. Break it and . . . comes back.*

I find myself stopping there. A word is smudged, and no amount of staring will clear it up. Something comes back . . . What? A person? An animal? Nightmares?

I flip the page, my heart thundering, hoping the answer is found elsewhere.

The pages are full of sketches. Some are in the margins at the top and bottom, some fill the page. Most are stick-figure girls with Xs over their mouths. One drawing shows a girl in a basement with tall stairs leading up, and a woman — *Mother* is written above her — standing at the top, watching with empty eyes.

I swallow hard.

The next few pages spiral, the sentences repeating in tighter, messier loops.

They made me do it. They made me stay. I tried to go, but the BAD is worse out there. She's the one who told me to stay. She's the one who said we had to die if we left.

I pause. Who is she?

The last line has been scratched out so deeply that it tore the paper.

She said we had to die if we left.

I lean back in my seat, staring at the book in my hands. Something about the phrasing triggers a memory I can't quite place.

She said we had to die if we left.

My phone buzzes. Unknown number.

I hesitate and clear my throat, forcing myself to focus. "Amber."

There's a pause on the line, and the sound of someone breathing. "You found it, didn't you?"

The voice is female, young, flat, but trembling.

"Who is this?" I'm careful to remain calm, to keep my voice as flat as theirs.

Another breath. "She left it for you."

I swallow hard. "Who did?"

Silence follows.

Then, the voice whispers, "We're all going to die now, aren't we?"

Click.

The call drops.

Immediately, I yank the phone from my ear and go to hit redial, only to realize it's an unknown number.

I stare at the notebook again. The spirals, the rules, the pact . . .

Something went terribly wrong years ago. The three girls survived something . . . and maybe not all in the same way. One disappeared. One stayed. One pretended it never happened.

Now, Ella is dead. Jade is missing. And Lila?

She's still in the walls.

The knot in my chest tightens. This isn't just another case. It has roots reaching into the one place I don't want to go.

My own past.

I open the notebook again and turn to the final page.

It wasn't an accident. She didn't fall. She was pushed, and they all LIED for her. Even me. Because we PROMISED.
But a promise means you STAY.

Beneath that, there's a final sentence in different handwriting, smaller and tighter.

If you're reading this, she's coming for you, too.

I snap the notebook closed and feel eyes on me. I look around, but there's no one there.

That niggling feeling doesn't leave. Not as I walk away from the house, not as I sit in my car and think about everything.

Not even as I drive to my old storage unit, where I keep my personal files, something an old partner had once suggested I do. I go through a few boxes, but it's not until the last box at the very back of the unit that I find what I need.

Avery Shaw's old file.

There's a clipping from a newspaper, yellowing with age, with a photo. She has the same eyes as Jade. The same haunted stare.

I spread out the photos from the original basement scene. Everything I see is similar to what we've just found — peeling walls, scattered toys, a single bowl, and *STAY* carved into the wooden beam.

My heart sinks. It's the same as the Shaw basement. The same atmosphere. The same symbols. The same heartbreaking truth.

It's not a coincidence. It's repetition.

It's a cycle.

I pick up the crime scene photo from Avery's room, the one showing the journal that had been found. The only difference — this journal's pages had only one line scrawled on every page.

She made us promise.

My fingers tighten around a page as realization sinks deep into the marrow of my bones.

This isn't one killer.

This is an ideology, a belief of three girls that's deeply embedded in trauma. It's the sick loyalty of best friends who have seen too much at too young an age.

I stare at Avery's photograph.

Then Jade's and Ella's.

Then Lila's name in the notebook.

"Why did you all stay?" I whisper. "Who made you believe you had to?"

Behind me, something clatters. I turn, my pulse racing as I frantically search the area.

It's nothing. It's no one. Just wind against metal siding, but my pulse doesn't slow, and my chest doesn't relax.

For the first time in years, this feeling is back. An unease. No one knows about this unit, though. No one would know I'm here.

Unless they followed me.

I think about the phone call and the warning as I stuff the file in my bag and lock the unit.

I stand there, my back against the metal door, and leave myself open. If someone is watching me, let them get their fill. I'm not afraid. I won't show fear.

And if they want to follow me, that's fine too. They can come join me where it all began.

There was one person I always believed had the answers, but I could never figure out how to get her to talk. Maybe now she will. Maybe now will be different.

It's time to talk to Jade's grandmother. Again.

CHAPTER 5: THE GRANDMOTHER'S SECRET

Jade's grandmother lives in a two-story brick colonial tucked behind overgrown hedges and a rusted iron gate. The house stands like a monument to a past long buried, just like everything else in this case.

I park at the curb, rain misting on the windshield, and take a moment to breathe. My knuckles whiten on the steering wheel before I remind myself to relax.

The front yard is silent. There are no birds, no wind. Just the soft drip of water from the eaves.

I climb the steps and knock.

She answers, and I'm taken aback by her appearance. She's shrunken, and her hair is now completely white. Her cardigan is buttoned wrong and hangs off one shoulder like it no longer fits.

"Mrs. Greer," I say gently. I see from the flash of recognition in her eyes that I don't need to reintroduce myself.

The old woman peers at me with eyes like fogged glass. "Detective Amber. Took you long enough."

"I'm sorry?"

She tuts before stepping to the side. "Come on in, child. There's no one left but me now. Just me and the ghosts."

I follow her into the dim foyer.

When she leads me into the front room, I notice a tea service already waiting on a silver tray.

"Are you expecting company?" I ask.

She gives me a sad smile. "Only you, child. Only you." She slowly reaches for the teapot, and with trembling hands, she pours tea into the cups.

"I'm here about Jade," I say.

Mrs. Greer nods and hands me a cup of black tea, one sugar cube on the side.

"She's missing," I add.

"I know."

"She was seen with Ella Shaw the day she died."

"I know that too."

Carefully balancing the cup and saucer, I lean forward. "Did you speak to Jade recently?"

That would explain how she knows all of this already.

"Not soon enough," her voice is soft, full of regret.

I freeze. "Do you know about their pact?"

Mrs. Greer looks up slowly. "Those girls, they were always making pacts and pinkie swears, writing in secret diaries. Girls think they can trap time that way and keep the bad things from following them." She glances away as if hoping to keep her secrets.

The time for secrets is over.

"What happened in that basement, Mrs. Greer?" I ask.

Silence.

I don't push. Instead, I wait.

The old woman sets her teacup down with a sharp clink. "You think you understand what happened, don't you? I can promise you don't. You don't know even if . . . well, even if you found those journals."

Her words catch me off guard, and tea splashes from the side of my cup. I set it down on the table in front of me and find a napkin to clean my mess.

"What do you mean?" I ask.

She lifts one shoulder in a shrug. "You need to realize things aren't as they seem. The house . . . that basement . . . it eats people. It has for generations." The corner of her lips twists as she gives me a glance. "Oh, I know you think I've gone crazy, that I'm losing my marbles. There's more to this world than what we see. Surely, in all your cases, in all you deal with, you understand what I'm saying, don't you?" She leans forward and lightly touches my knee with her bony hand. "What happened to those girls, it happened to others too. We just stopped writing their names down."

I stare at her, trying to read between the lines and understand the truth behind her words. "Are you saying someone hurt them?"

"Oh yes." Mrs. Greer's voice crackles. "But not always with hands." She heaves a sigh, as if the breath that leaves her body is one she's been holding for a very long time, a breath carrying secrets too hard to continue to carry. "Sometimes, the worst hurt is the kind you can't see. The kind that hides behind smiles and bedtime stories. The kind that whispers *stay quiet or else.*'"

"Who whispered that to them?" My tone hardens. "Who taught them to be afraid?"

The old woman reaches down, her fingers trembling, and opens a side drawer. She pulls out a photograph, one of three girls, their arms slung around each other, their faces shining in the summer sun.

Jade. Ella. And a third.

Lila.

"She never left," Mrs. Greer whispers. "They buried her without digging a grave and made her a ghost while she still breathed. Because of what she saw. Because of what she knew."

I stare at the photo, my chest aching. "She's alive." There's a hint of truth in my voice, a finality that wraps around my bones.

"I believe so," Mrs. Greer says, "but she's not . . . whole."

I nod, as if understanding, but the reality is, I don't. "And Jade?"

"She went back to finish it, to end the pact, but you can't undo that kind of promise. You can only die with it."

My heart pounds with a sense of urgency as I stand, my pulse thundering in my ears. "I need to find her," I say. "I need to find both of them and save them."

Mrs. Greer reaches out and wraps her hand around my wrist with surprising strength. "You'll have to go back there. All the way back. You'll have to ask the one question no one ever dared to."

I swallow. "What question?"

Mrs. Greer's gaze darkens. "Why did they make the pact in the first place?"

* * *

Outside, the wind picks up. I'm on the porch, my heart hammering. I don't quite remember how I got here. The pieces are sliding into place slowly, like glass fitting into a shattered window, but the center is still missing.

Why did they make the pact in the first place?

I glance down at the photo in my hands. Three girls. One basement and a promise.

A promise that is worth dying for if I don't find a way to end all of this.

Am I ready? I have to be.

CHAPTER 6: RETURN TO THE BASEMENT

I stand once more at the threshold of the Harris house.

It's been cleared by forensics and sealed for safety, but I managed to call in a favor. Technically, I'm not supposed to be here alone, and technically, Officer Lou Garland is on his way, but nothing about this case has followed protocol, and the truth doesn't live in reports or checklists.

The air inside carries a different smell now. The rot has settled deeper, or maybe I just notice it more. The scent reminds me of trauma and the residue it leaves, like fingerprints.

I flick on my flashlight and walk slowly down the hallway. The furniture is still in disarray, crime scene tape fluttering from the stair rails. A single lightbulb sways in the kitchen, casting slow, swinging shadows. I don't pause there. This isn't my destination.

The basement is.

I open the cellar door, heart thudding.

The air rushing up to greet me is thick and wet. It clings to my lungs and makes me forget how to breathe.

I descend the stairs one step at a time, flashlight trembling slightly in my hand.

The space looks the exact same, yet it feels different, as if something malevolent has awakened. A chill runs down my spine, and I force myself to move and head toward the far wall. My fingers dance along the concrete as I walk, pressing lightly, making my mark, feeling the indents and grooves.

I saw marks earlier and look for them now. Lines had been scraped deep into the wall. Lines that make a pattern, that mark a path.

Lines that reveal a hidden door.

I drop to my knees, pull out my knife, and jam it into the seam. The blade scrapes metal, then slips inside with a soft pop.

The panel gives way, revealing a hollow space.

I crawl in and flick on my flashlight, its beam cutting through the dark like a blade. The small space is a tight squeeze.

The first thing I notice is how rancid the air is.

The second thing I notice is a girl, curled into herself, her eyes wide and too bright in the dark.

"Lila?" I ask, my voice cracking.

The girl flinches but doesn't speak.

I drop the flashlight and raise both my hands. "You're safe," I say, keeping my voice soft, low, and kind. "I'm not here to hurt you. I'm here to help."

Lila stares, unblinking. She looks like she's aged and stayed young all at once. Her hair is matted, her skin pale, wrists bruised with time.

"You came back," Lila whispers, her voice cracking.

I nod. "I promised I would."

"No," Lila says, blinking slowly. "She promised."

My blood runs cold. "Who?"

Lila tilts her head, like she's listening to something only she can hear. "She said if we stayed, we'd be safe . . . but we're not safe. We're never safe."

I move closer, keeping my movements slow and fluid. "Lila, who said that?"

The girl's lips tremble. "Ella. She lied. They all did. She said if one of us left, the others would die."

"But you didn't leave," I say as gently as I can.

"She made the pact," Lila whispers. "Ella. Jade. Me. But I broke it when I told the truth. That's why I had to stay."

My heart cracks.

This isn't just fear.

This is indoctrination.

"You were children," I say gently. "You were trying to survive."

Lila closes her eyes. "She said it was the only way to be free, but now she's dead."

"Yes," I say, "and Jade is missing."

Lila opens her eyes again. "She's not missing."

I still. "Where is she?"

Lila doesn't answer. She just slowly raises her hand and points toward the far side of the crawl space.

I pick up the flashlight and crawl toward another wall. My hand brushes against something soft.

Cloth.

Hair.

Skin.

I jerk back, my stomach twisting.

Jade.

Curled like Lila had been, only she's still.

So still.

No breath.

No pulse.

No light in her open, staring eyes.

I drop my head against the cold wall.

I'm late. I'm too late.

Lila crawls beside Jade, silent tears streaking through the dirt on her cheeks. "She came back to trade places. She thought it would fix everything."

I wrap an arm around her. "Will you come with me? Leave here?"

Lila doesn't say yes, but she also doesn't say no.

By the time we make it out of the crawl space, Officer Lou is there, along with the medics. I stay close by as they place Lila on a stretcher and carry her up the stairs and then outside. She looks so young lying there, so young and so pale, limp but alive. Jade's notebook is pressed tight against her chest like armor.

"I remember you," Lila finally says. "From before. With Avery."

I swallow hard. "I remember you too," I say.

I want to ask about Avery, but I have a feeling I already know the answer.

"Avery wasn't the first," Lila whispers, her body relaxing as the truth she's been holding on to for years finally comes out. "Jade won't be the last either."

The ambulance doors close, and I find myself locked in place.

I'm thankful I found her. Broken that I wasn't in time for Jade. Disappointed that I missed something two years ago when Avery first went missing.

The rain falls harder, washing the porch and soaking the crime scene tape until it sags like tired ribbon.

Inside the house, the basement door stands open, and somewhere inside the dark, a promise still echoes.

One that someone made.

One that someone broke.

One that cost those girls their lives.

CHAPTER 7: THE HOUSE
WHERE SECRETS SLEEP

One week later, I return to the house where Ella Shaw's body was found.

The crime scene tape is still stretched across the door. This is a case that won't go away any time soon, and while I don't have any answers, I know they will be found.

Mrs. Greer, Jade's grandmother, suffered a heart attack after receiving word about Jade's death. She passed away a few days ago.

I still can't get that last question she'd asked out of my head. Why was the pact made in the first place? Who started it? Who is responsible?

I need to know. I need to know about the other girls and give their souls a sense of peace.

I pause at the front door and look back at the street behind me. It's empty and silent. Everyone is inside with lights off, curtains drawn. The neighborhood doesn't want to be reminded of the horrors that happened here.

Inside, the air is stale and sour. Dust motes float in thick shafts of light breaking through the windows.

I move slowly, every creak of the floorboards sounding like a breath, like someone whispering just out of reach.

My goal isn't the basement. Not this time.

Instead, I climb the stairs.

The second floor is less disturbed. The bedrooms are dressed in layers of normalcy — framed photos, laundry baskets, a clock blinking 12:00 endlessly. Ella's room is light and bright with hand-drawn pictures on the walls, photographs of her and Jade taped into place, books stacked neatly beside her bed, and a journal on the nightstand.

Strange that this journal was left behind.

My thoughts drift to another case involving teenage girls. I was young and new to the department, eager to prove I belonged.

A report had been tossed on my desk about a runaway girl, fifteen years of age. Her father said she'd snuck out after a fight about her coming home past her curfew.

Something about his statement and the shiftiness of his features hadn't sat right with me, but my superiors said I needed proof, and there was none.

Until that girl was found weeks later in a field, her body badly damaged.

A drifter with a record confessed under pressure, and I was told to close the case, now labeled transient assault.

But it never sat right with me. It felt too easy.

I think about the case files I'm responsible for, of the dozens of teenage girls like Lila and Jade, like Avery and Ella . . .

And now, looking at Ella's room, there's a pattern. I'm not seeing it yet, but I know it's here.

Fear gets passed down like an heirloom.

I rise and step to the window. Outside, the sky hangs low and gray. The trees sway gently, unaware or uncaring.

I think of Lila, brainwashed into believing she couldn't leave and that she couldn't get help for herself or Jade. I think of the lifetime of trauma that girl is going to endure.

I remember Lila's voice, raw and trembling. *"She said if one of us left, the others would die."*

It wasn't just fear that lived in this house. It was a belief taught by someone.

A twisted and violent fear, a belief born from trauma and secrets and silence.

The girls weren't just victims of abuse. They were believers in it.

That's what scares me the most. They believed that whatever happened to them was their fault. Who taught them that? Who brainwashed them into believing it?

I will find out. I will hold that person accountable if I'm able.

I turn back to the bed and finally pick up the notebook.

Ella's handwriting is precise, slanted, every word heavy, like she needed to etch her truth into the paper.

I flip through the pages and find pacts, a promise, and rules.

We don't speak about the man in the dark.
We don't wake the girl in the wall.
We never, ever leave each other behind.

I close my eyes.

Those girls lived in a prison. Why? And when one tried to escape, the others were dragged back down. By whom?

Jade sacrificed herself to save what was left of them.

Ella . . . maybe she never had a choice.

And Lila, she's alive but barely. She's broken, beyond reach, beyond sanity. Any hope of getting answers from her dwindle each day she remains broken.

After I tuck the notebook under my arm, I walk out, drive to the precinct in silence, and head down to the archives. I let these girls down, but I won't let another.

I pull out an old box and reach for a file. Which one doesn't matter. I will go through each file, page by page, line by line, and make sure I didn't miss something else.

Not all of these are mine. Many are from before me, but that doesn't mean they don't deserve a second glance, a second chance.

If there's one thing I'm realizing I'm good at, it's finding the missing. And maybe, just maybe, one day, I'll find my sister too.

The End

9.
A VOICE LIKE MINE

RULE #9

Every survivor has a tell.

It's in the flinch, the silence, the too-smooth story.

CHAPTER 1: BOX OF VOICES

The cardboard box lands on my desk like a dare. It's water-stained, the kind of thing offices shove into basements, intending it to be someone else's problem. There's a strip of tape across the top that reads *ARCHIVE — DO NOT DESTROY.*

Inside is a stack of old cassettes, a cheap tape player, and a memo from Records that reads, *Unresolved 911 Calls, Harlow's Edge, 2008–2010. Flagged for review after recent case activity.*

Clearly, Caleb Rusk's arrest stirred up some mud. Somebody higher up wants the appearance of diligence, so they kicked this box my way. *Let Amber listen to dead girls whisper into static.*

Not that I mind. It's what I do.

I close the evidence room door and lock it behind me. I imagine my board and everything on it — threads running from Caleb's Polaroids to Andy Rawlings' trucking routes, River's photo at the center. One Polaroid shows the Harlow's Edge Youth Center, its steps blurred but unmistakable.

I press play on the tape player.

The first call starts off with a hiss and muffled breathing. A girl whispers, *"Please. He said lights out. Please."* Then, there's a slam, and the line goes dead.

The second call is from another girl, her words rushed. *"She's still in the basement. We can hear her."* There's nervous laughter in the background.

The dispatcher sighs. *"Prank calls are a crime."* Then the line cuts.

By the fifth tape, my skin is crawling. Different voices. Different nights, but always the same plea: *"Someone is below."* *"Someone is ignored."*

But it's the sixth tape that changes everything.

The whisper is so soft I don't hear it at first. I rewind and play it again and again.

"He doesn't like the lights on."

The air leaves me.

River said that once, years before she disappeared. She said it about our father, her voice shaking under the covers. *"He doesn't like the lights on."*

My finger slams on the stop button.

These girls called for help, and the county wrote it off as a prank.

I dig through the box and find dispatcher logs with dates, times, and the durations of each phone call. Every single one was marked as *No units dispatched.* Some even scribbled with *repeat caller.*

The dispatchers were wrong. They weren't pranksters. They were survivors.

My phone buzzes. It's Valdez.

"Are you still at the station?" she asks.

"Yeah."

"Have you eaten?"

"No."

She sighs. "You're on something."

"I got a present." I lean back in my chair with a sigh.

"I didn't know it was your birthday."

I want to chuckle, but don't. "Someone sent me some tapes." My voice is hoarse. "Harlow's Edge. Girls calling and begging for help. Everyone ignored them."

Valdez takes a moment. "Is that place still running? It's probably a graveyard by now."

I can't argue with her, but I see it differently. "Or a crime scene."

"Same difference."

"They'd probably disagree since it's still open."

She swears. "You need backup?"

"Not yet. Just jurisdiction."

"You've got it, but, Meri . . ." Her voice lowers. "Be careful. That place eats people."

I hang up and pull Caleb's Polaroid down from the board. The youth center in 2009. He was there.

And Rawlings . . . My gaze lands on his truck log. He passed through Harlow's Edge twice that same year.

There's too much overlap, too many coincidences, except I no longer believe in coincidences. Only truth has been left out in plain sight.

And the truth I know is this — the girls didn't vanish. Their voices are still here.

Tomorrow, I go to Harlow's Edge.

CHAPTER 2: HARLOW'S EDGE

Harlow's Edge looks like a place that decided to stop halfway through being a town.

When Valdez called it a graveyard, she was right. There's a diner with a burned-out *Open* sign on one side and a school that forgot its students and let the windows cloud over. The youth center lives in the school's old shell. A cinderblock once painted cheerful yellow now resembles mildewed leaves left too long in a garden bed.

The sign out front — *Harlow's Edge Youth Transition Center* in blue letters — needs a good repainting.

I park under a cottonwood that leaks fluff into my hair as I walk to the front steps, the same steps that have seared themselves into my memory from staring at Caleb's Polaroid for too long. They're smaller than the photo made them look, which tends to happen to places you've stared at too long on a board. They shrink when you finally stand there. The truth doesn't.

The lobby smells like lemon cleaner fighting a war with old gym mats and institutional air. A corkboard holds a scatter of faded flyers thumbtacked over older layers — *MENTOR NIGHT, ART THERAPY, GROUP 6 @ 7 P.M.* A pay phone hangs near the door, its cord frayed and wrapped in gray tape where the plastic split. There's a piece of paper taped above it with the local area code and 911 handwritten in Sharpie as if someone needed the reminder.

A receptionist behind bulletproof glass looks up from a cross-word. "Can I help you?"

The question lands like a challenge.

I show my badge. "Detective Amber. I'm here about historical 911 emergency calls placed from this facility."

Her jaw tightens at the word *historical*. "We're under county oversight," she recites. "All safety concerns are logged and reported."

"That's why I'm here," I say. "To read the logs and speak with staff who were on during the years 2008 to 2010."

A pause. "Most of that staff are long gone."

"Then I'll speak to whoever kept their keys."

She buzzes the inner door with a sigh. "Director Harrow will see you."

Director Harrow arrives the way administrators do, with his shoulders squared, his tie perfect, his apology smile practiced. He's in his mid-fifties with buzzed gray hair, hands soft from paper instead of rope. He extends one. "Detective."

"Meri Amber." I keep my grip light and my eyes on his. "Appreciate the time."

He ushers me down a hall where the bulletin boards have been stripped and repainted so many times you can still see the ghosts of tape squares beneath the gloss.

"We do a lot of good work here," he says without prompting. "Kids land with us in crisis, and we move them toward stability."

"While you were moving them," I say, "they were calling 911."

He doesn't break stride, but the angle of his shoulders changes. "If you're referring to the prank calls—"

"I'm referring to the calls."

I stop at a door labeled *Recreation*. Through the narrow window, I watch two girls play ping-pong with the focus of surgeons. Laughter spikes then dims.

I turn to the director. "We'll decide if they were prank calls or not."

Harrow grimaces but motions me into an office with a wall map of the county and a motivational poster about resilience. He sits and steeples his fingers. "You need to understand context. Those years were . . . turbulent with funding cuts and staffing shortages. Teenagers can be theatrical. We got calls about monsters in closets."

I lean forward instead. "Dispatcher logs put the origin of the calls at your pay phone, girls whispering about *lights out, basement, please.*"

He only nods.

"And no unit was ever dispatched." I wait to see if he'll give me a reaction.

He doesn't. Instead, he opens a folder on his desk like it's supposed to calm me. "We instituted a policy after the first wave — phone supervision after curfew."

"That must be why the calls kept coming," I say, not buying whatever he's trying to sell.

He doesn't smile. "If you've come here to paint us as villains, I can assure you—"

"I've come to see your intake rosters," I say, "specifically during the years of 2008 through to 2010, as well as all incident reports and any basement access logs."

"There is no basement," he says too quickly.

I let the silence sit between us until the HVAC kicks on and fills the room with a tired hum. "Old schools have crawl spaces," I say. "Old gyms have storage pits. The girls said basement. If it wasn't a basement, show me what it was."

He stands, his posture stiff. "We keep cleaning supplies in a ground-level utility room. That's all."

"Then showing me won't be a problem."

Exhaling through his nose, he concedes the smallest inch. "Files first," he says. "Then a brief walk-through."

He takes me to the records room — a long room with metal shelves, the air stale with paper that knows more than it says.

A staffer with a lanyard that reads *MAYA* looks up, her eyes flicking from me to Harrow.

"Maya, we'll need all the intake rosters," he says. "'08 to 2010."

Maya rolls her chair to a cabinet, pulls three thick binders, and places them on the table.

I open the first and scan the columns — *NAME, DOB, DATE IN, DATE OUT, GUARDIAN/PLACEMENT*. The handwriting shifts across pages — blocky, rushed, or neat depending on who was on the desk that day, I'm assuming.

That part's normal. The patterns aren't.

"Why are there erasures?" I ask.

Maya leans in. "We reuse lines when kids transfer."

I point to a page where white-out blots a last name into a blank cloud. "And this one?"

Harrow clears his throat. "Some guardians objected to privacy breaches. We corrected."

"By removing names?"

"By sanitizing records," he says, clearly defensive.

I flip ahead. A cluster of entries for late summer 2009. Same birth year, three girls within two months of each other, all admitted within a week, all discharged the same day to "alternate placement." The receiving field reads only *STATE* in block caps.

"Where did they go?" I ask.

"State intake," Maya answers too fast. "I mean, they were transferred to a state-run facility."

"Which one?"

Silence.

I turn the page. There's a notation margin crowded with initials — *CR, LH, TR* — but no key to explain who those initials belong to. I run my finger along the column of staff initials until I land on curfew check. CR is logged again and again.

"Who is CR?" I ask even though I have a feeling I already know the answer.

Maya's gaze flicks to Harrow. He looks like he swallowed a lemon.

"Community responder," he says. "Volunteers from SAR occasionally provided overnight coverage when we were short."

"So this is Caleb Rusk then?"

Harrow recoils a fraction. "He was vetted."

"I'm sure he was," I say. "I'll need copies of every shift he worked and the incident reports that correspond."

Maya says, "We don't—"

"You do," I say, my voice softer than a knife, "because when this gets to court, you'll either look like the facility that helped us or the facility that hid him."

I scan the second binder. There are more white-outs, more transfers to state. One page is photocopied twice, as if someone wasn't sure which version to keep. The first shows a name — *Tansy Carr*. The second shows a white rectangle where her last name used to be.

"Who's Tansy Carr?" I ask.

Harrow shakes his head. "Old case."

"And . . ."

"It doesn't matter."

Are you kidding me?

"Old names matter," I tell him. "Names point to people, and people point to rooms that aren't basements."

He bristles. "We're not required to keep records past seven years."

"You kept these," I say, tapping the binder, "either out of diligence or guilt. I'll take both."

Maya prints copies with her jaw tight.

While the machine hums, I let my eyes drift to the corners of the room, the first places truth gets tired. A cardboard banker's box under the lowest shelf is labeled *MAINT*. A file folder slid half-way behind the copier, with an old logo for Harlow's Edge Public Schools visible. I crouch and tug the folder free. Inside is a map of the building from the 1970s, including the gym and auditorium. Under the west wing, in neat architect letters, is *MECH / BOILER RM (SUB-GRADE)*.

"No basement?" I call out, holding up the map with one hand.

Harrow's face goes carefully blank. "That's obsolete."

"Truth doesn't go obsolete," I say.

He takes me on the "brief walk-through" like a man offering a tour of a crime scene he believes he can narrate into innocence. The girls in REC pretend not to glance at us. A staffer stands at the dorms area with a tablet like a shield. We pass a door labeled Utility. Harrow keeps walking. I don't.

"What's in this room?" I ask.

He sighs. "Cleaning supplies."

"Let's open it to be sure."

He hesitates just long enough to confirm the answer. Then he fishes for keys, finds the right one, and turns it.

The room is full of cleaning supplies, like he's said, with shelves full of bleach bottles and mop heads along with folded rags stacked like prisoners. On the back wall, there's a metal grate near the floor, the bolts cleaner than the paint around them.

"Ventilation," Harrow offers, softer.

"For a sub-grade mechanical room?" I don't hide my sarcasm. "Which door opens to that?"

He blinks. "We sealed the lower spaces in the nineties."

"After the floods," Maya adds from behind us.

I squat and run my finger along the edge of the grate. Scratches mar the paint — small, vertical, regular — like someone dragged something metal across it over and over.

"What's this?" I ask.

Maya leans close and then jerks back a fraction. "Letters."

I bend farther. Once you see them, you can't unsee them. There's a short line repeated into a column then a longer one curving at the top. *I I I I I* then a *J* that misses its hook. Next to it is a slanted *A*. Child-carved, dull-tool, patient.

The paint tried to swallow them and failed.

Harrow's voice gets tight. "Kids graffiti."

"Kids leave names," I say, "and when they're running out of room to speak, they carve them where grown-ups never kneel." I look up at him and give him a cold, hard stare. "I'll need full access to sub-grade. If you've sealed it, we'll unseal it with a warrant."

"That's not—"

"Jurisdiction is mine," I say. "You can stand in the way and make the evening news, or you can show me the nearest external hatch and let me be the one who finds out what you forgot to hide."

We stare at each other long enough that the quiet grows teeth.

Finally, he exhales. "There's a hatch behind the old loading dock. It floods every spring."

"Which means it keeps secrets every summer," I say.

We circle to the back lot where there's a loading dock slumped under a warped metal awning. Behind it is a tangle of dead ivy and a steel hatch lies flush with the concrete, its hinges orange with rust.

The padlock, however, is bright and new.

"Who locked it?" I ask.

Harrow doesn't answer.

I crouch. The concrete holds a faint ring around the hatch where water dried slow. In the dust along the edge, there's a crescent of shoe prints, narrow and quite recent.

I pull out my phone. "Valdez," I say, keeping my eyes on the hatch. "Bring bolt cutters, a forensic kit, a sub-grade air monitor, and a camera to Harlow's Edge. We're going down."

Harrow swallows. "Detective—"

"You had years to go first," I say without looking at him. "I'll take it from here."

The cottonwood fluff tumbles across the concrete like slow snow. Somewhere inside, a girl laughs and then stops. The pay phone near the lobby door hangs quiet.

No one hid it, and no one believed it mattered, but the truth is still here, waiting where everyone stopped looking.

CHAPTER 3: BELOW THE HATCH

Valdez pulls up thirty minutes after I call, lights off, engine ticking as it cools. She steps out with a duffel bag slung over one shoulder and a look that says we're doing this now because we should have done it years ago. Behind her, a CSU tech in coveralls wrestles a Pelican case out of the back.

"Evening stroll?" Valdez asks.

"Why not?" I answer. "Lots of fresh air."

We all look at the hatch. There's a new padlock attached.

Director Harrow hovers at the edge of the loading dock stairs, his arms folded. I think he's trying to look authoritative instead of obstructive. Maya stands a step behind him, her eyes flicking between us and the metal like she's waiting to hear what's been living underneath her feet.

Valdez snaps on gloves. "Bolt cutters."

The tech passes them over. Valdez lines the jaws on the lock. There's a pause, a breath, and a clean metallic pop that makes Harrow flinch.

She kicks the hasp free with the toe of her boot. We heave the hatch. The hinges shriek like they're alive. A smell wafts up — wet concrete, old iron, and the thin sting of bleach that can't quite kill what it tries to cleanse.

"Air monitor," I say to the tech, who lowers a sensor on a cord. The numbers glow green. The oxygen level is okay, and there are no explosive gases. Mold, sure, but not enough to drop us.

He nods. "You've got an hour before I start nagging."

Valdez clicks on her headlamp and hands another to me. "After you, Sherlock."

"You're too kind," I say, and I swing my legs over.

A metal ladder clings to the wall like a spine. I test the first rung. It holds.

Valdez's light sweeps past me into the dark. The air cools a degree with each step down. I count them, one, two . . . thirteen, and land on a lip of concrete that becomes a narrow corridor.

I aim my beam down the corridor. It runs twenty feet west, turns, and widens. Pipes hang low and sweat into the silence. Labels peel — *BOILER SUPPLY. RETURN. DRAIN.* Water whispers somewhere, but I don't think it's the river.

Valdez drops beside me, then the tech with the case. Above, Harrow mutters something about liability insurance. Maya shushes him.

We move.

The corridor opens into a room that used to matter. A boiler the size of a truck crouches in the center, its paint flaking like old skin. The floor is stained in rings where the water once stood. On the far wall, someone bricked in an archway, but the bricks don't match. They're newer.

A Band-Aid over a broken bone.

"It was sealed in the nineties," Harrow parrots from above, his voice echoing down, "after the floods."

Valdez says nothing. She sweeps her light left and illuminates shelves bolted to the wall. Cleaning supplies, sure, but not just bleach.

"Bag and tag," I tell the tech.

I step closer. There are folded twin blankets here, faded cartoon prints of astronauts, stars, and kittens with crescent moons, all threadbare from excessive washing. Next to them is a bucket of zip ties. Next to those is a flat coil of chain with a hook like a question mark.

Damn it.

I run my palm over the shelf and come away with dust and something gritty. I pinch it in my glove and bring it to my light. Sand from the river? Or tracked here by feet that went there? Either way, it shouldn't be on this shelf.

I swing my beam lower. Along the base of the wall, near the floor, and bolted into the concrete is a vent grate like the one upstairs. The paint here shows scratches, too. Deeper. Longer. Letter shapes that fought harder.

I kneel. *I I I I I* in a careful row. A backward *E* as if the carver learned letters from a mirror. A line that could be the start of an *R* or a *K*. The gouges are old, the edges softened by time, but they're there, defiant.

My chest tightens. The space smells like panic that dried and went to ground.

Valdez's light pauses on the opposite wall. "Amber."

I cross over to her. She's found a corner where the concrete has been scratched white. Words this time, not just letters, in all caps.

I read them aloud because the air needs to hear them, or else they'll fade again. "'Lights out isn't sleep.' 'I was here.' 'Tansy.' 'Lea.' 'No one answered.'"

Under those words are short marks, tallies grouped by five. Seventy-eight of them.

"Photos," I say.

The tech is already snapping, each flash a flat clap. He works methodically, angles and scales, the monotony a rhythm that keeps us from shaking.

"Mechanical room," Harrow calls down, like renaming it redefines its use. "You see? No basement."

"Right," I say softly. "That guy is an idiot."

We move past the boiler to the bricked archway that someone wanted shut. The mortar is sloppy, smeared in fingerprints that have fossilized.

My beam finds an old seam where brick meets cinderblock. The tech taps it with a knuckle. It's hollow on the other side.

"Get me the hammer drill after we've cleared the rest," Valdez says without looking up. "If there's a space behind, it's part of our scene."

I follow a second corridor to a second room. It's smaller and square-shaped. It would've been storage with old desks, folding chairs, and boxes of uniforms. Now it's a closet for what the upstairs didn't want to remember.

A covered plastic tub rests on the table. I pop the seal. Inside, there are Ziploc bags full of bracelets, hair ties, and cheap pendant necklaces shaped like hearts, stars, and initials. Contraband, someone would call them. Personal effects, I call them. A hand-scrawled label on masking tape reads *CONFISCATED — DO NOT RETURN*.

Here, they didn't hide the truth. They labeled it in block letters and then shoved the bin where only the dark could read it.

I lift one bag. A beaded bracelet with blue glass. A cracked bead with an *L*. Another with an *E* rubbed thin. Lacey Quinn had one like it. So did her friends.

"Inventory all of that," I say. "Cross-reference names we can prove. We'll show Mrs. Quinn when the time is right."

Valdez calls me back with a note in her voice I don't hear often. Not fear. Not quite. Respect for something terrible.

She's found another door. It's made of steel and set into the cinderblock like an afterthought. No handle, just a slide bolt that's been cut and rewelded. The weld is newer than the rust.

"Somebody shut this," she says.

I try the bolt. It sticks. Bracing my boot on the wall, I give a good haul. It gives with a jerk that shudders through my arms. The door swings in a few inches and stops against grit. I push harder. It scrapes over a lip. The smell of wet earth that hasn't seen daylight in a decade deepens.

My light illuminates the narrow space. It's no more than eight by ten. The ceiling is so low that the kids would've had to watch their heads. The walls are close, and the floor is damp. There's a crate in the corner with the lid half off, like someone left in a rush and didn't bother to make it neat.

I put my shoulder into the door. It opens enough for us to slip in sideways. The tech mutters about air quality. The monitor says we're still green.

I don't want to think about how many bodies a space this size could hold. I think instead about breath, girls counting theirs in the dark to keep panic at bay.

At eye level, a phrase has been scratched deeply into the wall, lettered like someone had time. *HE DOESN'T LIKE THE LIGHTS ON.*

I touch the words with my glove, and my throat closes. River's ghost stands beside me, not as a specter but as a sentence that keeps finding new mouths. Tansy said this. A caller said it. My sister said it. Men who wanted control said it without speaking.

Rule #9 isn't a comfort. It's a blade. *The first thing people forget to hide is always the truth.*

They left the truth here. They wrote it down for me.

"Look," Valdez says. She's crouched by the crate.

Inside are a stack of composition books swollen with damp, their marbled covers bleached gray. A bundle of floral cloth strips is torn on one side, as if teeth did the work. Next is a roll of duct tape and a pair of scissors with dried adhesive along the blades.

Underneath is a clipboard with a plastic sleeve and water damage that somehow spared the ink.

I pick up the clipboard. It's a delivery manifest for Harlow's Edge Youth Transition Center — Receiving. There are dates in a column, a half dozen in 2009, more in 2010. Items listed: Disposable linens, cleaning chemicals, bulk food, misc. At the bottom: Carrier: Prairie Star Freight. Driver Signature: A. Rawlings.

My heart stumbles and rights itself.

The same weeks he passed through on my board. The same spring when the calls spiked.

Valdez's eyes cut to me. "Bag it," she says softly, like the air might bruise us if we speak louder.

I slide the manifest into a sleeve and tuck it into an evidence bag like it's a live thing. Because it is. It's the first paper link I've seen between this floor and the truck I've been chasing. Not proof of a crime by him here, not yet, but proof he knew this place. Proof that he came to this town. Proof he put his hand on a pen and left A. Rawlings, where Harrow forgot to scrub.

I exhale slowly.

The tech flips open a composition book with a plastic wedge. The pages cling together before surrendering with a wet sigh. The ink is a wash, the words turned to weather, but in the gutter of the spine is the last thing the paper remembers, *Tansy. C.* Next to the name is a drawing of a phone, a crude rectangle with a coiled cord.

"We have a witness," I say. "We have artifacts. We have a sealed room. We have a route. We have a name."

I stand in the center of the little room and listen. No, not for ghosts. For air moving through vent lines that connect spaces not meant to talk to each other. For water in a pipe that connects here to the river like a vein. For the click of the tech's camera, each flash an insistence.

In one corner, something catches my light. A circle of scuffed concrete. I crouch. It's a ring, lighter than the surrounding floor, like a bucket sat here a long time before being moved. Around it, rust flakes, and in the flakes is a strand of hair, long and brown.

I point.

The tech collects it with tweezers and slides it into a tube. "Maybe," he says. "Maybe not."

"Everything is a maybe until a lab says otherwise," I tell him, "but truth doesn't need the lab to exist."

We work the room for an hour. Photos. Measurements. The tech maps each carving. We find more names, some I recognize from intake, some I don't. We see a small plastic charm wedged between brick and mortar, half a star, the gold paint chipped. We find a strip of blanket hem where someone picked thread loose until it made a rope thin enough to bite the skin and leave a mark.

When we're done, we back out. The door resists closing then does. I slide the bolt because the chain of custody is jewelry we can't afford to lose. The space behind the bricked arch will wait for the morning, for the right tool and the right paper.

At the base of the ladder, I tilt my head and stare up. The square of night at the top looks small, as if the world narrowed while we were below. I climb. Halfway up, voices filter down — Maya's low and strained, Harrow's sharp and too cheerful.

". . . see?" he's saying. "Mechanical. Storage. It proves—"

I pull myself over the lip and stand. "It proves there's a sub-grade space where girls were locked and kept," I say. My voice isn't loud, but it doesn't have to be. "It proves you knew enough to lock it."

Harrow opens his mouth and closes it. His gaze darts to the CSU labels on the bags. He sees the clipboard. He sees the floral cloth. He sees the bracelet pressed against clear plastic.

Maya's hand covers her mouth. Her eyes are wet, furious, and ashamed at once. "I didn't know," she whispers.

"I believe you," I say. "I also believe you can help fix it."

She nods hard. "Tell me what to do."

"Start with copies of every vendor contract from 2008 to 2012," I say. "Every receiving log. And the names that got whited-out."

Valdez comes up behind me, her breath a little high from the climb, the duffel bag's strap carving a line in her shoulder. "We'll post a deputy at the hatch," she tells Harrow. "We'll post one at Records. Nobody touches anything. You do, and you're part of it."

Harrow's face reddens. "You have no idea what this will do to our funding."

"You have no idea what this already did to kids," Valdez says.

I feel an old, familiar heat in my chest that isn't anger so much as calibration. We're aligned, and we're pointing at the same thing.

We secure the hatch with our lock. We tape and tag the perimeter. The cottonwood fluff falls in lazy spirals, landing on the metal and sticking to our fingerprints. The evening is moving toward night. A wind comes up from the west, carrying the smell of the river, the mill, and a greasy diner.

I look at the pay phone in the lobby through the glass of the locked door. The tape on the cord gleams dully under fluorescent lights. I glance at the paper above it. Someone wrote the emergency number big enough for fear to find it in the dark. That someone did their part. We didn't do ours.

I tuck the manifest bag against my chest without meaning to.

Valdez nudges my elbow. "You okay?"

"No," I say. I don't have to lie to her. "But I will be when we break the arch."

She grins fiercely. "Tomorrow, then."

"Tomorrow," I echo.

We leave the loading dock and walk past the sign with its chipped letters. *TRANSITION CEN—*

A word that didn't finish.

Maya locks the main door. She hesitates. "Detective?"

"Meri."

"Meri." She swallows. "What you said about the truth . . . I think we forgot how to look at it."

"Then we'll make it so you can't look anywhere else," I say. "That's what happens next."

When I slide into my car, the manifest rides shotgun. I key the ignition, but don't shift out of park. The hatch is behind me. Under it is air that remembers breathing. Ahead is the road toward my house. Toward the room where I keep everything that won't let me go.

The Polaroid of the youth center on my board flashes in my head. Caleb in the background. Rawlings on the route.

I rest my hand on the evidence bag, lightly tapping the plastic, and whisper not to the building, not to the river, not to the men who thought paper was camouflage, but to the girls. "I see you," I say. "I hear you."

And the truth answers, the way it always does when it's finally given a mouth.

It doesn't shout. It doesn't need to.

It merely waits until you open the door.

CHAPTER 4: THE RUNAWAY

I find her at a halfway house two towns over, the kind of place the county labels *transitional housing*, even though they really mean *don't ask too many questions*. Her name on paper is Darla Knox, but she used to be Tansy Carr.

The erased name from the intake roster. The one they tried to white-out.

She answers the door, letting me in once I show her my badge. It's a small house, barely taking any time to walk from the door through the living room to the kitchen. It smells like reheated chili and Lysol. A TV murmurs in the corner with subtitles on, ignored. A man snores on the couch under a quilt stitched with ducks. I sit down at her kitchen table.

She knows why I'm here.

"Someone finally listened to those tapes," she says, her eyes on the coffee mug between her hands. Her nails are bitten to the quick, the skin around them raw. "Took you long enough."

"You were one of the callers," I say.

She nods once. "Not the first. Not the last. Just the loudest, maybe." She smirks without humor. "Didn't matter. They never sent anyone."

"Tell me what happened after curfew."

Her eyes flick up, her gaze wary. "You'll write it down?"

"Yes."

"Then I want it clear. It wasn't all the staff. Some were decent. Some looked the other way because they didn't want to lose the only paycheck they'd had in years, but some . . . some used that place like a cage."

"Who?"

She swallows. "Night staff. A couple of volunteers. One guy — Caleb — showed up sometimes. He said he was keeping us safe. He was worse than the rest. He would walk the halls and shine his flashlight under the doors just to watch us flinch."

I don't move. Don't let the rage shift my face. "The basement?"

"It wasn't supposed to be open. They said it flooded, that it was sealed, but the hatch behind the dock still worked. They used it when they wanted to punish us or hide us. Lock us down there with no light until we stopped crying." Her voice dips. "You could hear the water under the floor. Like the river was waiting."

"The 911 calls—"

"We took turns," she says quickly, "calling from the pay phone by the lobby. If you timed it right, you could call before the staff made their rounds. Whisper quick then hang up. We thought that if we said 'basement' or 'lights out,' somebody would come, but nobody ever did." Her fingers tighten around the mug. "After a while, we stopped calling. What's the point of telling the truth if nobody cares?"

"What happened to the other girls?" I ask.

She shakes her head. "Transfers. That's what they called it. One day, you'd eat breakfast together. The next, their bed was stripped, and the staff said they were 'state-placed.' No goodbye. No paperwork. Just gone."

I show her the photocopied page with her name and the white-out square. "Like this?"

Her breath hitches. She touches the paper with one fingertip, tracing where her last name should be. "That's me. That's when I ran."

"You didn't transfer."

"No." She leans back, her eyes faraway. "They said I was next, that Caleb had plans. I didn't wait to find out what they meant. I climbed the fence and broke my ankle when I landed, but I kept running until the trees hid me. Nobody followed, or maybe they just didn't care enough to chase." Her mouth twists. "I thought the truth would protect me, that if I told someone and showed them, they'd believe me, but when I limped into town and begged for help, the sheriff wrote me up as a runaway and said girls lie for attention."

My heart breaks hearing her story. It shouldn't have been like that. We let her down.

"What happened next?"

"I made it to my aunt's. She hid me until I aged out. Changed my name. Told me to keep quiet."

"And you did," I say.

"I was too scared not to." She looks at me sharply. "And if you hadn't come, I still would be."

I nod. "I believe you."

She studies my face like she's measuring if that sentence means anything. Finally, she asks, "Why now?"

"Because the river gave something back," I say, "and because the truth never stays buried. Not forever."

She leans forward. "Then you need to look in the basement for bones. For the ones who didn't make it to a transfer, or a fence, or an aunt's house. You need to see what's still down there."

I slide a recorder across the table. "Will you give me a statement?"

Her lips twitch. "You think my voice will matter now?"

"It matters to me," I say, "and I don't stop until the truth is louder than the lies."

She stares at the recorder, then presses the button. Her voice trembles at first, then steadies. She says her old name. She says the year. She says the word basement with the weight of someone who lived it.

I let her talk until the truth sits solid in the room, undeniable. When she's done, I stop the recorder. "Thank you."

She nods, exhausted. "You're going to drag it into the light, aren't you?"

"Yes."

"And if they try to shut you up?"

I almost smile. "They'll fail."

She looks down at her bitten nails, then back at me. "Find them. The girls who never ran. Find their names."

"I will."

CHAPTER 5: THE HATCH

Tansy thought the truth was hidden. It wasn't. It was written in rosters, carved in grates, whispered into phones, waiting for someone to notice.

I have.

The morning crew sets up flood lamps like we're filming a crime drama instead of standing in the middle of one. CSU wheels in a hammer drill that howls against brick. Dust pours into the air, a chalky fog that settles on our coats, our lashes, and the skin around our masks.

Valdez stands with her arms crossed, her eyes on the widening hole. "Place smells like a grave already."

I nod grimly. That smell has been earned.

The last brick tumbles with a thud that echoes for far too long. When the dust clears, the opening gapes black. Cold air spills out, a cold no one needs to feel.

The techs go first, their headlamps bobbing with each step. Their silence carries up the tunnel until one calls out, "Clear for entry."

I duck inside.

The room beyond is low and rectangular, maybe fifteen by twenty. The ceiling drips, and I can't help but shiver. The floor is a patchwork of damp concrete and rust stains. In one corner, metal cots lean in a stack, their frames tangled like bones. In another, a row of plastic chairs sits broken, backs scrawled with marker names.

The walls tell more than the furniture between the scratches, carvings, and pencil notes rubbed half away. One section is covered in overlapping dates — 2008, 2009, 2010 — each line thick, carved over and over as if someone wanted to make sure the year wouldn't vanish.

On the far wall, a single word is gouged deep. *ENOUGH*.

Valdez exhales behind me. "Jesus."

We move carefully while CSU photographs everything and tags every scrap of cloth and every scrap of paper.

I find a shoe under the cots, a child's sneaker. It's too small for anyone over thirteen. The sole is split, the laces stiff with mold. A sticker still clings to the side — half a star.

"Bag it," I say.

Valdez crouches by the chairs and shines her light on one of the seats. "Look at this."

A message has been etched with a nail or a screw. *CALEB WATCHES*. The next chair says *CALEB COMES*.

My jaw tightens. "That's our link. He wasn't just a volunteer. He was part of the routine."

"And he knew the basement wasn't sealed," Valdez adds. "Son of a . . . He used it."

We push deeper. The far corner holds a plastic bin. Inside are spiral notebooks, the pages warped, ink bled. CSU flips through them with tweezers. Most are ruined, but one page holds up. Names have been written over and over. Some are crossed out, but others are underlined hard enough to rip the page. At the bottom is a lie written in ink.

"They weren't transferred," I say despite what's written on that page.

"No." Valdez straightens, eyes hard. "They were erased."

A tech approaches with a warped clipboard in an evidence bag. The paper inside is still legible under its plastic sleeve. Another manifest. Different month. Different load. Same carrier name — Prairie Star Freight. Same driver signature — A. Rawlings.

My throat dries. It's not proof he stepped inside this room, but it's proof he was here at this building, with access.

I take the bag and hold it up to the light. The ink has bled into the paper fibers, but the signature is unmistakable.

The river gave me Caleb. This building just gave me Rawlings.

* * *

Later, upstairs, we gather in Harrow's office. He sits stiff, his tie knotted, his hands folded like he thinks his posture will make a shield. Maya perches near the door. She's pale as she wrings her hands.

I drop the evidence bag on his desk. The clipboard thuds. "Your vendor."

He blinks. "What am I looking at?"

"Freight logs signed by a driver tied to multiple disappearances in this county." I tap the clipboard. "Deliveries here during the years you claim you had no basement." I tap again. "No issues." Another tap. "No missing girls." I tap yet again.

His throat bobs. "We don't screen drivers."

"You do now," I snap, "because this one connects your center to every board I've got on my wall. I want every contract. Every invoice. Every signature you've filed away since 2005."

Maya whispers, "I can get them."

Harrow glares at her, but she doesn't look at him.

I lean across the desk. "You wanted to sanitize records. You wanted to white-out names. That's obstruction. What you didn't erase is worse because every lie you tell leaves the truth sitting right beside it."

His face cracks then, just a hairline. Not guilt. Fear.

Valdez steps in. "We'll post deputies here until we have every file. If you interfere, we'll take you in for obstruction today."

Maya finally meets my eyes. There's something desperate in hers. "Detective . . . the girls who called . . . do you know their names yet?"

"Some," I say. "Not enough. But I will."

She nods once, like that's the only promise she's been waiting for.

* * *

That night, I sit at my kitchen table.

I pin a copy of the manifest to my wall and red string from it to the copied Polaroid of the youth center, to the map of his trucking routes, to River's photo.

For years, I've been building this web, threads thin and fraying. Tonight, one of them has been pulled taut.

Rawlings knew this place. He stood on those steps where Caleb grinned at a Polaroid camera.

The girls were telling the truth all along. They shouted it with knives on walls and whispers in phones. We were the ones who didn't listen.

"I'm listening now," I whisper into the room, to River's photo, to the voices still trapped on those tapes.

For the first time in weeks, the house doesn't feel empty.

CHAPTER 6: THE ONE WHO DIDN'T VANISH

Maya's email lands in my inbox after midnight.

> *Found these in an old finance box. The director never saw them. Please move fast.*

The first attachment is a typed vendor ledger with misaligned columns and cigarette burns along the edge. The second is a photocopy of a property inventory stamped *STATE INTAKE*. Half of the entries have been redacted by a marker. The third is a transfer list, two pages, with a case number repeated where it shouldn't be.

I print them, lay them on my kitchen table, and trace the pattern with my finger like I'm following a river on a map. The ledger shows monthly confiscated effects shipments to state storage labeled *Batch C*. The inventory lists bracelets, hair ties, journals, and dozens of personal items. Next to one line, the clerk wrote a note that never made it to the retyped copy. *Caller — Lea (lights out).* The transfer list takes the same case number and assigns it to two different girls on the same day, only one of whom is redacted.

Lea. A name carved on a wall under a room with no light.

I call Valdez.

"Tell me you're not at your board," she says, her voice thick with sleep. "Tell me you're horizontal like a human."

"I have a name," I say, not feeling one ounce of guilt for waking her up, "and a case number duplicated to make a person vanish twice."

By eight in the morning, we're shoulder to shoulder in a gray government cubicle at Family Services while a supervisor clicks through a database built in the era of dial-up and never rebuilt. Valdez stands behind me with a second cup of coffee and the look she gets when she's not in a good mood.

"Here," the supervisor says finally, tapping the screen. "Case J-09184. Intake at Harlow's Edge, 2009. Transfer to state holding then to county adult services at age eighteen. Name on file is Leona J. She goes by Lea. Current residence is St. Francis Transitional in Charlton."

"Charlton's our county," Valdez says.

The supervisor nods absently, already bored now that the puzzle's solved for her. "Traumatic mutism, likely. She communicates in writing. Why are you looking at this again?"

I pocket the printout. "Because she called for help, and no one came."

The supervisor blinks like I spoke in a foreign language and waves us off with the practiced indifference of someone who files people for a living.

* * *

St. Francis Transitional sits on a sloped lawn behind a church the color of old chalk. The entry smells like mop water and canned soup. A woman at the desk looks up, looks down, and then looks up again when she sees our badges.

"We'd like to speak with Lea J—" I start.

"Lea Jameson," she fills in, with the pride of someone who knows the names of the people she's paid to keep alive. "She's in the sunroom."

The sunroom isn't sunny. The windows face a stand of trees that block the light, but there are plants on every sill and a radio turned to a station with slow songs.

Four residents sit in mismatched chairs. One stares at a puzzle. One sleeps with her chin on her chest. One talks to a plant, and the plant is gracious enough to listen.

Lea sits in the corner, her ankles crossed, a notebook on her knees. Her hair is long and dark, pulled into a low braid. She glances up as we enter, then drops her gaze to the paper like we're a rainstorm she has to wait out.

"Lea?" I say softly. "I'm Meri. This is Valdez. We're here about Harlow's Edge."

Her pencil stops. She doesn't look up. Then she writes on the top line, *No police*.

"We're not here to arrest you," I say. "We're here to listen."

She still doesn't lift her head. Her hand moves. *Too late.*

"It wasn't too late for you," I say.

There's a long pause. Then her eyes flick up to mine and hold. Her mouth doesn't move, but something in her face does, a shift that feels like someone inside leaning toward the door.

"I've heard your voice," I say.

I slide a small player from my pocket, thumb the volume down to a whisper, and press play. *He doesn't like the lights on.* It's not her voice, not necessarily, but it's a voice like hers, born in the same darkness.

Her hand clenches around the pencil. She presses the tip to the paper hard enough to snap the lead. She stares at the break. I hand her a pen. *Basement. Phone. No one came.*

"I've come now," I say, "and I can come with you into a courtroom if you want, or I can come into an office and watch you write a statement, or I can simply sit here and honor that you tried."

She studies me. Then she tears the top sheet free, folds it into a square, and hands it to me. On the next page, she writes, *Ask.*

"Okay," I say. I sit.

Valdez stays standing just behind me, watchful and quiet.

"Do you remember a man named Caleb?" I ask. "He volunteered at nights."

He watched. He came.

"And a truck driver," I say. My throat tightens, so I make my voice a stranger's. "Tall. Dark hair. Chrome truck. Star on the door."

She looks past me at a corner of the glass where a leaf has pressed itself flat and left its print for the sun to read. Then she writes: *He signed the paper. He laughed.*

If the room tilts, it's only inside me. Outside, the world holds.

Valdez shifts her weight.

"Do you remember his name?" I ask.

Last name R.

That's enough.

"Did he ever go downstairs?" I ask.

Lea's mouth hardens. *No.* She underlines it. *He talked to the man with keys. He waited.* She draws a rectangle with a line under it. A door. Then a circle by the side. A lock.

"Harrow," I say. "The director?"

Her eyes lift slightly. It's not a nod, but it's not a no.

"Did he take anyone?" Valdez asks gently.

Lea writes slower now, like every letter is heavy. *He picked. Caleb carried. Van.*

I see the loading dock, the hatch, the flood lamps, the ledger. I see a clipboard with a signature that has curled in my dreams for two decades.

"Do you remember the night you called?" I ask.

She starts to write and stops. The pen hovers. I wait a full minute. Then she writes one line that hurts more than I expect — *I wanted your voice.*

A sound cracks somewhere inside my ribs, and it's a struggle to contain the grief building inside me.

"May I ask you a cruel question? If it is too much, put your hand up, and I'll stop."

She doesn't nod, but she doesn't shake her head either. I'll take that as a yes.

"Do you know names I don't?" I ask. "The girls who didn't make it past the hatch or who made it and were called 'state' instead of 'alive.'"

She writes five in a tidy column, *Tansy. Me. Joy. Maira. Ana.* Then she flips the page and writes three more on the back, the letters getting smaller as if she's trying to make room for all of them, *Beth. Nessa. R.*

"R?" I ask.

She taps the letter, then writes: *She said he didn't like the lights on.* A pause. *Gone before me.* A small, hard line beneath the next word. *Truck.*

I keep my face still because if I don't, the floor will move.

"We found notebooks," I say. "We found your names on the wall."

Her eyes shine. She doesn't wipe them.

"Would you write a statement?" I ask. "We'll take as long as you need. We'll go as slow as you want. We'll never put you where you can't see the door."

She studies my face for a long time. Then she writes: *Not here.*

"Where?"

Where you keep the strings. She underlines it like a joke that's not a joke.

I nod. "Okay. My office. The room where I won't let anyone else in."

I can feel Valdez agreeing behind me. She knows the door, the key, the wall.

Lea tears the sheet free again, folds it, tucks it into her pocket like it's a pass, and stands. She's taller than I expected, her spine straighter than the notes said. She takes the cassette player from my hand, rewinds, presses play, listens to the whisper that is hers and isn't, and then presses stop with her thumb like she's closing a small, unnecessary door.

"Tomorrow," I say.

She leans down and writes, *Tomorrow*.

* * *

In the parking lot, the wind carries the smell of rain that isn't here yet.

Valdez leans against the cruiser and stares at the sky like it's part of her case file. "She gave you his name," she says. "You didn't feed it to her."

"Only the initial, but I'll take it," I say.

"You think she'll testify?"

"I think she'll choose where to place her voice, which is more than anyone's let her do in fifteen years."

Valdez nods. "Harrow?"

"Arrest for obstruction today. More soon." I tap the folder under my arm. "Maya handed us a bridge. I say we walk across it."

"And Rawlings?" she asks carefully.

"He's closer than he was yesterday." I look out past the church at the road that leads to Charlton, to Harlow's Edge, to the river that knows more than it tells. "He's always closer than he looks."

We stand there a minute with the engine cooling and the grit of the day under our nails. For once, the air doesn't feel like it's all taken. There's some left for us.

On the drive back, Lea's list rides in my pocket like a pulse. *Tansy. Joy. Maira. Ana. Beth. Nessa. R.*

At a red light, I take out my notebook and add a line I should have written years ago.

Find their mothers if they have them. If they don't, be one.

The light changes, and I put the car in gear.

Tomorrow, Lea will sit at my table in the room I don't open for anybody, and she will write words that stay. Maya will run copies until her fingers go gray. Valdez will stand at a door and dare anyone to knock.

And somewhere, a man who signed a clipboard will wonder why his name is suddenly worth less than ink.

CHAPTER 7: THE DOOR THAT STAYS OPEN

Lea sits at my table, the one in my locked evidence room. The wall of threads looms behind me — Rawlings in the center, Caleb's Polaroid to the left, the youth center map taped crooked beside them. She doesn't look at it. She looks at the paper in front of her, her pen poised, eyes steady.

Valdez leans in the doorway with her arms crossed. She's not in the room, but she's not leaving either.

"Ready when you are."

Lea nods. Her braid rests over her shoulder like a cord. She begins to write.

My name is Leona Jameson. They called me Lea. I was thirteen. Harlow's Edge said I was a ward of the state. I was a girl. I called 911. No one came.

The scratch of her pen on paper is loud in the room. Every written word lands heavy, not because it's new but because it's survived. She writes about the hatch, the dark, the chairs with names carved. She writes about Caleb's flashlight beam cutting across her blanket, about the way he carried girls under one arm like they weighed nothing. She writes about the man with the clipboard who smiled too much and signed his name too large.

Rawlings.

She underlines his name twice.

I breathe through it. Not because I doubt her, but because if I let my body do what it wants, it will tear through walls and drag men into the street by their collars. I need steadiness. She needs it more.

When she pauses, Valdez brings her water. She drinks, swallows, and then sets the glass exactly in line with the edge of the notebook before continuing.

Harrow knew. He had the keys. He told us if we didn't behave, we'd go back down. Caleb laughed when he said it. Rawlings waited. He picked. I don't know where they took the girls who didn't come back.

The pen slows. Her hand shakes. She presses harder.

I do know the calls were true. Every story we told was true.

She sets the pen down and looks at me, her eyes wide, maybe waiting to see if I'll flinch.

"I believe you," I say.

Valdez speaks up, her voice soft. "We both do."

Lea nods once, sharply, like she's scored a point on a tally she's been keeping in her head for years.

We sign and date the pages. I seal them in an envelope with her initials across the flap. She presses her palm flat against it like she's blessing a grave.

* * *

Two hours later, Harrow sits in an interview room with his tie undone and sweat slicking his temples. He thinks Lea won't talk. He probably thinks Lea hasn't talked since silence kept her safe for fifteen years, but silence won't keep him safe now.

I push the envelope across the table. "She spoke."

His face blanches, then stiffens. "She's unstable."

"She's consistent," I say. "Her statement matches the rosters, the graffiti, and the manifests. She named you. She named Caleb. She named Rawlings."

His lips press white.

Valdez leans forward. "Want to explain how a freight driver ended up with a key to your facility?"

"I—" His voice cracks. He clears it. "He donated supplies. Food. Clothing. We needed support."

"You gave him access to *children*," I say, barely able to contain my anger.

He doesn't contain his. His fist slams on the table. "We were drowning. The state cut funding every year. We had two staff members for thirty kids. If we didn't take help, we would've lost them all."

"You lost them anyway," I snap, "piece by piece through the hatch you swore didn't exist."

Silence swells. The fluorescent light buzzes. His hand trembles against the steel tabletop.

"You can either cooperate," Valdez says, low and even, "or you can ride this all the way down with Caleb."

His eyes flick to the envelope, and he swallows hard. "What do you want?"

"Everything," I say, like it isn't obvious. "Every vendor, every log, every volunteer list, every key holder, and the truth about who walked through your doors while you looked the other way."

He exhales. He knows the fight's over.

* * *

By nightfall, CSU trucks have emptied the basement. Evidence fills crates — journals, scraps of clothing, the manifest with Rawlings' signature, Lea's written testimony. Valdez oversees the chain of custody. Harrow signs his statement with a pen that shakes.

Outside, the cottonwood tree sheds white fluff across the dock like mock snow. Lea stands with me, watching deputies load the last of it. She's quiet, but her shoulders are straighter than they were this morning.

"You opened the door," she says. Her voice is low and cracked from disuse.

I freeze.

Valdez's head snaps toward us, but she doesn't speak.

Clearly startled, Lea touches her throat then lets the hand drop. "Thank you," she whispers.

I nod, my throat tight. "You opened it yourself. I just cut the lock."

She almost smiles. Almost. Then she turns back to the dock, watching the hatch close under a deputy's seal.

* * *

Back home, I pin Lea's statement copy to my wall. Red string ties it to Caleb's Polaroid. Another string runs to the manifest with Rawlings' name. Another to River's photo.

The board hums like a web catching wind. Every new thread makes it stronger.

Lea's voice echoes in my head. *Every story we told was true.*

River's photo stares back at me, as if to say *mine too.*

"I haven't forgotten," I whisper into the room.

CHAPTER 8: THE WALL OF VOICES

The house is dark when I get in. I don't turn on the kitchen light. I don't stop for food. I go straight down the hall, key in hand, to the locked door.

The lock turns, and the hinges sigh. My room waits.

The board glows faintly under the desk lamp I left burning. Threads stretch across it, red and white, a map of voices and vanishings. In the center, Rawlings' face — grainy, smiling, blurred by photocopy. Beside him, River's photo, the only one I've never pinned through for fear it'll feel like nailing her down.

I stare at Lea's statement copy, three pages thick, taped neatly against the cork. The manifest signed in Rawlings' hand. The Polaroid of Caleb outside the youth center, pinned so the steps line up with the manifest's address.

The wall is crowded now, but crowded feels right. It should be.

I sit at the desk and open my notebook. The room is still, but it hums with the memory of scratches carved into walls, numbers tallied to prove time passed, and a voice whispering into a pay phone that no one came to answer.

No one until now.

I lean back. River's smile catches the lamplight. I remember her whisper at night when our father's footsteps creaked the floor, *"He doesn't like the lights on."*

The girls said the same thing. Lea carved it into stone. Voices overlap across time, proving they weren't echoes.

They were warnings.

For years, I've built this room like a cathedral to silence. Tonight, it feels louder. Lea spoke. For the first time in fifteen years, her voice crossed a table. She said thank you, and in that thank you, I imagined every other girl who called and never heard the knock of boots on the stairs.

I whisper back, not to Lea because she's safe now but to River, "I'll find your voice too."

The clock ticks in the hall. The house stays quiet, but it doesn't feel empty.

I thread a final string from Lea's statement to River's photo. The line hums under my finger. The web holds.

Rawlings is still out there, but he's closer now. He touched the youth center, signed its papers, and stood on its dock. His name is no longer a shadow. It's ink, and ink stains.

I close the notebook and click off the lamp.

The wall waits in the dark, but it's not silent. It's never silent.

Because voices like theirs don't vanish. They wait until someone listens.

I'm still listening.

And I won't ever stop.

THE PATTERN

Cold coffee sweats on the desk between us, forgotten long enough to turn bitter.

Valdez flicks her pen across the blotter and lets it roll. "Ever think it's not one monster?" she asks. "Not one house, not one manager? Just the same playbook with different hands writing the rules?"

Her words land like a stone in a well, and I picture dolls sealed in basements. Pact sisters stitching their secrets shut. A birthday room that smelled of cake and cruelty. A girl who learned to break her own smile. And now this apartment, dressed like it's empty but hiding its loss between the walls.

"It's never just one," I tell her. "That's the point."

Valdez studies me. "And you'll keep chasing them all?"

"As long as there's someone to find," I say. "As long as silence is being taught. As long as there's even a chance my sister's still out there."

Her eyes flicker. "You're relentless, Meri. One day, it's going to break you."

"Maybe," I say, "but I made a promise when River disappeared. I was fifteen. Everyone told me to accept she was gone. I swore I wouldn't stop until I knew the truth. I haven't stopped since."

The words hang between us.

* * *

Hours later, back in my office, the board glows under a single lamp — lines crossing, faces blurred, scraps of evidence that shouldn't belong together but do. It's a web, a pattern, and patterns don't let go once you see them.

The city's hum is a far-off tide against my window. My eyes burn from staring. When I close them, the girl's wide gaze stares back — alive, disbelieving, refusing to be erased. For tonight, that's enough to keep me upright.

I spread the files like an unwanted deck of cards. *House of Dolls*, broken, porcelain, hidden bodies. *The Pact*, secrets stitched between friends like scars. *The Birthday Room*, innocence traded for control. *The Apartment Above*, with too many unanswered questions. *What the River Took*, nothing stays buried. *The Widow's Game*, the widow who knew but wanted to forget. *The Girl Beneath the Glass*, River's shadow. *The Girl with a Broken Smile*, Luce learning to unlearn what was forced on her. And now *A Voice Like Mine*.

Different addresses. Different predators. Different methods. All spun from the same thread — places built to disappear the lost, including River.

Above the board, my rules hang in chalk, one through ten. Fingerprints smear the edges where I pressed them into service.

I flatten my palms on the desk. Each item hums the same question. *How many more?*

The answer writes itself in thick marker across the top of the board. *I WILL NOT STOP.*

Because I can't. Because somewhere, River's face is still out there. Because every rescued girl is one less voice gone to silence.

The End

THESE WERE FOR YOU . . .

Hey fellow booklover . . .

For all of you who read *The Sister Under the Stairs* and *The Girls in the Basement*, and sent me messages asking to know more about Meri Amber . . . this is for you.

I loved getting to know Meri better. She intrigued me in The Sister Under the Stairs when she stood beside her car, sucking on a Halls candy. She grabbed hold of my heart in *The Girls in the Basement* when I recognized her tenacity and drive as she refused to give up on finding her sister.

In this book, my goal was to dive into the cases before we first met her. I wanted to discover how she became who she was when we first met her, and personally, I love that she's always been about finding those everyone else forgot about, don't you? It was also important to show that not every case file was closed as cleanly as Meri would have liked. Some linger, some got passed on, and some revealed a larger pattern. Kind of like life, right?

I have one more story for you.

Here's the link to download the story — you'll be joining my mailing list, and we can keep the conversation going about our love for stories and where they take us.

Link: https://steenaholmes.myflodesk.com/qsj1byxl7h

Or just head to my website and click on the "Get a Free Read" tab at the top! Chat soon!

THE JOFFE BOOKS STORY

We began in 2014 when Jasper agreed to publish his mum's much-rejected romance novel, and it became a bestseller.

Since then, we've grown into the largest independent publisher in the UK. We're extremely proud to publish some of the very best writers in the world, including Joy Ellis, Faith Martin, Caro Ramsay, Helen Forrester, Simon Brett, and Robert Goddard. Everyone at Joffe Books loves reading, and we never forget that it all begins with the magic of an author telling a story.

We are proud to publish talented first-time authors, as well as established writers whose books we love introducing to a new generation of readers.

We won Trade Publisher of the Year at the Independent Publishing Awards in 2023 and Best Publisher Award in 2024 at the People's Book Prize. We have been shortlisted for Independent Publisher of the Year at the British Book Awards for the last five years, and were shortlisted for the Diversity and Inclusivity Award at the 2022 Independent Publishing Awards. In 2023, we were shortlisted for Publisher of the Year at the RNA Industry Awards, and in 2024, we were shortlisted at the CWA Daggers for the Best Crime and Mystery Publisher.

We built this company with your help, and we love to hear from you, so please email us about absolutely anything bookish at feedback@joffebooks.com.

If you want to receive free books every Friday and hear about all our new releases, join our mailing list here: www.joffebooks.com/freebooks.

And when you tell your friends about us, just remember: it's pronounced Joffe as in coffee or toffee!